CUTS

RICHARD LAYMON

LEISURE BOOKS NEW YORK CITY

A LEISURE BOOK®

March 2008

Published by

Dorchester Publishing Co., Inc.
200 Madison Avenue
New York, NY 10016

ISBN-10: 0-8439-5752-2
ISBN-13: 978-0-8439-5752-5

The name "Leisure Books" and the stylized "L" with design are trademarks of Dorchester Publishing Co., Inc.

Printed in the United States of America.

10 9 8 7 6 5 4 3 2 1

Visit us on the web at www.dorchesterpub.com.

This book is dedicated to Don Cannon.

Thanks for the many years of
encouragement and support.

You keep selling them,
I'll keep signing them.

RAVE REVIEWS
FOR RICHARD LAYMON!

"I've always been a Laymon fan. He manages to raise serious gooseflesh."
—Bentley Little

"Laymon is incapable of writing a disappointing book."
—*New York Review of Science Fiction*

"Laymon always takes it to the max. No one writes like him and you're going to have a good time with anything he writes."
—Dean Koontz

"If you've missed Laymon, you've missed a treat."
—Stephen King

"A brilliant writer."
—*Sunday Express*

"I've read every book of Laymon's I could get my hands on. I'm absolutely a longtime fan."
—Jack Ketchum, author of *Offspring*

"One of horror's rarest talents."
—*Publishers Weekly*

"Laymon is, was, and always will be king of the hill."
—*Horror World*

"Laymon is an American writer of the highest caliber."
—*Time Out*

"Laymon is unique. A phenomenon. A genius of the grisly and the grotesque."
—Joe Citro, *The Blood Review*

"Laymon doesn't pull any punches. Everything he writes keeps you on the edge of your seat."
—*Painted Rock Reviews*

CUTS

PART ONE

OCTOBER, 1975

ONE

NORTH GLEN, ILLINOIS

"Do you want to get in the backseat?"

"Hmm?" Albert asked, not listening, too entranced by the smooth feel of her breasts against his face.

She pushed him away. "The backseat. Do you want to get in the backseat with me?"

"What for?" Albert asked, wanting only to get back to her breasts. They looked pale in the darkness, their nipples almost black.

Though seventeen and a senior in high school, he had never seen actual breasts until tonight. He'd seen them only in photographs and paintings—except for his mother's breasts that one time when he was just a little kid. He hadn't touched them, but he'd wanted to. In spite of the blood. Or maybe because of it.

But he was sure touching these. They felt even more wonderful than he'd imagined. So smooth and soft and springy. The nipples weren't smooth. They were rumpled and hard and the way they stuck out . . .

"So we can *do* it, stupid," Betty said. "You want to do it, don't you?"

"Sure. I mean, I guess so. Of course I do."

"We aren't gonna do it in the front seat, that's for sure."

"Okay."

She looked at him and didn't move.

"I'll get the door for you." Albert leaned across her. Pressing the side of his face against her breast as he reached for the handle, he felt a nipple slide into his ear. It tickled and made him squirm.

She gripped his arm.

"What's wrong?" he asked. "Somebody out there?"

He looked out the windows. He was parked at the end of a dead-end street. In front of the car was a small patch of woods, the trees nearly bare of leaves, their branches reaching into the October moonlight. If anyone was lurking among those trees, Albert couldn't see him. Nor did he see anyone on the sidewalks or lawns of the nearby homes. Except for a few porch lights, most of the houses looked dark.

"I don't see anybody," Albert said.

"That isn't the problem, darling."

"Huh?"

"You're really something."

"Don't you want me to open your door for you?"

"Not yet. I want my twenty dollars first."

"What?"

"Twenty dollars. I never do it for a penny less. It's more for lots of guys. I'm giving you a break because I like you. You're a little weird, but I think you're *awfully* cute." She put a hand into his shirt and rubbed his chest.

"If I'm so cute, you shouldn't make me pay."

"I wouldn't, but I've gotta go to college next year."

"So what?"

"That's a lot of cost. The dorm, the books, not to mention tuition."

"Twenty dollars, though. That's a lot of money."

"It'll be worth a lot more than that," Betty said. She pushed a hand down the front of Albert's pants. He moaned at the cool touch of her fingers. "Ooo, no underwear. You *are* a naughty boy."

"How about ten dollars?" he asked.

"Twenty."

He felt her hand glide slowly up the length of his penis.

"But I've only got . . . I don't know, maybe fifteen. On me."

She pulled her hand away.

"Let me see." He dragged his wallet out of a seat pocket of his jeans, spread it open and removed the bills. He held them close to the windshield and peered at them in the dim light from outside. A ten and four ones.

"How much?" Betty asked.

"Fourteen dollars."

"Not enough."

"Come on."

"No dice, Albert."

"I can give you the rest tomorrow."

"Sure. You do that, and maybe tomorrow night we can get it on."

"Let's do it now, okay? Come on, I'm only like six dollars short. Please."

"Didn't Stan tell you the price?"

Stan hadn't mentioned anything at all about paying her. He'd said, "She's hot to trot, man. I already talked to her. She *wants* you. Told me so. Man, this is your chance to score."

"What do I have to do?" Albert had asked him.

"Just invite her out. Call her up, take her out for some pizza or something and a movie, then just stop somewhere good and private on the way home and have at her. She'll be all over you."

Frowning at Betty, Albert said, "He didn't say I'd have to pay you."

"Well, he should've. The dork. It's twenty bucks and not a penny less."

"Come on, Betty."

"If you don't have it, you can take me home now."

"Take you *home?* Why should I take you home? Shit! You can *walk* home."

"Don't be a bastard."

"Just get out of my car," Albert said.

"Are you kidding?" She bent her arms behind her back and fastened her bra. "Don't be ridiculous. Just drive me home. Dig up the rest of the money tomorrow and give me a call." She buttoned her blouse. "We'll have a great time tomorrow night."

"Shit," he muttered.

"Be nice. It isn't the end of the world."

Feels like it, he thought.

He started the car and backed up with a sudden lurch that threw Betty forward. "Hey!" Her hand caught the dashboard. "Damn it, calm down!"

Albert didn't calm down. Speeding along the narrow road, he took the curves so fast his tires sighed. Betty held tightly to the dashboard.

As he raced around a bend, his headlights gleamed on the rear end of a parked Porsche.

He jerked the wheel.

Not quite fast enough.

With a grinding scrape of metal, he sideswiped the Porsche.

"Now you've done it," Betty said.

"He shouldn't have parked there," Albert said, flooring the accelerator.

"Aren't you gonna stop?"

"Why should I?"

"Christ, Albert! You've gotta. It's against the law."

"Fuck the law," he said, and raced past a stop sign.

"Okay," Betty snapped. "That's enough. Let me out. Right now!"

Albert didn't stop.

"Let me out *please!*"

He looked at her and made a smile. "No."

"Albert!"

He came up fast behind a station wagon, crossed the double yellow lines and rushed past it.

"You'll get us killed!"

"So?"

"Damn it!"

He swung around a corner, the car skidding, the tires shrieking, and sped up a sloping street. On both sides were houses with wide driveways. Expensive, two-story homes.

"Which one's yours?" he asked.

"The middle of the block. The white one on the right."

In front of it, he jammed on his brakes. He said nothing. Staring straight forward, he didn't move until the door thudded shut.

Then he watched Betty walk up the driveway. Her skirt was very short. A breeze fluttered it. Her legs were pale in the moonlight.

"Bitch," he muttered.

Nothing but a dirty whore, he thought. Nobody but a dirty whore wants money for it. She'd probably give me the clap or something. Lucky I *didn't* have twenty bucks.

But if I'd had it, I'd be screwing her right now.

He watched her enter the house and shut the door.

"Good riddance," he muttered.

Then he gripped the steering wheel tightly with both hands and threw himself forward. His forehead hit the top of the wheel. He did it again. Again.

For a long time after that, he sat without moving. Then he started the car and drove slowly away. When he reached Washington Avenue, he turned right and drove into the business district.

The North Glen Theater must've just let out. Its marquee announced the same double-feature that Albert had seen last night: *The Texas Chainsaw Massacre* and *Race With the Devil*. He supposed that most of the people heading back to their cars were probably feeling a little freaked.

He'd *loved* those movies. Both of them, but especially *Chainsaw*.

The audience had screamed like hell last night.

But not Albert.

He'd wanted to be *in* those movies, chasing down those gals . . .

Albert suddenly realized that if he hadn't gone to the movies last night he would've had enough money for Betty. His ticket had cost two fifty and he'd spent at least four dollars more on snacks.

He let out a sour laugh.

Then he noticed a dog trotting along a sidewalk. It seemed to be alone.

He parked his car and climbed out.

The October wind was strangely warm for this time of the year. It felt good blowing against him, and carried a faint, tangy aroma of burnt leaves.

He walked quickly, watching the shadows and listening.

He knew what he wanted to hear.

A few minutes later, he heard it.

The collar tags jangled like keys on a chain.

At first, he saw no sign of the dog. Then it appeared from behind a tree a few yards ahead of him: a short-haired, spotted dog like a Dalmatian except for its short legs.

Albert walked toward it.

The dog paid him no attention. It wandered through the grass by the roadside, nose low, sniffing loudly.

When Albert walked up behind it, the dog glanced over its shoulder.

"Hi, fella." Albert crouched. "Come here."

The dog watched him but didn't move.

Albert looked all around. A car passed him on the street. Another pulled away from the curb and drove off. The nearest pedestrians were a couple of blocks away and seemed to be walking in the opposite direction.

He smiled at the dog. "Come on, fella," he called softly. "Come here." He patted his knee. "Come here, boy."

The dog took a step toward him, then hesitated.

"It's okay, fella. Come on. Come here. I've got something for you."

He reached toward it with a closed hand.

An empty hand, but the dog didn't know that.

It stepped closer.

"That a boy. That's a good boy."

When it started to sniff Albert's left hand, he reached out with his right hand and scratched the fur under its chin.

"You like that, fella? Huh?"

Then he opened his left hand. The dog pressed its wet snout against his palm and snuffled as if trying to locate the mysterious treat. Albert used the hand to rub it behind the ears. It hung its head low, eyes half-shut. Its tail swept slowly from side to side.

"Yeah, you like that, don't you."

Continuing to pet the dog with his left hand, he lowered his knees to the wet grass and worked his right hand into a front pocket of his jeans.

Tail wagging, the dog flopped onto its side.

Albert scratched the fur of its chest. When he scratched its belly, its left hind leg jerked in quick circles.

"Yeah, you like that."

He pulled the switchblade knife from his pocket. It had cost him twelve dollars from a Mexican kid on the Chicago subway. He pressed the button. A six-inch blade snapped out, making the handle jump in his grip.

The dog, suddenly alarmed, tried to flip over.

"Oh, no you don't."

Albert held it down with his left hand.

With his right, he jammed the knife into the soft flesh below its ribs.

The dog's shriek split the silence.

Albert pulled out the knife.

He was excited, tight and hard and aching.

He punched the knife in again.

The dog's shriek stopped.

He pulled out the knife and plunged it again into the animal's belly and this time his tight ache broke, throbbing with heat and wetness.

TWO

GRAND BEACH, CALIFORNIA

Janet Arthur woke up on Saturday morning with a hand slipping between her thighs. She moaned with sleepy pleasure and nestled her face deeper into the pillow.

Soon, the hand pulled away.

A breeze stroked Janet's bare back as the covers were thrown off. She took a deep breath. The breeze held the fresh, exciting smell of the ocean a few blocks away.

She rolled over and saw Dave kneeling next to her. His black hair was thick and tangled. His sleek, trim body still kept its summer darkness and he looked starkly pale where his trunks had been during long days by the pool.

"Good morning," she said. Smiling, she reached out to him.

He was erect. "How come you always wake up like that?"

"I see you in my dreams."

"Oh, is that it?"

"That's it." He climbed between her knees and lowered himself.

"Let's not just . . ." Janet twisted and Dave went with it, rolling onto his back.

Janet straddled him. Smiling, she leaned down. She let the rigid flesh of her nipples brush against his chest as she lightly kissed his lips. "First we've got to talk," she said.

"This is no time to talk."

"This is a fine time."

"To screw."

She felt his hands slide over her buttocks. "It's serious."

He gave them a gentle squeeze. "Okay."

"How would you feel about having a kid?"

"Can't have one. I'm a guy. Biologically unlikely if not impossible."

"Let me rephrase that," Janet said. "How would you like to be a daddy?"

"Eventually, maybe."

"I had in mind sooner rather than later."

His hands, gently massaging her buttocks, suddenly stopped.

"You're not pregnant, are you?"

"Yep."

"Tell me you're kidding."

"That'd be a lie," Janet said as something inside her began to sink.

"How can you be *pregnant?*"

"If you don't know . . ."

"But you said it'd be *safe.*"

"It's never *completely* safe. Maybe I miscounted the days or . . ."

"Maybe you *miscounted?*"

"It's not an exact science, Dave. And you *wouldn't* use a rubber."

"It's no good with a rubber on."

"Well, then . . ."

"If you'd stayed on the pills . . ."

"They're *dangerous*. I'm supposed to give myself cancer so you don't have to wear a *rubber* on your dick? Get real."

"Shit!"

"You knew there was a risk of this."

Shaking his head from side to side, he let out a long, low

moan. "Have you been to a doctor? You haven't just missed your period or something?"

"I'm pregnant, Dave. One hundred percent, fully guaranteed. I found out yesterday."

"Great," he said. "Just great. Absolutely fucking *terrific*."

Pushing at his shoulders, Janet sat up straight. "I thought you might be happy about it," she said.

"Sure. Happy. Okay." He closed his eyes and took a few deep breaths. Then he said, "No problem. What'll it run to get it taken care of?"

"Well, it isn't due for about seven months so we've got plenty of time to save up."

"I don't mean delivery costs."

Her throat tightened. Heat rushing to her skin, she asked, "What do you mean?"

"You know what I mean."

"You want to *kill* it?"

"Oh, for the love of God."

Janet made a quiet, whimpering sound and smashed her fist into his cheek. Her other fist caught the side of his nose. Blood rushed from his nostrils.

He twisted sharply beneath her, grabbed her arm and threw her off the bed. She hit the floor hard, shoulder first, feet in the air.

Dave looked down at her. "You damn near broke my nose!"

She rolled over and got up.

"What do you want to hit me for? Shit! All I said . . ."

"I know exactly what you said." She stepped into a pair of brown corduroy trousers.

"So what's all the fuss about? It's perfectly legal."

"Sure. Legal." She pulled on a big, loose sweatshirt.

"What the hell's wrong with you?" Dave blurted.

"I'm leaving," Janet said. She shoved her hands into the front pockets of her cords and leaned back against a wall.

"You can't leave!"

"The hell I can't. I'll be back Monday for my things.

While you're at work. Don't worry, I won't take anything that isn't mine."

"You're not being rational."

"Screw rational. I'm pregnant. You want to murder my baby."

"It's not *murder*. Murder's what Idi Amin does to his political enemies. Murder's what Manson did. Murder's what Nixon did in Vietnam. Murder isn't aborting a god-damn fetus."

"When it's *my* fetus, it is."

"You're nuts."

"Go to hell."

"What'll you do for money?"

"I'll manage."

"Easier said than done."

"I'll teach."

"Sure you will. This is October, in case you haven't noticed. They hire teachers in the *spring*, not in *October*, for God's sake. *Halloween's* in a couple of weeks. You're not gonna get a *teaching* job. Who do you think you're kidding?"

"Good-bye." She grabbed the straps of her purse. As she walked toward the door, she heard a soft thump—Dave kicking something, probably a wall.

"You'll be back!" he shouted.

Janet didn't answer.

"You'll come back *begging*."

The hall carpet felt stiff and cool under her bare feet. With each step she took, the floor seemed to give the way ice gives on a thinly frozen pond.

She trotted down the apartment-house stairs and hurried across the foyer.

Outside, the sun felt good on her face. She climbed into her Ford, did a tight U-turn and headed for Grand Beach Boulevard. Meg would be glad to see her. And glad that she'd split up with Dave. "That guy's a creep," Meg had said after meeting him. "Beautiful, but a creep."

"You hardly know him."

"Oh, I know him. I've known plenty of guys like Dave. Hotshots. Think they're God's gift. What they are, they're assholes disguised as men."

Meg wasn't home.

Janet sat on the front stoop. The shaded concrete felt cool through her corduroys. She was too hot in the sweatshirt. With nothing on underneath it, she couldn't take it off. So she fluttered its front to get some air inside.

For a long time, she stared at her engagement ring. Then she pulled it off. It left a band of pale skin around her finger.

She put the ring in her purse and looked inside her billfold.

A twenty-dollar bill and six ones.

She opened her checkbook. Her bank account contained a grand total of one hundred and thirty dollars and twelve cents.

"What wealth," she muttered.

It was all that remained of the stipend she'd received for her teaching assistantship at the university last spring.

At the bottom of her purse, she found a ballpoint pen. She couldn't locate any scratch paper so she tore a deposit slip out of her checkbook. On its back, she wrote, "Meg, I'll be back this afternoon. Must see you. Janet."

She left the note under the heavy brass door knocker and went back to her car.

THREE

THE SUPERMARKET

That morning, Albert looked at his reflection in the window of the North Glen Safeway.

Pretty as a girl.

Makes me wanta puke.

A mustache would probably help.

Good luck, he thought.

He didn't even need to shave more than a couple of times a week. Growing a halfway decent mustache would probably take him months. Maybe years.

I'll just have to put up with it, he thought.

"You're awfully cute," Betty had said. The dumb bitch.

Twenty bucks!

When the automatic door sprang open, Albert stepped into the supermarket. He went directly to the cookie aisle, pulled a package of Oreos off the shelf, and headed for a checkout line.

How'll I get my hands on twenty bucks? he wondered.

Six, he reminded himself. I've already got fourteen, so . . .

It'll be less than that after I buy the Oreos.

Screw it.

His cheapskate father only forked out two bucks per week in allowance. At that rate, it would take three damn weeks just to save up six dollars.

And that's if I don't spend any.

He tore open the sack and ate a cookie. It made the emptiness in his stomach hurt less.

Maybe I oughta get a job.

Yeah, like doing what? Bagging groceries after school?

Babysitting?

He sort of *liked* the idea of babysitting. Maybe someone

would hire him to take care of a cute little gal, and he'd be alone with her . . . Maybe give her a bath . . .

He felt a hardness start to grow in his jeans.

Yeah, but who's gonna hire me as a babysitter? Nobody, that's who.

Albert stepped into line behind a woman with a shopping cart. "Would you like to go ahead of me?" she asked. She had a gentle voice and an open, friendly smile.

Albert glanced into her shopping cart. There wasn't much in it. No more than a dozen items, at most. "Naw," he said. "Thanks anyway. It's all right."

"You sure? I don't mind at all."

"Yeah. I'm in no big hurry. But thank you for the offer." He ate another cookie and watched the woman start piling her groceries onto the conveyor belt.

The clerk rang up each item on the cash register. Then the woman's total came up.

Munching a cookie, Albert watched her unsnap a checkbook and flatten it out on the counter close to him.

The check had a snowcapped-mountain design.

Against the rich blue sky to the left of the mountain peak, Albert saw a block of letters and numbers:

Arnold Broxton
Rita M. Broxton
3214 Jeffers Lane
North Glen, IL

Was this woman Hank Broxton's mother?

No, she looked too young to have a kid in high school.

Albert was prying open a cookie when he saw Rita make out a check for thirty-two dollars.

The cookie parted cleanly, leaving all the vanilla filling on one side. With his upper teeth, Albert scraped an uneven furrow through the whiteness.

He tried to take a closer look at the checkbook, but Rita was already folding it shut.

What was her last name? Jeffers? No, that was the street.

Broxton! That's it! Same as Hank. Remember Hank.

Albert paid for his cookies, then watched Rita walk toward the exit.

She looked nice in those tight slacks. Smooth and curved without any seams showing through.

Maybe she's got nothing on underneath!

Following her outside, Albert wondered if he should offer to carry her shopping bag to her car.

No, don't.

Don't want anybody seeing me with her.

FOUR

GRAND BEACH

Janet tucked her purse under the front seat of her car, locked the door and put the key chain into a pocket of her corduroy trousers. Hands free, she walked half a block to the beach.

The breeze was stronger there, and cooler, and had a sea taste that made her breathe deeply and feel good. She bent down to roll up her cuffs, and the breeze filled the front of her loose sweatshirt.

She glanced ahead. Nobody seemed positioned for a good look down the neck hole of her sweatshirt so she stayed low, letting the breeze roam around inside, drifting over the hot skin of breasts and belly, while she rolled up both the cuffs of her corduroys.

Then she straightened up and strolled down to the shore. The breakers were rolling in, one after another, their bellies translucent green with the sun behind them, their heads glinting and frothing as they fell.

The first cold lick of water made Janet flinch. Then she stepped out farther and let the water climb her ankles.

With a lifeguard tower as her landmark, she started strolling south.

Each time a wave retreated, it sucked sand out from under her feet.

The water slipped back into the ocean, leaving the hard-packed sand bare for a few seconds before it came swirling back, curling between her toes, rising and soaking the rolled legs of her trousers, then sliding away again.

Sometimes, she watched how the water played around her legs and feet. Other times, she watched the surfers, the sailboats far out, or the diving, squealing gulls. Much of the time, she watched what was happening to her left where the beach was dry.

Lots of joggers, both men and women. Children digging in the sand. Dogs chasing each other and sticks of driftwood. Lone sunbathers. And couples.

Couples running together, walking, sitting or lying close to each other in the sand. Many held hands. Some embraced as if they were alone.

She was glad she'd never been to the beach with Dave. The one time she'd suggested it, he had said, "The beach? My God, you've gotta be kidding."

If he'd come to the beach with her, it wouldn't be the same now. It wouldn't be so totally her own. It would've been ruined for her.

It's all mine, she thought. Completely mine.

The water felt *so* good.

She wished she were wearing a swimsuit under her heavy sweatshirt and cords.

Her only swimsuit, a blue bikini, was back at Dave's apartment.

That gonna stop ya?

Letting out a soft, quiet laugh, Janet waded out. The water climbed her trousers, making the fabric cling to her legs and groin and buttocks. When it reached her waist, she dived beneath a wave. The cold water washed over her, soaked and pulled at her sweatshirt, pushed her, tumbled her, sucked her forward, tossed her backward.

Again and again, she stood up to meet the inrushing waves.

She dived into them, swam under them, rode them toward the beach, then waded out again to meet new waves.

Finally, exhausted, she waded for shore.

Her sweatshirt, stretched and pulled askew, drooped from her shoulders. Her corduroy trousers felt so heavy with water that she feared they might fall around her ankles. She hung on to the waistband with one hand as she walked.

When she reached dry sand, she lay on her back and gasped for air. Her breath soon began to come more easily.

That was nice, she thought. Very nice.

But what am I going to do?

Just take it one step at a time. I'll be all right. The baby'll be all right.

We'll both be better off without Dave.

Who needs him, anyway.

The world's full of guys, she told herself. They're *always* after me. The trick'll be finding one who isn't an asshole.

I sure was wrong about Dave.

Better be more careful next time.

Maybe just the right guy will come along this morning. He'll see me sprawled here on the sand and fall madly in love with me. The way I'm dressed, maybe he'll think I got washed ashore after a boating accident.

I'll wake up and find him standing over me, smiling.

As her mind played with the idea, she drifted into sleep.

She woke up some time later. Nobody was standing over her, but the front of her sweatshirt and corduroys was nearly dry. She rolled over and shut her eyes.

The second time she awoke, she was still alone on the beach. She felt as if she were baking inside her heavy clothes. Her mouth was parched.

She got up, brushed sand off her clothes, then headed

back toward the lifeguard tower that she'd earlier used to mark her way.

It was a long walk.

When she reached the tower, she sat in the sand to rest. She felt tired and gritty, hot and sweaty. She shouldn't have stayed out so long. She was probably dehydrated.

I'll have to make up for it, she thought, when I get to Meg's.

She struggled to her feet, then walked the rest of the way to Meg's house.

The front door stood open.

Janet went to it and raised her hand, ready to knock, when Meg's rough, husky voice called, "Come on in, hon."

"Okay. Just a second." Bracing herself against the door frame, she brushed sand off her feet and ankles.

"Don't worry about it," Meg said. "A little sand never hurt anyone."

Janet went inside and saw Meg sitting on the couch, a copy of *T.V. Guide* lying open on her lap, her bare feet resting on the coffee table.

"Been waiting long?" Meg asked.

"Since about eleven this morning."

"Wish I'd known. I was off playing volleyball at church."

"Meet anyone interesting?"

"If I had, I wouldn't be here now. So what's the word, anyway?"

"I left Dave."

Meg shook her head. "Sorry to hear it."

"But not very?"

"Sorry for you. I know it's gotta be tough."

"Well . . . Do you have something to drink?"

"Sure. Something hard?"

"Not too hard."

"How about a beer?"

"Yeah, that'd be great. In the refrigerator?"

"Right. Bring me one, too, will you?"

With two cans of Hamms, Janet returned to the living room. She gave one can to Meg, then sat on a wicker chair and popped open her lid.

"Did you catch him stepping out on you?" Meg asked.

"Huh-uh." Janet took a swallow of the beer. It was cold and sharp and slightly sweet. She breathed, then drank some more. "He doesn't want the baby," she finally said.

"Baby?"

Smiling, Janet nodded.

"Terrific! How far along are you?"

"About seven weeks."

"Wow! That's fabulous! How're you feeling?"

She rubbed the cold, wet can across her forehead. "Not bad right at the moment."

"You know what I mean."

"I'm a bit shaky in the morning once in a while. And sometimes I don't feel too perky. Aside from that, though, I feel great."

"A baby. Wow!"

"A baby without a father," Janet said. "I'm finished with Dave. He wants to kill it. Like it's a fly or mosquito or something to be swatted."

"Maybe he'll change his mind."

"He can go to hell."

"He won't let you off that easy, hon."

"He doesn't give a damn about me."

"Even if he doesn't," Meg said, "he for sure gives a damn about himself. His ego's way too big for him to let you off the hook."

"I hope he rots."

"Until he does, do you want to stay here?"

"That'd be great. Will I be in your way?"

"Not a chance. We'll have a great time."

"Well, thanks. Thanks a lot."

"Hey, what are pals for?"

FIVE

THE SOCIAL COMMITTEE

A bunch of lushes, Lester thought.

Well, maybe not all of them.

For the most part, however, the Grand Beach High School social committee seemed like a group devoted to liquor, laughs, opinionated posturing and flirtation.

Lester had heard plenty about their meetings from Helen, but this was the first he'd attended.

Because Helen had decided to host it at their home.

Thanks a bunch for wrecking my Saturday night, he thought.

After spending a couple of hours hatching plans for the faculty Halloween party nearly two weeks away—the alleged *purpose* of the meeting—they had scattered to begin some serious drinking and frolicking.

There seemed to be no end in sight.

Time for me to split, Lester thought. Nobody's talking to me, anyway. I'm just Helen's poor loser of a husband. Not even a teacher.

Around this crowd, you're shit if you aren't a teacher.

Bunch of pretentious bastards.

Drunk, pretentious bastards.

Figuring to hole up in the bedroom until the fun was over, Lester began making his way across the living room. But someone caught hold of his arm from behind. Annoyed, he frowned over his shoulder.

And found Emily Jean Bonner smiling at him.

Emily Jean, the aging and pathetic Georgia belle of Grand Beach High. Fifty if she was a day—probably closer to sixty—but still sporting a blaze of flowing red hair and a flamboyant spirit.

"You're *just* who I was looking for, Mr. Bryant," she said, her voice a soft drawl.

More of a drawl than usual, he imagined, due to the martinis she'd been consuming.

"What do you think of our plans for the Halloween party?"

"They seem fine."

"I believe they do, myself. Of course, I would *prefer* that costumes be mandatory rather than optional. I think *everyone* should come in costume. It's so much more festive that way. It's so much more *Halloween*, don't you think so?"

"Yes, I do," Lester said.

"*You'll* be coming in costume, won't you?"

If I have to attend the damn thing at all.

"Oh, probably," he said.

"I haven't decided *what* to wear yet. Do you have any suggestions for me?"

"How about a Georgia peach?"

Laughing, she patted his shoulder. "You *are* a card, Mr. Bryant. Perhaps I *shall* come as a peach." Resting her left hand on his shoulder, she raised her right to her mouth and sipped her martini. "And what'll be *your* costume?"

"I might come as the Invisible Man."

"Ah! That would be . . . unusual." She removed her hand from his shoulder and looked around as if searching for someone.

"Well," Lester said, "I'll see you around. Nice talking to you, Emily . . ."

She reached out and took hold of his wrist. "Oh, you needn't run off. I've been admiring your house. It's really very charming."

"It's okay," Lester said, and thought he would like it a lot *more* if it hadn't been a gift from Helen's parents. Okay, not exactly a gift: they'd loaned her the down payment. Same difference.

"This is a good location for Helen," Lester explained. "And it's only twenty minutes to Blessed Virgin."

"You're the libararian there?"

Lester wondered if that was what Helen had been telling all her faculty cronies to save face. "No, actually, I'm the library secretary. I still need to finish my M.A. before I can be a real librarian."

"Does it require a master's degree?"

"Well, almost. It takes about thirty semester hours."

"Are you taking them at U.C.L.A.?"

"U.S.C."

"Ah, a fellow Trojan."

To Lester, Trojan would always be a brand of condoms. He didn't mention this, however, to Emily Jean.

"How long will it be before you're done?" she asked.

"Another two years, probably."

Another two years with Helen making three times as much money as him. And even *with* the degree, what guarantee did he have that he would find a librarian job?

"It must be marvelous working with all those books," Emily Jean said.

"It's not bad," he told her. Why mention that the only books he currently worked with were accounting ledgers?

"I *love* books," said Emily Jean. "Do you love books, Mr. Bryant?"

"Some of them."

"I just *adore* Tennessee Williams. Are you familiar with his works? I find them *so* grand and tragic and . . . lyrical."

"Yeah, they are. But I've really gotta get going. I'll see you later, okay?"

"Oh." She blinked and seemed puzzled as she removed her hand from his arm. "Certainly. We'll see each other later, I'm sure."

Forcing a smile, Lester turned away and headed for the bathroom.

He was glad to get away from her.

The woman was over the hill, a sad case.

In the restroom, he locked the door and stepped over to the toilet.

I shouldn't be so hard on her, he thought as he un-zipped his trousers. At least she's *nice* to me.

Nobody else is.

Except maybe that Ian guy. He seemed like a pretty good fellow.

But the rest of them were snobs who preferred to ig-nore Lester.

Just because I'm working at some lousy job for peanuts.

Bunch of assholes.

Lester finished urinating and flushed the toilet. Before opening the door, he made sure his zipper was up.

That'd be just what I'd need, he thought. Wander around with my fly open.

As if anyone would notice, anyway. I am *the invisible man.*

In the living room, he looked for Ian. He spotted the tall, solemn man in the corner talking with Helen and Ronald.

Helen looked good standing there. Pert with her up-tilted nose and Peter Pan haircut. Sexy in her tight skirt and turtleneck sweater. The sweater *really* emphasized her breasts, clinging to each of them.

She stood so close to Ian that her right breast was almost touching his arm.

On purpose?

Of course it's on purpose, Lester thought.

But Ian didn't seem to be aware of her breast's proximity.

Unless he's putting on a good act.

Ronald was the one paying attention to Helen's chest. He was an English teacher, but not at the high school. A few years ago, after marrying Dale, he'd transferred out of Grand Beach High and taken a position on the faculty of the community college. But he'd kept an honorary mem-bership on the social committee and showed up at every function. Apparently, he liked to party as much as he liked to educate people. He considered himself the expert on every subject, and was always holding forth on something. Now, as he nodded sagely, talking and listening, Lester could see him sneaking glances at Helen's breasts.

He'd probably like to rip that sweater off her, Lester thought.

Good luck, pal.

Because underneath the sweater he would find a big stiff bra with four hooks at the back, and underneath the bra he would find a pair of very lovely icebergs.

Or maybe not, Lester thought. Maybe she's only an ice-cold bitch with me.

Feeling squirmy inside, he looked away from his wife and the two men. He saw Emily Jean sitting on the couch, sipping her martini and talking to Dale.

Her back to Ronald, Dale was unaware of the way her husband was ogling Helen.

Maybe she wouldn't even care.

She sat there listening to Emily Jean, a rather smirky look on her face, a Scotch in one hand and a cigarette in the other. As always, her cigarette jutted from the end of a long, slim holder that appeared to be gold-plated.

Tall and sleek and elegant, Dale was *almost* beautiful. But she had a hardness about her.

Don't they all, Lester thought.

No, they don't *all* have the hardness. Emily Jean doesn't. She seemed a little lost and vulnerable, certainly not hard.

But Helen had it. And Dale had it. *Most* of them had it, especially the women.

Maybe it comes with the territory.

Feeling very depressed, Lester went out to the patio table where the drinks were. He filled his glass with ice and poured himself a screwdriver from his plastic pitcher. Then he went inside again. He sat on his recliner. He sipped his drink.

Fuck them all, he thought, and wished they would all go home.

SIX

THE TOAST

"The problem starts in the lower grades," said Helen. She said it as fact, not opinion.

Ian realized that he was gritting his teeth, irritated by her words. He'd known Helen Bryant for three years—ever since she first joined the faculty of Grand Beach High School—and the tough, humorless, defensive way she stated her opinions never failed to scrape his nerves.

"You're passing the buck," Ronald told her, grinning and nodding and glancing down at her breasts—which seemed to be jutting out more than usual, maybe because of her tight-fitting white sweater.

Why does she dress like this? Ian wondered. If it's not a tight sweater, it's a blouse you can almost see through or a miniskirt hardly long enough to cover her butt.

She wore such revealing clothes not only to parties, but even to school.

It seemed incongruous to Ian that a cold fish like Helen would want to flaunt herself that way.

Maybe she's *not* the cold fish she seems to be, he thought.

Or maybe she's oblivious of the way men react to such displays. Off in her own world of lesson plans and preparing tests and grading homework.

"I'm merely explaining," Helen said, "that most kids can't read or write worth a damn by the time they get to us. They're so far behind that . . ."

"Why, Helen, you sound like a doctor complaining because his patients come in sick. Well, let me tell you what you can do. You can get your rear in gear and *cure* the poor blighters."

"That's more easily said than . . ."

"I get kids coming into my classes who don't know a noun from a verb. They think a period is what women get once a month. And that's *college*, for God's sake!"

"That's *city* college," Helen pointed out. "The ones who can read go elsewhere."

Ronald blurted out a laugh. *"Touché!"*

"Besides," Helen went on, "we only have the kids for three years."

"Only three?" Ronald asked with heavy sarcasm.

Helen narrowed her eyes at him. "We can hardly be expected to overcome a dozen years of ignorance in three."

"Oh, please."

"Especially when half of the kids don't even speak English in their homes."

"Violins, please."

Helen nudged Ian's arm with one of her breasts. The stiff cup of her bra seemed to cave in slightly and he felt the soft springiness underneath it. "You know how it is. Tell him."

Ian realized he was blushing.

Why'd she do that?

He shrugged and said, "I don't see any way we can justify graduating illiterates."

"Bravo!" From Ronald.

"Thanks a heap." From Helen.

"With those new competency tests for the kids," Ian said, "we probably won't be *able* to graduate them."

Emily Jean Bonner, delicately holding a fresh martini, strolled over and joined the three of them. Ian nodded a greeting to her and she smiled back as if surprised at being noticed.

"I suppose," Ronald said, "you'll have to spend more time on sentence structure than on Shakespeare, for a change. It's about time, if you ask me. Leave literature for college."

"Thou dost protest too much, methinks," declared

Emily Jean, smiling at Ronald and lifting her scarlet eye-brows. To Ian, the remnants of her Georgia drawl always sounded a bit sad. She made him think of an aging Scarlett O'Hara torn from Tara's halls but clinging to her pride and, with the help of a beauty parlor, her flaming hair.

"How does a sixteen-year-old kid," Ronald asked Helen, "grasp the significance of 'living in the rank sweat of an enseamed bed, stewed in corruption, honeying and making love over the nasty sty'?"

"Marvelous!" blurted Emily Jean. "You do know your Shakespeare, Mr. Harvey."

"It comes with the territory," he told her, and winked.

Emily Jean laughed in her high-pitched, fragile way. "Did you know that I played the role of Linda Loman at the Wilshire Playhouse? To this day, tears fill my eyes whenever I hear the words of Willie's funeral. Such a strong, sorrowful . . ."

"So you think," Helen interrupted with a wry, challenging glance at Ronald, "that we should give up teaching literature entirely?"

Emily Jean looked hurt for only a moment. Smiling strangely, she drifted toward the rear door.

"Not entirely, perhaps," said Ronald. "Matters would certainly be improved, however, if you focused on reading material that isn't *miles* over the heads of the students."

"Excuse me," Ian said. Not waiting for any response, he went to the back door, slid it open and stepped onto the lighted patio.

To his left, a picnic table was cluttered with paper bags, wet spoons and a stack of plastic drinking glasses. Bottles of liquor and mix, mayonnaise jars and pitchers containing drinks concocted at home, stood among the bags. The ice chest lay on the concrete floor.

Emily Jean was kneeling beside the ice chest, holding her plastic glass in one hand while she fumbled with the latch. Ian watched her as he set his glass down on the table. Her white blouse was pulled taut across her back, showing the narrow straps of her bra and the prominent, jutting points of her spine. She looked damn breakable. He put his hand on her shoulder.

"Let me get that for you," he said.

"Why, thank you, Mr. Collins."

"My pleasure." He opened the ice chest. "How many would you like?"

"I believe I could be quite happy with three."

He dropped three ice cubes into her plastic glass, then filled his own and secured the lid.

They stood up. They were alone on the patio. "Shall I mix you a drink?" Ian asked.

"Thank you for the thought, Mr. Collins, but I've already seen to that." She tapped a fingernail on the lid of a half-empty mayonnaise jar. "My homemade martinis. I see that I'm getting a tiny bit low. I'm a naughty girl tonight, aren't I? Am I not?"

"Oh, I shouldn't say that," Ian told her, pouring vodka into his glass as he watched her unscrew the lid of her jar.

"I shouldn't either, really. I view overindulgence in gin as a trifling sin and a major solace. Mr. Collins, this may seem peculiar to a young man of your energy and talent, but I have been teaching for twenty-eight years and I feel that I've wasted my life."

Her eyes flashed a proud, painful look that defied Ian to contradict her.

"I could have done so many things. I could have remained on the stage. I could have written books. I could have gone into business. So many things, so many opportunities. All thrown away, all lost."

"Teaching isn't the most fulfilling of jobs," Ian said.

"As trite as the analogy may sound, Mr. Collins, teaching is like living one's life on a merry-go-round down at the amusement pier. A teacher climbs onto his horse—or hers—and goes around and around, around and around, year after year. The Calliope makes charming music, but it repeats itself. It plays the same few tunes over and over.

The scenery never changes. The faces do. Yes, the faces do change, unfortunately. That's part of the tragedy, too. Some of the faces are so charming, some so full of pain and need. Some, you even grow to love. But they all go away after a while and you stay on your horse, going around and around, and they're gone."

She gazed for a long time into her drink. "All the golden rings, Mr. Collins, are only brass. And the merry-go-round turns out, after all, not to be so very merry." She laughed sadly. "That rhymes, doesn't it? Very merry."

"Have you thought of climbing off the horse?" Ian asked.

"And what would I do then?" Suddenly, her smile became less sad. "I have a daughter. Did you know that? I have a very fine, beautiful, talented daughter. She's on the stage, did you know that? Quite a fine little actress. May Beth Bonner? Perhaps you've seen her performance as Laura . . ."

Laura!

The name, a blow to his heart, sent a jolt of pain and longing through Ian.

". . . *Glass Menagerie* at the Stage Door?"

"I'm afraid not," he said, forcing a smile. "But I'd *like* to see her perform sometime."

"I would like that, too. I would love for *everyone* to see her perform. Unfortunately, she ended her run last week. If you wish to see her as Laura . . ."

Again, the name tore at his heart.

His mind flashed an image of Laura's face above his own, smiling at him, her soft auburn hair flowing straight down like curtains enclosing her face and his, hiding them from the rest of the world.

Get over it, he told himself.

I can't. There's never been anyone else and never will be. You only get one chance at love, and she was mine.

Not necessarily, he thought. You never know. I might meet someone tomorrow . . .

Not like Laura.

Knock it off.

Emily Jean opened her purse, took out her wallet, and flipped through several photos under frosted plastic. "Isn't she lovely?"

Ian looked at the snapshot. It showed a slim, attractive redhead in her early twenties. "She is beautiful," he said. "She looks a lot like you."

Emily Jean chuckled softly. "Oh, Mr. Collins. And who *said* chivalry is dead? Though I must say, in all honesty, I *did* look almost exactly like May Beth when I was much younger. We might've been twin sisters. But that was long ago."

"Well, you're *both* striking women."

"May Beth certainly is, at any rate. This picture, of course, does her no justice. Don't you think she would look *splendid* on the big screen?"

"She would."

"Some day, I'll *see* her on the big screen. We all will."

"Does she have any film projects coming up?"

"Oh, not that I'm aware of. It's terribly difficult to break in, I understand. Terribly difficult."

"I've heard that, too," Ian said.

"But she'll get into films one day. I know she will."

"I'm sure she will."

"And I shall be very proud, shan't I? Shall I not?"

"Very." He frowned into his drink.

"Is something the matter?"

"I'm . . . just thinking. I know a few people in the movie business. If you'd like to give me May Beth's phone number . . ."

Smiling, Emily Jean reached out and squeezed his arm. "Why, Mr. Collins! No need to prevaricate. I would find it absolutely *lovely* if you wish to call on May Beth."

"Prevarication and I are sworn ememies," he said.

"Ha! I do despise mendacity, myself."

"I really do know people who might be able to help your daughter break into films. I'll see what I can do. It's possible nothing will come of my efforts, but . . ." He shrugged.

"Any efforts along those lines, Mr. Collins, would be *most* appreciated."

"I'll do what I can," he said. He pulled a note pad and pen out of his shirt pocket. "Do you know her phone number?" he asked.

"Why, yes, I certainly do. She lives at home with me. I suppose I know my *own* phone number." She giggled softly. "Unless my mind has grown too befuddled by demon gin."

She recited the phone number. Ian wrote it down.

"That's May Beth Bonner?" he asked.

"Indeed, it is. *She* is. Shall we drink a toast to her success?"

"Let us," said Ian.

They raised their glasses.

"To May Beth," said Emily Jean. "May she become a true star of the silver screen."

"To May Beth," said Ian.

They bumped together the rims of their plastic glasses, then drank.

SEVEN

NIGHT MISSION

Albert wished he could take his father's car, but starting it inside the garage would make too much noise. He took his bicycle instead, wheeling it out of the garage, climbing on and coasting down the driveway.

At first, he was cold without his jacket. His turtleneck offered little protection from the night's chilly wind. His only jacket was bright yellow, though. Such a color wouldn't do at all for a night operation.

Soon, the cold no longer bothered him. He enjoyed the

feel of the wind in his face. It smelled fresh and clean like Betty's hair.

"I've got twenty dollars for you," he had told her on the phone that afternoon.

"Are you sure?"

"Yeah, I'm sure. I wouldn't have said it if I wasn't sure."

"I just mean, I don't do it on credit. If you have a down payment in mind, and small monthly installments . . ."

"Hardy har. Very funny."

"I'm serious."

"I've got the twenty dollars."

"Okay then. How about eight o'clock?"

"Tomorrow night."

"Tomorrow?" Betty had asked. "What's the matter with tonight?"

"I've got a previous engagement."

"Previous engagement, huh?" She sounded suspicious. "With whom, may I ask?"

"That's my business."

"If it's Suzy Hayden, forget it. She's a pig. Besides which, I happen to know she's got a contagious disease."

"You're not very friendly to your competition."

"*Competition?* Suzy Hayden? Oh, honey, you're pulling my leg. She's not competition, she's a bargain basement."

Albert turned onto Jeffers Lane and started pedaling up the slope. At the fourth house from the corner, he climbed off his bike. He lowered it quietly to the grass and ran to the front stoop. The address on the door was 3212. The next house on the left should be the Broxton's.

It had lights on.

Crouching, Albert dashed across the space between the two houses. He knelt against the wall. Above him was a window. He paused for a few moments, catching his breath and waiting for his heart to slow down. Then he raised himself.

He peered into the window.

The living room. Lamps were on at each end of a long,

blue sofa. The television screen was blank green. He saw no people.

Maybe nobody's home.

He ran along the side of the house and across the backyard to an elevated stoop. At the top of its concrete stairs, he peered into the windows of the door.

The kitchen. Dark.

He hurried down and ran to the garage. Its side door had windows. He pressed his face to the glass. By the dim moonlight, he could see an expanse of emptiness. The two-car garage appeared to be carless.

How convenient.

Albert quickly returned to the kitchen door. He pulled a thick mitten over his right hand. With a quick, sharp blow, he punched through a corner of the glass. Then he reached inside and opened the door.

The soles of his tennis shoes crunched bits of glass and made scratching sounds against the kitchen floor. He thought about taking his shoes off. That might put him in a fix, however, if he had to make a quick run for it.

Keeping them on, he entered the lighted hallway.

The front door of the house was straight ahead.

Walking toward it, a wall on one side and a staircase on the other, he felt as if he were trapped in a narrow canyon. He didn't like it. But there wasn't much choice—not if he wanted to go upstairs. He felt like running, but that would mean noise. So he walked slowly and silently forward, staring straight ahead at the door, half expecting it to fly open.

By the time he reached the foot of the stairway, he needed to crouch down to ease the cramps in his bowels.

What's going on? he wondered.

Maybe that fried chicken I had for supper.

But he figured it was more likely fear. He'd gotten cramps before when he was scared.

Nothing to be scared of, he told himself. Nobody's here.

Probably.

But this was the first time he had ever broken into

someone's house. Only natural to have a little indigestion at a time like this.

Soon, feeling better, Albert hurried up the stairs.

To his right was a bedroom with model airplanes strung across the ceiling in dogfights. The bed was empty. He started to enter the room, then stopped as he was gripped by more cramps.

He leaned against the door frame and shivered.

Getting worse! What'm I gonna do?

Gonna crap my pants . . .

Turning around, he saw the doorway of an upstairs bathroom only a few feet away. He hurried over to it, slapped the light switch, rushed to the toilet, jerked his jeans down and dropped onto the seat just in time.

After the explosive diarrhea, he felt much better.

He wiped his rear end. Then he wiped the sweat off his face. Then he stayed on the toilet and wondered whether to flush.

Better wait. If I flush and somebody's in the house, I'll be up Shit Creek.

He pulled up his jeans and fastened them. After washing his hands at the sink, he resumed his search of the house.

There were two more bedrooms. One seemed to be a guest room, the other the master bedroom. Albert found nobody in either of them, so he returned to the bathroom, flushed the toilet, and sprayed the area with pine scented air freshener.

Then he went into the boy's bedroom. Using his penlight, he checked the cluttered top of the dresser. No money. He went through the drawers. He scanned shelves that were loaded with books, model ships, and Indian souvenirs: a tom-tom, a miniature teepee, a headdress full of colorful feathers, a tomahawk with a rubber head.

He picked up the tomahawk.

Too bad it isn't real.

On its handle was printed, WISCONSIN DELLS—VACATION WONDERLAND.

Albert put down the tomahawk and continued his search.

He found an ashtray filled with foreign coins, but no other money.

On the bedstand, beside an empty drinking glass, was a Boy Scout sheath knife.

All right!

Keeping it, he went to the desk. The pencil holder held pencils, a gum eraser, an old crayon, and two pennies. He gave the top drawer a tug. Locked.

"What have we here?" he whispered.

Using the Boy Scout knife, he pried open the drawer and found a tattered copy of *Playboy*. He set the knife aside and pulled out the magazine. It was the September, 1973 issue. On its cover, a naked gal was crouching. Her right breast actually showed. Even her nipple.

Hands trembling, Albert flipped through the magazine. Miss September was a great-looking blonde.

Wow!

He searched the small print for her name: Geri Glass.

He started to grow hard, staring at Geri's photos.

I'll take this with me, he thought. The little Boy Scout shouldn't have a nasty magazine like this, anyway. I'll be doing him a favor.

Chuckling softly, Albert left Geri behind and searched the magazine for more treasures.

Near the back, he found an article about a movie called *The Naked Ape.* It had a photo of Johnny Crawford stark naked.

The kid from The Rifleman*?*

Holy shit, that's him, all right! And you can see his peter!

Not interested in *any* guy's peter, Albert moved on and found that the article had a pretty good layout on the movie's other star, a brunette named Victoria Principal.

Not bad, he thought.

But he liked Miss September better. Something about Miss September really got to him.

He flipped back to the center section and gazed at her, then shut the magazine and slipped it under his arm.

He resumed his search by trying another desk drawer. This one wasn't locked. Inside, he found flat tubes of model airplane glue, bottles of paint, a few instruction sheets and an assortment of spare airplane parts.

The third drawer was a catchall: it had caught just about everything except money. But in the bottom drawer, Albert came upon a tobacco tin. He shook it and grinned.

Inside were eight dollars.

That'll do it! That'll put me over the top for Betty!

"Thank you, kid," he whispered. "Wherever you are."

With eight dollar bills in his pocket, the sheathed knife in his hand and the *Playboy* under one arm, he stepped into the hallway and headed for the master bedroom.

That's when he heard a thump and rumble.

Familiar sounds, but he couldn't quite . . .

The garage door was opening!

His heart jumped with fright.

He rushed to the guest room and knelt beside one of the twin beds.

A door thudded. Then another.

The bed was too low. Just as well. They made great hiding places because adults never looked under them, but he always felt trapped under beds. Flat on his belly. The box springs pressing against his back. No room to turn. No way to get out fast. Under beds, he had to fight off panic. Especially after the night his mother was killed just above him and the blood kept dripping onto the toe of her slipper just inches from his face. It had been exciting but awful, and he had rarely hidden under beds after that.

From downstairs came quiet sounds of voices.

And footsteps.

Albert got up. He tiptoed to the closet. Then he pushed back the sliding door, stepped inside the closet and slid the door shut.

Wire hangers pinged together when he hit them with his head. To free a hand, he pushed the blade of the boy's sheath knife under his belt. Then he reached out to the side. His fingers pushed against flimsy plastic. He edged his foot sideways. It stopped against a box.

Better not try burrowing in, he thought. Too much other stuff.

Even if he could manage to hide himself more deeply in the closet, it would only make getting out more difficult.

And he might have to get out fast.

More sounds of footsteps. Voices.

One was a woman's voice. He supposed it probably belonged to Mrs. Broxton, but he couldn't be sure. After all, he'd only heard her speak a few words at the Safeway that morning. He couldn't quite make out what she was saying, either.

The man's voice was smooth. He laughed at something.

From the sounds, Albert supposed the man and woman were climbing the stairs.

He knelt down to keep his head from knocking against empty hangers.

Now they seemed to be coming up the hall. In a few more seconds, they would be entering the master bedroom.

Wait till they're in there, Albert thought, then get the hell outta this place.

Or stay and try to watch them?

That wouldn't be very smart, he told himself.

Might be worth the risk.

He'd never actually watched anything like that. But he'd always *wanted* to.

The bottom edge of his closet door lit up.

What? This is the guest room! What're they doing in here?

On the other side of the closet door, there was a long silence. Then came a moan from the woman. "You don't mind, do you?" she asked.

"No, it's fine," said the man. "Who needs all that room, anyway?"

"This might not be as comfortable, but I'll feel so much better. I just wouldn't feel quite right in there."

"Hey, don't worry about it. I don't care which bed, I only care which woman."

There was another long silence. Albert wondered if they were kissing.

"You're my first Boy Scout widow," the man said. They both laughed. "I always knew there was a lot to be said for campouts."

"Shush."

More silence.

"I'll be right back," the woman said.

"Going to get into something more comfortable, I presume?"

She laughed softly. "How did you know?"

"I'm psychic."

"I won't be long."

"I'll be waiting."

Albert heard her leave the room. Then he heard the man walking on the carpeted floor.

Coming closer.

He slid the knife out of its leather sheath.

Closer.

What's he gonna do, hang up his clothes?

The door slid open, flooding the closet with light.

Albert crouched in the shadow of the man, who was holding a blue sports coat in one hand. As he reached for a hanger with his other hand, he let out a quiet gasp.

He stared down at Albert with shocked eyes.

Albert slashed.

The man sucked in a quick breath and stumbled backward, grabbing his gashed thigh. Blood pumped through the cracks between his fingers. He dropped to the floor. Gasping and squirming, he clutched his wound with both hands.

Keeping the *Playboy* clamped tight against his left side, Albert crouched over him and slit his throat.

"Charles, what's going . . . ?" Mrs. Broxton came in from the hall. As she stopped in the doorway, her eyes leaped from the crumpled body to Albert. *"You!"* she gasped. Then her back hunched. She spun around and ran.

Albert dropped the magazine and raced after her.

Halfway down the hall, he got close enough to drag the knife down her back. The blade split her slip open to her waist—her slip and the skin beneath it. Crying out, she fell.

Albert clenched the knife between his teeth. Grabbing her ankles, he twisted until she flipped over onto her back.

When he tore away her underpants, she moaned and covered herself.

"Move your hands."

"Don't," she gasped. "Please."

"Move 'em or I'll kill you."

She shook her head and didn't move her hands.

Albert took the knife from his mouth. "Think I'm kidding?" he asked.

Before she could answer or take her hands away, Albert pounded the knife deep into her belly.

She grunted, sat halfway up, and fell back.

Albert slipped the blade out and shoved it in again, sliding it into the same slit, shoving it deep.

Convulsions jerked her body.

He pulled out the knife.

She had a raw, vertical split just below her naval. It was three inches long and pumping blood.

She no longer struggled, just lay there sprawled out, sobbing and groaning.

Albert crouched down and slit open the front of her slip. He spread it, exposing her breasts. They were smaller than Betty's.

More like Miss September's.

"Nice tits, Mrs. Broxton," he said.

He watched them rise and fall as she sobbed.

Cupping one of her breasts with a bloody hand, he felt

its nipple push against his palm. He squeezed the breast. The blood made it slippery.

His penis was stout and aching in his jeans.

Holding the knife in his teeth, he pulled his zipper down and freed himself.

EIGHT

THE REQUEST

The roar of his Jaguar still rang in Ian's ears after he was inside his dark house. He stepped cautiously through the kitchen. Once in the living room with its glassed-in side facing the backyard and pool, he could see well enough to avoid collisions.

For a moment, he considered going outside and sitting quietly in the fog.

Enough time for that later.

He went into his study and turned on a light. It took a few seconds for his eyes to adjust to the sharp brightness. Then he moved them slowly over the desk, the file cabinets, the card table, the two television trays, and the chair and lamp table in the corner. "It's gotta be somewhere," he said.

A simple matter of spending the rest of the night searching through clutter.

What he should do is spend a while thinking.

He went to the easy chair, cleared its seat of three thick file folders, and sat down.

Now, reconstruct it. When was the last time you talked to him? Monday, from the faculty lounge. No, he called me. Wednesday? I phoned him Wednesday from here. From where exactly? The desk.

Ian walked to the desk. The telephone didn't seem to be on it. He stepped behind the desk and rolled the swivel chair back to the wall. There, on the floor, was the telephone. But not flat on the floor.

A frayed, black corner of his address book protruded from beneath it.

The phone bumped the floor and jingled once as he pulled out the book.

The index card with Arnie Barrington's phone number jutted like a bookmark from the top of the address book.

Ian glanced at his wristwatch. One-fifteen. That made it four-fifteen in New York.

Much too late.

Or too early.

He propped up the card on the carriage of his typewriter and headed for bed.

But sleep wouldn't come. He lay there looking at the darkness, thinking of Emily Jean who felt she had wasted her life and of Laura who never got the chance.

Laura.

My God, was it really seven years? Had he actually survived so long without her?

He told himself to change the subject.

He thought about his work and became calm and sleep finally came.

When Ian woke up Sunday morning, he folded his hands behind his head and took a deep breath. The cool air smelled of autumn. How does autumn air smell? Of burning leaves. But there was no aroma of burning leaves, so what made him think of autumn air?

Simply because he knew it was October? Or because he planned to see a football game at City College after lunch?

It had to be more than that.

The air had a silence to it. And a sadness. It had a quiet, mildly disturbing quality of loss. But of excitement, too.

Laura would have smiled and said, "You're loony. California's got no seasons."

She didn't last long enough to find out about them.

Ian glanced at the empty side of his bed. Then he got up fast and put on his old flannel robe. On the dresser, he found the notepad that he'd taken with him to last night's social committee meeting. He carried it into the study.

8:45. In New York, it would almost be noon.

Arnie oughta be up by now.

Ian picked the index card off the carriage of his typewriter and dialed Arnie's suite.

He let the phone ring ten times.

Nobody answered.

Come on, Arnie, where are you? It's Sunday morning, you oughta be lounging around in your suite.

After swimming, Ian dressed and sat down at his desk with a cup of coffee. He wrote three pages of his novel. Then he fixed himself a Bloody Mary and dialed Arnie's suite again.

The phone rang twice before it was picked up.

A nasal, male voice recited, "Arnold Barrington Associates."

This obviously wasn't Arnie's secretary, Bernice.

Of course not, Ian thought. It's Sunday. This must be Arnie's current boyfriend.

"I'd like to speak with Arnie."

"And who may I say is calling?"

"Ian Collins."

"Oh, *Ian!* Evan Chandler, I presume?"

"That's right."

"Oh, it's such a pleasure to finally *speak* to you. I simply *adore* your novels. They're so *hunky*. And *Some Call it Sleep!* What can I say? A marvelous book. I do hope the film does it justice."

"Well, it better. Arnie and I are co-producers, so it'll be our fault if the thing stinks."

"I'm sure it'll be absolutely wonderful. I'm Dennis, by the by."

"How you doing, Dennis?"

"Oh, I'm just *super*. You've absolutely *made* my Sunday morning. But I'm sure you don't want to spend all day chit-chatting with little ol' me. I'll call Arnie to the phone. Hang on just a sec. Don't go away."

"Sure. Thanks."

He sipped his Bloody Mary. It needed more Tabasco.

Dennis's voice returned. "Arnie will be right along."

"Thanks, Dennis."

"Anywho, it's been *splendid* talking to you. I'm *such* a fan. And I'm *so* looking forward to meeting you in the flesh, so to speak. We'll *all* be at the premiere, of course."

"Yeah. Probably see you then."

"Here's the man himself. *Ciao*, Ian."

"So long, Dennis."

"Ian?" Arnie said.

"Hi, Arnie. Sorry to bother you on a Sunday."

"You're never a bother, my friend. How are things in sunny Los Angeles?"

"Nice and sunny."

"Oh, sometimes I could die of envy."

"You'd probably die of boredom if you ever stepped out of New York City."

"You're so right, you know. I think I would shrivel up and blow away if I were exiled from this place. Of course, I have no intention of that happening. What can I do for you?"

"I've got a big favor to ask."

"And should I grant it, will you do me the favor of abandoning your foolhardy obsession with the bending of young minds—and *write* full-time?"

"But I *enjoy* bending young minds," he said.

"We'd be able to *double* your income, you know."

"So you keep telling me. But I think I'll stick with teaching. At least for now."

"It's selfish, you know. Your public *hungers* for more books."

"They'll just have to be patient."

"Don't think I don't *know* why you insist on staying in the classroom."

He doesn't know, Ian thought. He can't possibly know.

"You simply can't bear to tear yourself away from all those nubile young maidens."

Ian chuckled. "That's certainly part of it."

It *is* part of it, he thought. the daily contact with the girls, not just with the nubile young maidens but with *all* of them, the cute and the plain, the sexy and the dumpy, the sweet and the snotty, the smart and the dull. Part of it, too, was the daily contact with the guys: the studious shy ones, the wiseasses, the jocks, the know-it-all jerks, the sneering bullies.

And part of it, too, was his contact with the faculty and staff of the school. There were the secretaries and clerks who generally seemed much more friendly and down-to-earth than the teachers. And there were teachers of every variety: the eager, often-frightened young ones; the dedicated pros; the loafers who spent most of their classroom time showing films; the arrogant pedants; the kid haters; the tired and the surly and the disappointed.

The disappointed, like Emily Jean.

"Are you still there, Ian?"

"Huh? Yeah. Sorry. My mind wandered."

"Daydreaming about your classrooms full of Lolitas?"

"Something like that. Anyway, the reason I called . . ."

"Ah, the favor."

"I'm wondering if you might contact Hal for me. Or give me a number where I can reach him."

"He's already on location in Denver, you know."

"Yeah, I thought he might be. Do you have a number for him?"

"Well, of *course* I do. We talk *daily*."

"Ah, good. Next time you talk to him, could you mention that there's a young actress I think might be perfect for the role of Lilly?"

"One of your Lolitas?"

Ian smiled. "I don't *have* any Lolitas, and you know it."

"More's the pity."

"Her name is May Beth Bonner. She's the daughter of a friend. She's a slim, very attractive redhead, early twenties. She *is* Lilly."

"But can she act?"

"I imagine so. She just finished a run of *The Glass Menagerie* at the Stage Door Theater here in L.A."

"Hal *has* been having a difficult time finding an appropriate Lilly."

"Well, why don't you let him know about May Beth? If he's interested, he can give her a call." Ian read the number from his notepad.

"Got it," Arnie said. "You do realize we begin principal photography at the end of the week."

"I know. But I'd like to see her get a break, if it's possible. I'd *really* like to see her get the role."

"I'll talk to Hal about it. We'll see what we can do."

"Real good."

"I can't guarantee anything."

"I understand that. Just do what you can."

"Will do. Now, how's the new novel coming along?"

NINE

THE BIG GAME

Lester didn't want to go to the City College football game. He wanted to spend his Sunday afternoon at home watching the Rams on television. He told that to Helen.

"I thought you were a big fan of Buster Johnson," she said. It sounded like an accusation.

"Who?"

"Buster Johnson. The quarterback you thought was so great last year."

"We didn't go to any College games last year."

"He wasn't *at* College last year." She didn't finish her statement with, "you stupid idiot." She didn't have to. The clipped impatience of her voice said it for her. "He was at High School."

"One of your students?"

Helen nodded.

"Isn't everyone," Lester said.

"Not everyone."

"Everyone who counts."

"Do you want to go to the game or not? Buster's first-string quarterback."

"I'd rather stay here and see the Rams."

"Do whatever you want," Helen said. "I'm going to the game."

"That figures."

He watched her put on the brown sweater he'd given her for Christmas last year.

"If you're coming," she said, "you'd better get your shoes on."

"I'm coming," he muttered. He stepped into his loafers, found a sweater and walked out to the car behind Helen.

"Are you driving?" she asked. "Or do you want me to?"

"I'll drive."

He drove, but he didn't talk. His stomach felt sick with emptiness, an ache that food couldn't cure. Maybe nothing could cure it. Helen had taken something from him. He didn't know for sure what it was, but he needed it back.

Helen reached forward and turned up the radio's volume. The music was John Denver singing, "Goodbye, Again."

Lester wasn't sure why, but he almost felt like crying.

Janet and Meg arrived at the City College football stadium in plenty of time to find good seats near the fifty yard line.

"Do you come to these games very often?" Janet asked.

"I come to them all. My duty, you might say. I know

everybody and they expect to see me. I know most of the players and all the faculty and all the administrators. Et cetera, et cetera. How would you like to hear the first eight bars of 'Getting to Know You'?"

"Oh, I'd love it. Maybe they'll let you use the public address system. You can do the national anthem as your encore."

"There's a thought."

"If you're good enough, they might even forget the game entirely. We could have an open air Meg Haycraft concert."

"Wouldn't that be great? Fantastic publicity for the student store."

"It might go to your head."

"As long as it doesn't go to my rear end. That's where everything *else* goes." She bounced on the seat. "Come the fourth quarter, though, I'm always glad to have the extra padding. The bleachers get mighty hard. I pity all those skinny-ass babes who haven't got anything to sit on but their butt bones."

"You mean like me?" Janet shifted her weight, trying to get more comfortable. "I should've brought my . . ." She stopped and thought about the foam-rubber pad that she always took with her to U.S.C. games. It was propped on a shelf in Dave's apartment.

"Your what?"

"I used to . . ." Her throat tightened. She turned away.

"Hey, hey, cheer up! What've you got to be so down about? Smile!"

"Sure," Janet said, and smiled for a moment. She couldn't hold it, though. Shaking her head in frustration, she said, "Sorry. Sometimes, you know, it just hits me. No more Dave. Like he died, or something. I go along feeling just fine, then bam! No more Dave."

"If you miss him, go back. Nobody's holding a gun to your head."

"Just to my baby's."

"Oooo."

Janet tried to smile, but couldn't.

"If I were in your shoes," Meg said, "I'd go back to him so fast my head would swim."

"You can't stand him."

"I know." She unwrapped a stick of chewing gum, folded it into thirds, and tossed it into her mouth. "He's everything I despise in a man." She chewed the gum, scowling. "But I'd go back to him, anyway."

"Sure you would," Janet said. "Back to the creep, the asshole?"

"In fact, truth is, I never would have left him in the first place. You see, hon, he's a man. He's everything I despise, but he *is* a man. In case you haven't noticed, *I'm* what's called a 'dog.' As the old saying goes, 'Bow-wows can't be choosers.' "

"You're not . . ."

"Don't try to tell me I'm not a dog. I've seen mirrors. Shoot, my face *breaks* mirrors. I used to trick-or-treat without a mask." She laughed and snapped her gum. "Always went as a troll."

"Hey, come on, don't put yourself down like that."

The smile left Meg's face. "The point is, hon, a gal might be glad to have a shit like Dave *if* she didn't stand a chance in hell of doing better. But you're no dog. Far from it. Fact is, you're a fox. So be glad you're rid of that turd and get yourself someone better. You can do a *lot* better."

Ian waited for "The Star-Spangled Banner" to end before heading toward the seats above the fifty yard line. He rarely had a difficult time finding one seat, even in crowded theaters and stadiums; most people tried to keep one open between themselves and whatever strangers were sitting nearby.

He nodded a greeting to Lester and Helen Bryant, several rows higher. They waved. Neither looked very happy.

"Is anybody sitting there?" he called down one of the rows. The people on either side of a vacant space looked at each other and shook their heads.

"It's empty," one of them called.

Ian sidestepped down the row. Just as he reached his seat, the cheerleaders on the track below flung up their arms and yelled, "Everybody up for the kickoff!"

Meg nudged Janet with her elbow, silently mouthed, "Look at *that* guy," and wiggled her heavy eyebrows in a way intended to appear lecherous.

Janet didn't need the signals. She had already seen him. He was about thirty, tall and slow-moving, with wind-blown hair that was shorter than most men wore. His face had a calm, confident look.

"Will you get a load of those dreamy eyes?" Meg whispered.

"Dreamy?" Janet laughed.

She didn't watch the kickoff. She watched the man and wondered who he was.

He sat down directly in front of Meg.

The second cheerleader from the end had a way of walking that made Lester feel sad. Mostly, she skipped or did bouncy sidesteps facing the crowd. But when she walked, she took long strides and swung her arms high with the joy of moving.

Nikki used to walk that way.

Nikki had been a great one for walking. During the five months Lester went with her, they had walked every-where together: to classes, to the student union, to movie theaters and coffee shops, through the park. The park most of all.

In the park, they always walked slowly and held hands.

They sat on swings in the sunlight, swaying just slightly as they talked. Or they perched atop the monkey bars. Or on fallen tree trunks by the stream. Some afternoons,

Nikki sat against the birch on the slope above the river and he lay there with his head on her lap, smoking his pipe.

Several times, they made love in the park at night. The grass was nearly always wet. Except when there was rain, he spread out his topcoat for a blanket. On rainy nights, he covered them with it. Nikki always liked making love in the rain. Afterwards, her face was cool and wet and she would be smiling and holding out her tongue to catch the drops.

He glanced at Helen.

"Something wrong?" she asked.

"What could be wrong?" he said.

Helen turned away.

The cheerleader, bowing down and tiptoeing backward as she thrust out her open hands, was shouting, "Push 'em back, push 'em back, waaaaay back!"

Twice, he'd had sex with Helen in the park. Then she had complained that the nights were too cold, the grass too wet, the ground too hard. Besides, someone might come along and see them. Why not go somewhere safe and comfortable like a motel?

It was all right with Lester.

He'd never liked the park much, anyway, after Nikki left him for that minister.

He'd never again liked a *lot* of things so much.

Helen suddenly jumped up and waved. "Charles, over here!"

A boy with curly brown hair and a mustache waved back.

"Another former student?" Lester asked.

She gestured for the boy to join her, then said, "You've heard me speak of Charles. Charles Perris. He's in my X-L class. Remember the Halloween party last year? Emily Jean was telling us about him."

"I don't remember."

"The poet," she explained as Charles made his way toward them. "He won second prize in the state poetry contest?"

"I still don't recall, but consider me impressed."

"Go to hell."

"A poet, huh?" He huffed out a laugh.

Helen looked at him with contempt and said, "Why don't you try acting your age?"

"He looks like a queer if you ask me," Lester said and smiled at the approaching boy. He tried to make his smile look friendly when Helen introduced him. "How are you?" he said, and offered his hand.

"Just fine, thank you." The boy's grip was firm, not the feeble touch that Lester expected. "And you?"

"Pretty good."

Charles sat down on the other side of Helen. They talked and laughed through most of the football game. Lester tried to ignore them.

When the game ended, Charles shook Lester's hand and said, "I enjoyed meeting you, sir."

"Enjoyed meeting you, too."

"Guess I'd better be off."

Helen patted Charles on the back and said things to him that Lester couldn't hear. The kid blushed and smiled. Then he wandered off into the crowd.

"I could use a stiff drink," Meg said. "How about you?"

"Sounds fine by me," said Janet. She fastened her seat belt as Meg backed out of the parking space.

"Let's have it—them—at my place. Then we'll go hunting."

"Hunting for what?"

"Men, of course."

"On a Sunday night?"

"You'd rather go to a prayer meeting?"

"I'd rather stay home and read a good book."

"Do that, you might end up old and alone and desperate."

"I'll take my chances."

"It's your life, hon. We sure as shootin' whupped those bums, didn't we?"

It took a moment for Janet to realize that Meg was suddenly talking about the game. "Sure did."

"But you know what we didn't do?"

"I know."

"Well, you'd rather read books anyway."

"Maybe not *all* the time."

"One of us," Meg said, "should have nailed the guy with a knee."

"That would've impressed him."

"Or spilled a Coke down his back."

"Better yet," Janet added, "you or I should've tapped him on the shoulder and said, 'Excuse me, but I couldn't help noticing your dreamy eyes.'"

"Oh, rich!" Meg blurted. "That would've been rich!"

Home from the game, Ian fixed himself a vodka gimlet and sat outside on a folding chair by his pool. The sun was blocked by palm trees. A cool breeze wrinkled the water and raised goose bumps on his bare arms.

There was no smell of burning leaves.

TEN

THE LIFT

"You got a whole life in front of you for seeing the world, Billy. A whole life." The scrawny old man used his tongue to shift the cigar stub to the other side of his mouth. The glowing tip jostled and half an inch of ash dropped onto his lap. He didn't seem to notice. "Take it from a guy that knows," he continued. "Not that I've done poorly by myself, 'cause I haven't. But I'm not a fella that kids himself. I'm a fella that could've done a damn sight better in life if I'd had myself a sheepskin."

"You coulda been a contenduh?" Albert asked.

"Huh?"

"You know. *On the Waterfront.*"

"Yeah, whatever."

Albert looked out the cracked passenger window of the man's car. The telephone poles stood out clearly against the Illinois night, but he could barely make out the cornfields. The fields just looked flat and empty and dark.

"If I was in your shoes, Billy, I'd make sure and get me that sheepskin. I'd say, 'Thanks for the lift, Milton, but you better just let me off here.' Then I'd hightail it back home."

That's what Albert had done before dawn that morning: hightailed it home. After getting done with Mrs. Broxton.

He had run down the stairs two at a time and rushed out the front door. His bike was just where he'd left it lying on the next-door neighbor's lawn. He'd grabbed the handlebars and swung the bike over the curb with such force that it almost flew from his hands. Then, all that pedalling. And all that wind. The wind had made the bloody front of his turtleneck turn cold.

He should have changed clothes *before* leaving the Broxton house. Borrowed some from the father or son. If he'd done that, he wouldn't have needed to hightail it home to change. But the idea of taking clothes from the Broxtons occurred to him too late. By that time, he was already halfway home and couldn't bring himself to turn back.

Leaving his bike hidden in bushes near the side of his house, he'd gone into the garage. It was warm and stuffy in the garage, and far darker than the night outside. His breath had trembled as he undressed. Standing only in his socks, he'd rolled his clothes into a tight ball and stuffed them into a duffle bag beside the workbench. The bag was already full of old rags. He'd pulled a few out, used them to cover his stained clothes, then clipped the bag shut.

The garage was too dark, so he'd opened the side door to let in more light. There still wasn't much, but enough came through the doorway for him to spot the irregular shading of his chest and belly. Must be blood.

"Well?" Milton asked, interrupting Albert's thoughts.

"What?"

"Don't you think I better let you out so you can head on back home 'n finish your education?"

"I'd rather stay with you."

"Can't see why."

"I can't go back home. Ever. Nothing could make me go back there."

"Get into some trouble with your folks?"

"I just live with my father," Albert said. "He's a drunk. And nuts. He gets himself chased around the house by the Angel of Death, and he's always beating up on me."

"That don't sound too good," Milton allowed.

"He even locked me up in the tool shed behind the house. I was in there for two weeks and I nearly starved to death, but finally I dug my way out and escaped."

"Is that so?"

"That's so," Albert said.

"If it *is* so, I'd say you oughta bring the *law* down on your old man."

"He said he'd kill me if I ever told. I shouldn't have told *you*. You won't tell on me, will you?"

"Well, I don't reckon."

"Thanks, Milton. You're a godsend."

"I try to do what I can to follow the Lord's way."

"Bless you," Albert said.

Milton nodded, leaned a little closer to the steering wheel, and scowled out at the empty road ahead.

Closing his eyes, Albert returned to his memories of the early morning hours. Where was I? he wondered.

In the garage.

He'd just hidden his clothes in the duffle bag.

I'm naked and bloody.

He brought up an image of himself leaving the garage and sneaking across his back lawn. The wind was strong. It made the moonlight sifting down through the elm leaves dance wildly on the grass. It mussed his long hair. It swept between his legs and touched him like a woman's cold fingers and made him stiff again.

The water that streamed from the hose was cold. It splashed against his chest and ran down his belly. With his spare hand, he rubbed his body everywhere.

After turning off the hose, he rushed to the warm shelter of the garage and shut the door. He put on his socks and shoes. Then, very slowly and silently, he left the garage again, crept into the house and made his way up to his room. There, he put on a clean shirt and jeans. He took his yellow parka off a hanger and found his folding Buck knife.

He slid the loop of the knife's black calfskin case onto his belt. The weight of it felt good at his side. He stuffed a second knife, his switchblade, down a front pocket of his jeans. Then he zipped up his parka and tiptoed downstairs.

He pedalled southward on his bicycle until the sun came up. The sunlight showed that his hands were faintly stained the color of rust.

The first two gas stations had no customers, so he wheeled past them and didn't stop until he came to one where a pickup truck was parked beside the pumps. The attendant was busy talking to its driver.

In the restroom, Albert washed his hands and forearms clean with grainy soap. He opened his shirt. More ruddy stains. The garden hose had taken care of the worst of the blood, but a subtle red-brown mottling remained.

It would have to wait. Nobody could see it, anyway, if he kept his shirt buttoned up.

He climbed onto his bike and headed for the road.

The bike would soon become a problem, but not for a while. Not until his father got out of bed and discovered it was gone. On Sundays, he never moved before ten. Give him an hour to get worried. Then he might call the cops and report Albert missing. Might or might not, the bastard.

At eleven o'clock, Albert ditched his bike just to be on the safe side. Once rid of it, he walked for nearly an hour.

At an A & W, he had a root beer, a cheeseburger and fries. It was nearly two o'clock in the afternoon before Milton stopped to give him a lift.

"Hungry?" Milton broke in, and flicked his cigar out the window. Its red tip trailed sparks through the night.

"I'm starved," Albert said.

"Sign we just passed says Litchfield's just up ahead. We can stop . . ."

"A hitchhiker!" Albert blurted.

She was only lit for a moment. Before the headlights left her in darkness, Albert saw that she was walking backward, her thumb out. She seemed to be about sixteen, slender and blonde. She wore an Indian headband, a big loose shirt that wasn't tucked in, and jeans.

"Give her a lift, Milton."

"Not much chance of that."

"Why not?"

"One thing you learn, Billy, you never pick up a hitcher of the fair sex."

"Come on, go back and get her. This road's really deserted. She might be standing out there all night."

"Tough titty. I don't stop for gals."

"Why not?"

"I'll tell you why not. You get one in your car and you're at her mercy. At her *mercy*, Billy. She can do whatever weird shenanigans come into her mind. Why, she might even up and decide to blackmail you."

"How can she blackmail anyone?" Albert asked to disguise the sound of his sheath snap popping open.

"She threatens to say you raped her. Easiest thing in the world. Happens all the time. Her word against yours. And what's more, she can go to the cops and describe you down to a T, your car too, even give 'em your license plate."

The knife was in his lap now, hidden under his crossed hands. "Are you talking from experience?" he asked.

"You betcha."

With a swift pull, the blade hinged open and locked upright.

Milton's head snapped sideways. He started to say something, but the point nipped the stubbled flesh beneath his chin. He shut his mouth and tipped his head backward.

"Stop the car," Albert said.

Milton took his foot off the gas pedal. His thin, leathery face was blank. Albert could see only one eye: it glistened with light and kept darting sideways.

"Pull off the road and stop."

Slowly, the car lost speed. Gravel on the road's shoulder crunched under its tires.

When the car stopped, Albert took the ignition key.

"Get out," he said, lowering the knife.

"You gonna leave me here?"

"Open the door and get out."

"Aw, come on, Billy. I mean, I do you a good turn and look what you're giving me back. How'm I gonna get to St. Louis without my car?"

Not answering, Albert prodded him in the side.

Milton opened the door. "Okay, okay! You don't gotta poke me." He climbed out.

Albert scooted across the seat and climbed out behind him.

"Last time I do a fella a good turn, you can bet your bottom dollar on that."

"Bet it is," Albert said.

Milton in the lead, they walked past the front of the car.

"It just don't pay to be nice anymore."

"Guess not," Albert said. "You can stop here."

They stopped a few paces past the front of Milton's car.

Turning to face Albert, Milton said, "Tell you what, I'll pick up that gal for you. That hitchhiker gal. Okay? How's that? I got no problem with that."

"You'd be in the way," Albert told him.

Then he slashed through the side of Milton's neck. With a quick jump to the left, he dodged the spurting blood.

Headlights appeared down the road. Far off. But how far? The road was as straight as a ruled line, so it might be a mile or more.

Or maybe a lot less.

Albert looked at Milton. The old man was down on his hands and knees, the white headbeams of his car skimming across his back.

The cut was in darkness, but Albert could hear the blood splashing on the dirt and gravel.

He reached inside the car and killed the headlights. Then he hurried to the front. Bending over, he grabbed Milton's ankles. He tugged them and Milton flopped flat.

Then he dragged the old man to the edge of the roadside drainage ditch and shoved him with his foot.

Milton tumbled down the steep slope.

Being careful not to lose his footing, Albert followed him.

At the bottom of the ditch, he crouched by Milton's side.

The guy was sprawled face down, silent and motionless.

Dead yet? Albert wondered.

He pounded his knife into Milton's back.

The first couple of times, Milton grunted. After that, he was quiet.

The stabbing didn't excite Albert very much, so he stopped after five or six times.

As he waited for the car to pass, he went through Milton's pockets. He found a stiff, wadded handkerchief, a comb, a rabbit's foot, two books of matches, a few coins, a wallet with eighteen dollars and a gasoline credit card, and another wallet. The second wallet, made of flimsy plastic, contained eighty dollars in traveler's checks.

Up on the road, the car sped by without slowing.

Albert waited until its sound was faint with distance, then rushed up the slope to Milton's car. He did a quick U-turn and headed up the road.

His heart raced as he thought about the girl.

She'd looked really cute.

It had only been a glimpse, of course. Maybe she was a dog if you got a good look at her.

Nah, I bet she's cute.

Find out pretty soon.

Albert imagined stripping her naked, then plunging his knife into her belly, watching the blood gush out, spreading the gash wide . . .

But five miles later, he realized that she was gone.

Maybe that other car . . .

Okay, Albert thought. No big deal. I'll just have to find someone else.

The world's full of women.

ELEVEN

RETURN TO DAVE'S

Janet woke up and stretched, enjoying the smooth warmth of the sheets next to her skin. She felt chilly air on her bare shoulders and neck. Under the covers, though, she was warm and cozy.

She felt good. This morning, there was no nausea.

Sleepily, she reached a hand sideways. She expected to find Dave's bare chest. Instead, her hand found only the edge of the mattress.

She was in a single bed.

Opening her eyes, she realized that she was in Meg's guest room.

Monday morning? Must be.

Her second morning without Dave.

Thinking of him, Janet's throat constricted. She tried to swallow the tightness away. He's nothing to cry about, she told herself. Don't cry. He's not worth it, not worth a damn . . .

Except that she had been in love with him and she had lived in his apartment and slept with him every night for three months and woke up in bed with him every morning. Every morning, she would find him there beside her, naked and warm, and they would snuggle and sometimes—often— they would end up making love.

Never again, she thought.

It's over. All over.

I don't want to *see* him again, much less *touch* him, *much* less make love with him.

Janet used the edge of the sheet to wipe her eyes. Then she took a deep, shaky breath.

Forget the bastard.

Watch who you're calling a bastard.

Smiling slightly, she touched her belly. It was smooth and warm and flat. "Howdy in there," she whispered. "Your daddy wants to kill you, but I'm not gonna let him."

She suddenly felt guilty for saying such a thing out loud. She patted her belly. "Can you hear me in there?"

Nothing.

"Blink once for yes, twice for no."

Janet laughed.

"That's from *The Count of Monte Cristo*, honey. Your mother's a bookworm. Just for the record."

She sat up, letting the blankets and sheet fall across her lap. The bedroom door was open a few inches, but she heard no sounds of activity from the rest of the house.

Meg had probably already left for work.

Janet swung the covers away and climbed off the bed. Naked and shivering, she hurried over to the chair where Meg had left a robe for her to wear. A big, pink, quilted robe. She put it on. The fabric felt slick like satin. At first, if was cool against her bare skin. Then it took on her body heat and felt fine.

In the kitchen, the coffee pot was still plugged in. She poured herself a cup, took it into the living room, and sat down on the couch.

On today's agenda was a return to Dave's apartment for her belongings.

Not gonna be fun, she thought. But it has to be done.

Not just now.

On the coffee table in front of her was the *Los Angeles Times*. First, she read *Peanuts*.

Always good to start the morning with Snoopy.

Unfortunately, this morning's strip was about Lucy and Linus. Snoopy made no appearance at all.

Janet began reading the rest of the paper. By the time she was finished with the first section, her cup was empty. She filled it, returned to the couch, and started reading the second part.

An article near the bottom of the page was headed, STABBING DEATHS STUN CHICAGO SUBURB. She read the article. When she finished it, she took another sip of coffee and read about a man who was killed when his car stalled on railroad tracks.

By the time she was done with Section Two, her cup was empty again. "Better get the show on the road," she muttered.

Then she sat for a while and stared at the floor.

God, I don't want to do this!

It was eleven o'clock by the time she stopped her Ford at the curb in front of the apartment house. On the radio, Jim Croce was singing, "Time in a Bottle." It almost made her want to cry. She listened until it ended, then turned off the engine and the radio died.

For a few moments, she sat without moving.

She glanced at Dave's space in the carport. Empty.

Okay, what am I waiting for?

She climbed out of her car.

In the building's foyer, her eyes turned by habit toward the mail trough and the row of boxes. The mailman hadn't arrived yet. He was about due, though.

It all felt so familiar: hurrying up the stairs, walking

along the dim hallway with the floor springy under foot, stopping in front of apartment 230 while she fumbled for the key. Often, she had needed to set down bags of groceries while she unlocked the door. But not today. No more of that.

She opened the door, stepped inside, and closed it silently. Then she fit the guard chain into its slot.

"Is that in case *I* drop by?"

She flinched. Then she rested her forehead against the door. "What are you doing here?"

"I live here."

"You're supposed to be at work."

"I took the day off."

"Where's your car?"

"Around the block." He chuckled.

"You know what?" Janet said quietly. "It sounds like you set a trap for me."

"Sure I did, but you baited it. I noticed how careful you were to tell me you'd be coming here this morning to pick up your things. It was obvious you wanted me to be here."

"Obvious to you, maybe. It didn't enter my mind."

"How's the view?"

"Just fine," she muttered, eyes on the door an inch away.

"I've always had a fancy for doorknobs, myself."

"Very witty."

His tone became serious as he said, "Do you realize, Janet, how foolishly you've been behaving?"

She heard him approach.

"Don't touch me," she warned.

"A baby is an enormous responsibility. At this time, I don't feel that I—that *either* of us—is emotionally equipped to meet that responsibility." He put his hands on her shoulders. Janet stiffened under their touch. "Do you understand my concern?"

"I understand. Let go of me."

He rubbed her shoulders gently. "In a year or two, perhaps, if our relationship has developed to a point where we're both willing to make that commitment . . ."

"Shut up," Janet said. Shrugging off his hands, she turned around and looked up at his somber face.

"I'm sure you'll come to realize . . ."

"I'll tell you what I've *already* come to realize," she said. "I realize you don't love me. If you loved me, you wouldn't want to kill our baby. There's nothing else to know."

He frowned, then walked to the dresser and took a pipe off its rack. "And how do you define this 'love'?"

"Please, I wish you'd go. I want to get my things and leave."

"First tell me what you mean by 'love.' "

"Please?"

He smiled nonchalantly and started to fill his pipe. "Do you mean, by 'love,' a mutually satisfying relationship? One that fulfills the needs of both parties?"

"Boy, you're being suave this morning. I know your Hugh Hefner routine really wows the gals, but I'm in no mood so why don't you drop it?"

His eyes were amused. "Tell me exactly what you mean by 'love.' "

She leaned back against the door and folded her arms across her gray sweatshirt and said nothing.

Dave lit his pipe. "Trust? Is trust a part of this thing you call 'love'?"

"I'd like you to leave."

"You broke our trust, didn't you?"

"I what?" she asked, suddenly feeling a hot blush spread over her skin.

"You broke our trust, our understanding that you'd be careful. You broke *that* trust, didn't you?"

"I *was* careful."

"You *accidently* lost track of your period?"

"*You're* the one who wouldn't wear condoms."

"Because I *trusted* you to know when it'd be safe."

"I tried . . ."

"I think you *wanted* to become pregnant. I think you lost track *on purpose.*"

"I did not," she said.

Did I? she wondered. She'd sometimes gotten *careless,* that's for sure. There'd been times when they'd gone ahead and made love even though she'd known it would be more risky than usual.

But not because I *wanted* to get pregnant, she thought. We got carried away, that's all. Did it because we were too turned on to stop.

Those had been some of the *best* times, too.

Nevermore.

Looking down, Janet said, "I loved you. I thought you loved *me,* too, but I was wrong."

"Were you?" He grinned with the pipe between his teeth.

"I think that's pretty obvious now," she said.

"Is it?"

"Cut it out."

"Maybe I still love you *in spite of* your betrayal."

"I didn't betray you."

"You got pregnant."

"If you loved me, you wouldn't call it a betrayal. So go to hell. I'm having the baby and I'm *done* with you."

"But maybe I'm not done with *you.*" He blew smoke in her face.

Janet waved it away. "You are," she said. "Whether you know it or not." She unhooked the guard chain. "But don't sweat it," she said. "I'm sure you'll have no trouble finding an adequate replacement."

"Maybe I don't want a replacement." He blew more smoke in her face.

"The world is teeming with young women who would leap at the chance of having a mutually satisfying relationship with a man of your charm."

He laughed. "But I want you." He blew more smoke.

Janet slapped the pipe from his mouth. It hit the floor, throwing out ashes and smoldering shreds of tobacco.

Dave picked it up. His foot crushed the smoky pile. "You really should do something," he said, "about these violent tendencies."

Janet opened the door. "Good-bye."

"See you soon, darling."

"Please don't."

"Oh, I will. Count on it."

TWELVE

HAPPY HOUR

Done with work on Monday afternoon, Lester shut the high, oak door of the Doan Library at Blessed Virgin College and locked it. Watching his feet, he descended the front steps and walked along the curving road. He was in no hurry. No big reason for getting home. Helen would just be grading papers or preparing a test.

"Good afternoon, Mr. Bryant."

He recognized the voice and looked up. "Hello, Sister Eunice." He tried to make himself sound cheerful.

"Don't we have a lovely view today? So hazy and golden." She laughed softly. "It's the smog, of course, but isn't it lovely?"

"It's beautiful," Lester said.

"I've always found it a trifle ironic that a filthy poison like smog can look so beautiful when the sun is just right. One of God's little compensations, I suppose. Well, you must be eager to get home. Have a nice evening. Tell your charming wife hello for me."

"I will, Sister. Good night."

He walked down to his car and drove out of the parking lot. The road down the steep hill was narrow. It curved tightly around bends, so tightly that drivers trying to make good time often used both sides of the road. Not Lester, though. He never strayed from his own lane and, to be extra safe, he beeped before each blind curve.

He knew the danger of the road. Three times during his year at Blessed Virgin, there had been head-on collisions.

No, only twice.

He honked and eased his foot off the gas pedal before rounding a bend.

The third accident hadn't been a head-on. The downhill driver had swerved to avoid it—swerved off the road and dived two hundred feet off the hillside. Flames from the wreck had started a brush fire that burned a house. One student had been in that car.

And Sister Joan.

Sister Joan with the clear, green eyes like Nikki.

Lester was picking up too much speed for the next turn.

Suppose I just . . .

Why not? he thought. Why the hell not?

Serve the bitch right.

Which one? Helen or Nikki?

He pressed the brake pedal. The tires sighed against the pavement, holding.

"Both of you," he muttered. "Both of you. Fucking bitches."

Hell if I'll kill myself over a couple of fucking bitches like them.

They aren't the only women in the world.

World's full of women.

Plenty of them would give anything for a guy like me.

Not for the first time, Lester wondered why he was wasting his life with a cold, condescending woman like Helen. She only seemed to care about her career. She *certainly* didn't care about him. He ought to divorce her, get himself free and find a woman who would love him.

I really oughta. Before it's too late.

"Yeah," he said.

And decided to have himself a drink. A margarita.

The Willow Inn had good ones. He remembered them from a visit to the restaurant last spring. They'd met some other couples there for dinner: Ronald and Dale, Mary and her boyfriend . . .

Lester couldn't remember the boyfriend's name. And didn't want to. The guy had been like *all* of Mary's boyfriends: handsome as a fashion model, conceited and boring.

Helen, Ronald, Dale, and Mr. Charming.

The dinner would've been *painful* except for Mary and the margaritas.

Mary, a first-year teacher at Grand Beach High, might not have been the youngest member of the faculty, but she was sure the most beautiful. To Lester, she also seemed a bit shallow for a teacher. (My God, look at the *guys* she dates!) But that night at the Willow Inn, she was stunning with her flowing dark hair, her flashing eyes and wild laughter . . . and the dress she wore with its plunging neckline.

Lester would *never* forget that dress. Or the smooth, tanned tops of Mary's breasts. Or how, now and then during the meal, he'd been able to see all the way down her cleavage to the shadowy underside of one breast.

He'd caught Ronald stealing glances, too.

But not Mr. Charming. That creep probably figured he didn't *have* to peek. Slick operator that he was, he'd be having those babies naked and rubbing his face before the night was over.

Why can't I ever have something like that happen?

Gals like that don't *look* at guys like me.

But I sometimes get to look at *them*, he thought. I saw plenty of Mary that night.

Probably as close as I'll ever get.

Too bad she wasn't on the social committee.

But I bet she'll be at the Halloween party.

Last year, she'd shown up as a belly dancer.

Suddenly, Lester realized he was only a block away from the Willow Inn—and erect from his thoughts about Mary.

Stop thinking about her, he told himself. Think about something unpleasant.

Think about Helen, that'll take care of it.

He thought about Helen, and it did.

In spite of the dark interior, Lester felt conspicuous as he crossed the thick carpet to the bar. This was the first time he'd ever entered a cocktail lounge alone.

It's no big deal, he told himself. It's not like a *real* bar, just part of the restaurant.

Relax. Nothing to be scared of.

Just everything.

What if somebody sees me in here?

So what? It isn't against the law. And I'm not with *anyone.*

Feeling hot and nervous—but somewhat daring—he sat down on a bar stool. On the other side of the counter were lighted rows of liquor bottles.

The bartender came over. "What can I get you?" he asked. Nothing gruff or pushy about him. Just a pleasant, regular guy like a restaurant waiter.

"I'd like a margarita," Lester said. "On the rocks."

"Coming up."

"Thanks."

He watched the bartender make his drink.

Kind of exciting, he thought. I should come to these places more often.

When the martarita was ready, the bartender placed a cocktail napkin in front of Lester and set the drink on it. "Would you like me to run a tab?"

"Huh?"

"Run a tab for you?"

"Oh. Yeah, I guess so." Lester blushed. "Sure. Thanks."

Nodding, the bartender turned away.

Probably thinks I'm a moron.

Big deal, he thought. So maybe I'm not an old hand at barroom stuff.

He started to pick up his drink.

"Why, that *is* you," said a voice behind him. A woman's voice. With a soft, Southern drawl. "I *thought* I recognized you, Mr. Bryant."

Oh, my God.

He turned his stool and looked up at a shadowy, lined face. Its smile and sad eyes were framed by red hair. "Oh, hi," he said. "How are you, Emily Jean?"

"Well, I suppose I'm just fine." She laughed lightly. "You know, Mr. Bryant, I hardly recognized you at all without Helen by your side. Are you aware that we don't recognize one another so much by facial features as by context? Did you know that, Mr. Bryant?"

"I'd suspected it," he said, though he wasn't sure what she meant and didn't care.

What if she tells Helen about finding me here?

Maybe she won't even remember it, he thought. She *does* seem a little smashed.

"Are you here by yourself?" she asked.

"Yeah. Just thought I'd drop in for a quick one on my way home from work."

"Would you care to join me at my table?" Emily Jean asked. "Afternoon libations are *so* much more delicious when imbibed in the company of friends."

I'm a friend?

He felt himself blushing.

"You're right," he said.

"Splendid! Come with me, then. I have just the nicest little table over in that corner away from all the hustle and bustle. I don't care for hustle and bustle, do you?"

"I hate it," Lester said, though there seemed to *be* no hustle or bustle. The cocktail lounge was very quiet, almost deserted.

As he climbed off the stool, he waved at the bartender. "I'll be at a table," he called.

"No problem," the bartender said.

"Over in my special corner," Emily Jean announced.

"Gotcha."

She started walking toward her table, Lester close by her side.

"When I saw you come in," she said, "I thought to myself, 'My, but that does appear to be a familiar face.' You were out of your proper context, however, without Helen, so I had quite a problem placing you for a minute or two. Do you come here often?"

"No, not often."

She sank onto a booth alongside her table, scooted over, and patted the cushion beside her. "Wouldn't you like to sit right here, Mr. Bryant?"

"Why don't you call me Lester?" he suggested. "Or Les." He sat beside her.

"I should much prefer to call you Mr. Bryant," said Emily Jean. "It sounds so distinguished, don't you think? And so few people call one another by their proper names anymore. A great loss, Mr. Bryant, a terrible loss. Family names are so formal and dignified. They carry the weight of our ancestors. Now tell me, how are your students this semester?"

Before answering, he took a sip of his margarita. It tasted good and strong. He used his thumb and forefinger to rub salt crumbs off his lower lip. "I don't have any students," he explained. "I'm not a teacher."

"Is that true?"

Didn't she already know this?

"Oh, I used to teach," he explained, wondering if she had completely forgotten their conversation at Saturday night's social committee function. "That was a couple of years ago, though. In downtown Los Angeles."

"A high school, am I right?"

"You're right."

"Wasn't it a parochial school for girls?"

She *does* remember. Some of it, anyway.

"Right again," Lester said.

In a low, conspiratorial voice, Emily Jean said, "Why *ever* did you leave such a position? Teaching at a girl's school must have been a delight for a man of your good looks and charm." She placed her long, cool fingers on his forearm.

Blushing again, Lester shook his head. "I had big plans," he explained. "Ever since I was a kid, I wanted to have my own bookstore. A small, intimate kind of place, you know, with chairs and maybe a piano, and free coffee. I saw myself spending long nights talking with enthusiastic customers about Joyce and Camus. And Miller," he added, remembering Emily Jean's interest in theater.

"Arthur or Henry?" she asked, and giggled.

"Both."

"I *adore* Arthur Miller. Of course, he's no Tennessee Williams. Tennessee Williams whispers in the chambers of my heart. Because I'm a Southern girl, I imagine. But I didn't mean to digress. Please go on."

"Well, after a year at the high school, I quit my teaching job to open the bookstore of my dreams—my daydreams. Used all our savings, including a couple of thousand dollars that Helen had earmarked for a vacation in Europe. Then I proceded to lose my shirt. And hers, too."

Emily Jean's hand stayed on his arm. She patted him gently. "How dreadful," she said. "I *am* sorry."

"So is Helen. She said from the start that it was a crazy idea. I managed to prove her right—and cheat her out of that trip. I don't think she's ever going to let me forget it, either."

"I have a perfect solution for you, Mr. Bryant. Take her to Europe next summer."

A harsh laugh escaped from Lester. Shaking his head, he explained, "She already has plans for that. She signed up to take a group of students to England, France, Spain, the whole bit." He frowned and drank.

Emily Jean's martini was low.

"May I buy you another drink?" he asked.

"You surely may."

The bartender was nowhere in sight, but a barmaid was wandering among the tables. He signaled for her to come over.

"We'd like another round," he said. Feeling pleased with himself, he added, "The bartender's already running a tab for me."

"And what would you like?"

Emily Jean spoke up. "I'll have a double martini, dear. Very light on the vermouth, please."

"And I'll have another margarita."

When the barmaid was gone, Emily Jean squeezed Lester's forearm. "You're very kind," she said.

"My pleasure."

"Now, about your excursion to Europe. Will it be taking you to Wales? Such a lovely . . ."

"The excursion isn't taking *me* anywhere. I'll be staying right here in sunny—foggy—Grand Beach. I can't go. I don't have the summers off."

"And you're permitting Helen to go without you?"

He nodded.

"My ex-husband, Robert, would no more have permitted me to travel alone than he would have . . . paddled a raft to Peru."

"Helen does what she pleases."

"She *is* a headstrong woman."

"She's got balls."

"Mr. Bryant!" Emily Jean giggled. "Such a horrid thing to say of one's wife!"

"Yeah."

Neither of them spoke while the barmaid set full glasses down on fresh cocktail napkins and cleared away the used ones.

Lester waited until she was gone, then said, "There must be at least one or two women left in the world who don't pride themselves on being self-reliant and obnoxious."

"The world is overstocked with such women." Softly, Emily Jean repeated, "Overstocked."

"That's very good to hear," Lester said, watching her. "I'm not sure I believe it, though."

"It is the simple truth. If Helen doesn't appreciate . . . Most women, I should think, would feel honored to . . ." She quickly turned her face away. "Will you please excuse me, Mr. Bryant?" She pulled a tissue from her purse and pressed it to her nose. Then she scooted out of the booth.

Lester watched her move across the dimly lighted room. A couple of times, she lurched sideways and had to steady herself against a table.

He had never seen a woman with such thin legs. A wonder she could stand up at all. Of course, he supposed it was the liquor that made her stumble. Maybe he shouldn't have offered her another martini. She must've had a couple before he even arrived. A couple, at least.

And I come along and buy her another and make her cry.

He hated to see a woman cry.

Waiting for her return, Lester finished his margarita. Emily Jean's glass wasn't quite empty yet.

Would she want another refill?

She sure doesn't *need* another, he thought.

Who am I to say what she needs?

He signaled the barmaid. When she arrived at the table, he ordered a margarita for himself.

"Another martini for the lady?" she asked.

"I don't think so. Not yet. We'll see, after she gets back."

He sipped his new margarita slowly, thinking about Emily Jean. She seemed to be a sad case, coming straight from school to a place like this on a Monday afternoon and drinking alone . . .

Hoping to get picked up?

Why not? he thought. She sure seems lonely.

Makes two of us.

Then he began to wonder why she hadn't returned.

After finishing his margarita, he made a sign to the barmaid. She came to his table.

"Another?" she asked.

"Not just yet. You know the woman I was with?"

"The redhead?"

"Yeah. She went to the ladies' room . . . must've been half an hour ago. Do you suppose you'd mind checking on her? I'm a little worried something might be wrong."

"Sure, I'll check."

When the barmaid returned, she was shaking her head and holding her palms upward. "Your friend isn't there now, sir. I'm sorry."

He frowned and muttered, "That's odd."

"Kinda."

"She's *gone?*"

"Guess so. Sorry."

"Okay. Well, thanks."

"Hope you find her."

"Thanks."

When Lester got home, he followed the quick, flat tapping sounds to the spare room and found Helen typing a ditto master. "Sorry I'm late," he said.

She continued to type for several seconds. Then she squinted at the page. Then she looked around at him and asked, "What?"

"I said, 'Sorry I'm late.' "

"Oh." She looked at her wristwatch. "God, it's almost seven! I must've lost track of . . . I've got to change and get ready."

"Ready for what?"

"My U.C.L.A. seminar."

"A seminar?"

"I told you about it. 'Fundamentals of Adolescent Dysfunction.' "

"Great."

"You don't have to act that way. These things move me up on the pay scale, you know."

"I know. You keep telling me."

"Shit, you're in a crappy mood." She removed the ditto master from her typewriter. "There's taco casserole in the freezer, if you're interested."

"Thanks."

THIRTEEN

TRAVELING MAN

Albert drove through downtown Kansas City until he found a Holiday Inn. He liked Holiday Inns. The one in St. Louis, where he had spent Sunday and Monday compliments of Milton Shadwick, had been very big and comfortable. So comfortable that he'd conked out, Sunday night, and had slept till noon.

Well rested Monday afternoon, he had forged Milton's name on two traveler's checks and paid for the night in advance. He'd eaten a steak sandwich, onion rings and fries at the motel cafe. Then, with three of Milton's cigars in his shirt pocket, he'd set out to explore St. Louis.

Forest Park was warm and pleasant. He smoked a cigar beside the pond, then walked through the zoo. It wasn't much compared to the Brookfield in Chicago, but he enjoyed watching the monkeys.

And the women.

The zoo was thick with women, some alone; some with girl friends, a few with men, many pushing baby carriages and trying to keep track of two or three eager kids.

He only paid attention to the lone ones. Most were plain. Not ugly, just plain—the sort of girls he'd dated on those rare occasions, like the Junior Dance, when he'd needed to save his self-respect. Nothing to lose any sleep over.

Nothing to waste an afternoon over.

Not when you've got a knife.

He was beginning to think about dinner when a good one appeared. Maybe twenty-five years old, long blond hair that streamed behind her in the breeze, and a slender figure. She wore white slacks that hugged her rear end and thighs. Her flowered blouse was tied in front, leaving her midriff bare.

Albert followed her through the zoo. She was a fast walker, never slowing down and never turning her head to look at anything except, twice, her wristwatch.

Her slacks fit so tightly that he could see the outlines of her bikini-style underwear. The tight seat reminded him of Mrs. Broxton in the grocery store.

He wished he'd taken more time with Mrs. Broxton Saturday night. Much more time. After all, what was the big hurry? If he hadn't killed her all at once like that, he could've had a lot more fun with her. Maybe tied her up and . . .

The woman in the tight pants waved at a man in front of the Jefferson Memorial building. The man waved back, smiling. Albert stopped. He stripped cellophane off one of his cigars and watched the woman hurry to the man, embrace him and walk with him through the door.

Albert muttered, "Shit."

He lit up his cigar and returned to the zoo. He waited an hour, but no one interesting appeared so he left.

He drove across town and found a restaurant with a good view of the Gateway Arch and the river. The hostess seated him beside a window. When he ordered knockwurst and sauerkraut and a stein of beer, the waiter asked to see identification. He had to pass on the beer.

After dinner, he drove around the area looking for a movie theater. He wanted to find himself a good horror movie or two, but he couldn't find any. He had to settle for a Charles Bronson movie and a long, dull film about a Mafia double-cross.

Then he returned to the Holiday Inn. The television worked okay. He watched Johnny Carson until he fell asleep.

All in all, he'd had a pleasant time in St. Louis. But not very exciting. Not a single score. Of course, he hadn't tried very hard.

Here in Kansas City, he would try damn hard.

After checking into the motel on Tuesday afternoon, Albert took a shower. He tried to shave with his knife, but it only smoothed down his light whiskers. He decided to try Milton's injector razor. It was crusted and gooey with bits of gray whisker clinging to the blade.

"The slob," Albert muttered.

But he shaved with it, anyway, and nicked himself once. When he finished, his face felt smooth. It looked much the same as before, however, and he wondered why he ever bothered to shave at all.

He ate a cheeseburger in the motel coffee shop and washed it down with a chocolate milk shake. Then he began to drive. He drove south until he found a section of town with nice, two-story homes. For a long time, he cruised the area. He didn't know exactly what he was looking for, but he figured he would recognize it when he found it.

There it is.

A supermarket.

He parked in its lot and climbed out of his car. As he walked to the store, the chilly wind flapped his parka behind him like a cape. Apparently, the October heat wave was over—or he'd left it behind in St. Louis. He pulled his parka shut and zipped it.

The market's automatic door flew open. He hurried inside, escaping the wind.

One of the front wheels of the shopping cart wobbled. He took a different cart. It was more rusty than the first and held a torn corner of lettuce leaf, but all the wheels worked fine.

The first aisle to the left seemed like the best place to begin. Start there and work toward the right until he'd covered the entire store. That way, he would be sure to see all the women.

And there were plenty in this place.

Housewives with hair wound up tightly in curlers, most of them looking chunky and dumb. Slim women in well-tailored outfits probably picking up dinner on the way home from work, their faces stiff and merciless. Old women who walked carefully, holding tightly to their carts. And a few who were different.

One, maybe thirty, seemed very sure of herself. She left her cart at the end of each aisle, walked briskly to several areas of shelving where she grabbed items without a moment's hesitation, and returned with them in her arms. Her wire-rimmed, rectangular glasses and jutting chin made her seem almost masculine, but she had gentle eyes with delicate, arching brows.

Not her. She made him curious, but she wasn't the type he wanted.

Another, in jeans and an army shirt, was more like it. She walked by him with her hands stuffed inside her pockets and a bottle of red wine tucked under one arm. Her breasts were large and swung loose inside her shirt. She walked with a sensual sway as if she wanted everyone to know she had space available between her legs.

Albert pushed his cart behind her, watching the seat of her faded jeans. A red patch, shaped like lips, was sewn over one rear pocket. When she stopped to choose a package of cheese, Albert pushed his cart around her. He turned his head as he walked by and glimpsed, in a space between two shirt buttons, the white skin of a breast.

That's when his cart bumped a girl whose back was turned.

She sucked a quick, sharp breath, hopped forward and

started to reach down. Then, apparently deciding that her injured tendon didn't hurt enough to need clutching, she straightened up.

"I'm awfully sorry," Albert said.

"It's okay," she said.

She was about Albert's age, with flowing auburn hair and a face so smooth that he wanted to reach out and touch it. She was slightly shorter than Albert, and slim. Beneath her open coat, her blouse was spread apart at the throat. Next to the whiteness of the blouse, her skin looked very tanned. Through the thin fabric, Albert could see the lace pattern of her bra.

She turned away from him and walked to her cart, limping slightly.

Her brown loafers were scuffed. She wore forest green knee socks. The plaid cotton of her kilt reached down almost to her knees.

This is the one!

As the girl headed up the next aisle, Albert rolled his shopping cart to one of the checkout stands. There were four customers in front of him. He kept watch on all the other lines until, finally, the girl in kilts entered one.

He grinned as the checker rang up his pack of cigars, Swiss cheese, salami, and Oreos. He would be out of the store in plenty of time.

With the sack tucked under one arm, he zipped his parka and walked to the exit. He turned around. The girl was lifting her grocery items out of the cart and piling them onto the checkout counter.

He shouldn't have long to wait.

Outside, the wind threw itself against him. He leaned into it and trudged across the parking lot to his car. He waited in his car, the engine running.

Soon, the girl came out of the store with a sack in each arm, her hair trailing in the wind, her kilts hugging her thighs. She climbed into a red Mustang.

It was very easy to follow.

After no more than a mile, it made a left-hand turn and rolled onto the driveway of a large, two-story brick house. The garage door opened automatically. The Mustang rolled to a stop beside a large sedan.

Albert pulled into the driveway. His headlights rested on the girl as she climbed from her car. Turning around, she shaded her eyes and smiled toward him.

Probably thinks I'm someone she knows.

He gave her a friendly wave, though he doubted she could see it with the lights shining in her eyes.

Apparently unconcerned by his presence, the girl walked around to the passenger side of her Mustang, opened its door and ducked inside for her groceries.

Albert shut off his headlights.

He swung his door open, stepped down onto the driveway and called, "Hi." Walking quickly toward her, he asked, "How are you doing tonight?" as if she were an old friend.

"Just fine, I guess," she said. She came out of the car clutching both sacks.

"Can I give you a hand with those?"

She peered at his face. "You're . . . ?" She shook her head, frowning, as if trying to rearrange her thoughts and come up with his name.

"Billy," he said.

"Oh. Sure, that's right."

"We're in English together," he said, grinned.

Everybody takes English.

"Oh!" She laughed with relief. "Of course. Now I remember."

"Do you want a hand with the bags?"

"Well . . ."

"My mom and dad know your parents," Albert explained. "That's why I thought it'd be okay to drop by. I'm new in school, so I don't know many people yet. I was absent today. I wondered if you could give me the homework assignment for English."

"Well, sure . . . I guess that's okay. It isn't catching, is it?"

"Nah. I was kinda playing hooky." He held out his hands. The girl grinned and stepped toward him.

As he took the bags, his hands touched hers. She looked away from him quickly, pretending not to notice.

She smelled very fresh, more like shampoo or soap than like perfume.

"Do you live near here?" she asked, opening the back door of the house.

"About a mile."

"Which street are you on?"

Ignoring the question, Albert followed her into the kitchen. "Mmm," he said. "Smells like leg of lamb. Where should I set these down?"

"Oh, just anywhere. On the counter, I guess."

"Here?"

"Sure, that's fine. Thanks for the help."

"You're welcome. Glad to be of service."

"I'll see if I can find that English assignment. Do you want to wait here? My notebook's in my room. I'll be right down."

"Fine."

As she pushed through the swinging kitchen door, she called out, "I'm home!"

Albert reached into his jeans pocket and pulled out his switchblade. He put it into the pocket of his parka.

His heart was thumping so hard that he felt sick. His mouth was dry. He hurried to the sink, ran water from the faucet, cupped his hands and took a drink.

After drying his hands, he went through the swinging door to the dining room. It was empty and dark. Light came through an open door at the far end. With his left hand in the pocket of his parka, he moved toward the light.

He heard the girl's footsteps overhead. Her bedroom must be directly above him.

He paused in the dining room's doorway. To the left was the house's front door, to the right the staircase. Directly ahead of him was the living room. He walked forward.

The girl's parents were sitting on the couch watching television. Though it wasn't even nine o'clock yet, both were already dressed for bed. The man wore pajamas and a robe. The woman wore a robe over a nightgown. She looked good, even with her hair in curlers. She was a larger, less delicate version of her daughter.

They both smiled at Albert. The man stood up. "Charlene will be down in a minute," he said. "I'm her father."

"I'm Billy Jones," Albert said, walking toward the man.

He was big—over six feet—with broad shoulders and a strong, heavy-jawed face. He held out a hand.

Albert reached for the hand, gripped it, jerked it down and lunged forward, freeing his left hand from the parka pocket, snapping open his switchblade and ripping a gash across the man's neck. With quick straight thrusts, he punched the blade four times into the man's side.

The woman began to scream.

Albert shoved the man, dumping him onto her. He grabbed an ashtray from the coffee table and swung it at her forehead. When it hit her, the scream stopped. The heavy glass ashtray wasn't damaged.

Albert slammed it against the side of her head twice before it broke.

He stepped back, panting.

The woman was slumped on the couch, mouth slack, a dislodged curler dangling over one of her shut eyes.

Footsteps on the stairs.

"Charlene!" Billy yelled. "Come here!"

He climbed over her father, sat on the back of the couch and swung a leg over the mother's head. Knees spread wide apart, he pulled her head backward against his crotch. Then he pressed the knife blade to her throat.

"Charleeeeene!" he called in a teasing, singsong voice. "Come heeeere!"

Soon, he heard her rushing down the stairway.

"I've got a surprise for you," Albert called.

She lurched into the living room, saw her parents and abruptly stopped.

"Come here quickly or I'll cut your mother's throat."

Charlene stepped forward, pale and dull-eyed as if her mind was far away.

"Okay, stop there."

She stopped in the middle of the living room floor.

"Okay, now take your clothes off. All of them. Every stitch."

FOURTEEN

THE MORNING AFTER

The alarm clock blared. Albert rolled across the bed and grabbed it, his fingers searching its back until they found the plastic lever and pushed it.

Silence.

He looked at the face of the clock.

7:25.

Throwing back the blankets, he felt the chilly air wash over him. He hurried to the closet and found an old flannel robe. It was the father's, probably the one he'd worn for years before getting the new robe he'd been wearing last night. Its sleeves hung past Albert's fingertips. He rolled them up as he went to Charlene's bedroom.

The mother was just as he'd left her, face down and spread-eagled, each arm and leg fastened tightly with clothesline to a leg of the single bed.

"Pleasant night?" he asked.

She groaned.

"I'll take the tape off now, but if you scream I'll kill you and Charlene. Got it?"

She nodded.

Albert lifted her head off the pillow, reached under the side of her face and ripped the adhesive tape off her mouth. She gasped for air, but said nothing.

"Say 'good morning.'"

She said nothing.

"Say it." He rapped his knuckles against the matted, bloody hair on the side of her head. Her body lurched, straining at the ropes.

"Good morning," she muttered.

"Sound cheerful."

"Good morning."

"That's better." He put his hands on her back. The skin felt like ice. "Again."

"Good morning."

"Your husband Mike isn't feeling well this morning." He knelt and looked at her face. He could only see one eye. It blinked and a tear slid across the bridge of her nose. "Mike has the flu."

"You killed him."

"No, he's got the flu. A bad case of it, too. He'll probably be laid up for the rest of the week."

"You killed him."

Albert opened the wallet he'd left beside the telephone extension and pulled out the business card. It read, MIKE ABERCROMBE, MANAGER, APPAREL PLUS, gave the address on 3rd Street and a phone number.

"Is this the number you call when he's gonna be absent?"

"He calls. I never call."

"Well, he's much too sick today, don't you think? What time does he call?"

"Eight-thirty."

"You'd better not be lying."

"I'm not."

"Does he drive to work?"

"Yes."

"Alone?"

"Yes."

"No car pool, nothing like that?"

"No."

"You'd better not be lying. Which car does he drive?"

"The Buick."

"Okay. Now, what about Charlene's school? When does it start?"

"Eight-thirty."

"How does she get there?"

"Walks."

"With friends?"

"Yes."

"Do they come here?"

"No."

"You sure?"

"They're along the way. She meets them along the way."

"Okay. What about you? Do you work?"

"No."

"Got any appointments today?"

"No."

"Expecting any visitors?"

"No."

"Okay. I'll be back in an hour and we'll make a couple of calls."

He picked up the spool of adhesive tape he'd left beside the phone, tore off several short strips, and taped the woman's mouth shut.

In the bathroom, he opened his robe and urinated. As his pee splashed into the toilet, he stared at Charlene in the tub.

"And how are you this fine morning?" he asked.

She didn't answer.

Albert flushed the toilet, then returned to the master bedroom. He found a drawer full of socks and put on a pair. Then he went downstairs.

His bloody clothes were heaped on the living room floor. He picked up his jeans, reached into a front pocket and brought out the keys to Milton's car.

On the kitchen table, he found Charlene's purse. The Mustang keys were inside it.

He used the kitchen door to go outside. The morning was chilly. He shivered as he walked around the house, inspecting the area. A tall stockade fence enclosed the backyard. The front yard was open at the front and along one side. The other side, by the driveway, was sheltered from the neighbor's house by trees heavy with yellow and orange leaves.

The neighborhood seemed pretty quiet.

He saw no one.

He went into the garage and climbed inside Charlene's Mustang. When he sat down, the robe fell open exposing his legs to the cold. He adjusted it. His hands shook violently, but he managed to push the key into the ignition.

The engine's roar echoed through the garage.

Albert backed the Mustang out of the garage, stopped it on the driveway in front of Milton's car, then pulled forward, veering to the right. He parked the Mustang just outside the garage, directly behind the Buick.

After that, he drove Milton's car into the garage and shut the door.

So much for the hot car, he thought. Nobody'll think much of seeing Charlene's car out on the driveway.

Back in the house, he entered the storage room off the kitchen and raised the lid of the freezer chest.

At the far end, separated by a carton of Rocky Road ice cream, were the soiled bottoms of a pair of white socks. Albert thumped a fingertip against one of the heels. The foot inside felt solid like a frozen steak.

"And how are *you* this morning, Mike? I'm fine, thank you. Enjoying your hospitality. Yell if you need anything."

Chuckling, Albert lowered the freezer top and latched it.

FIFTEEN

A TROUBLED YOUTH

Ian, alone in his classroom, heard the door open and shut. Instead of looking up, he continued to read the theme.

"Mr. Collins?"

At the bottom of the last page, he wrote, "Good ideas, but watch your word choice. *Was* isn't the only verb in the English language." He drew a B at the top, set the paper aside and looked up. "Oh, hello, Charles. How's our favorite poet?"

"Okay, I guess. Would it be all right to talk to you?"

"Sure. Come on in."

The boy walked slowly, bent at the waist as if his bowels were cramped.

"Do you feel okay?" Ian asked.

Charles shook his head.

"Have you seen the nurse?"

"No. She wouldn't be . . . they told me at the office that this is your conference period."

"They told you the truth. Have a seat."

Charles sat at a desk in the front row of the classroom. His face had a moist, doughy look. There were gray smudges under his eyes. He rubbed his face with both hands.

Ian had noticed it often—how a boy can look so much like a tired old man.

"What seems to be the trouble, Charles?"

"It's a personal thing. I mean, it hasn't got to do with grades or anything. It's just some trouble I'm having."

"Must be serious, the way you look." Ian got up from his chair, circled to the front of his desk and sat on its edge. "Is there some way I can help?" he asked.

"I don't know, Mr. Collins. My head's all messed up. I mean, everything was going great until . . . a couple of days ago. Now I'm all messed up. I don't know what's happening. All of a sudden, everything's upside-down. I can't even study any more. I thought maybe if I talked to somebody about it . . ."

"Have you spoken to your parents?"

"Are you kidding me? They'd crap if they knew what was going on. But you're different. I mean, you understand stuff. You listen to people."

"What is it I'm supposed to understand?"

"Well." Charles hesitated. He glanced at the door as if considering whether to leave. Then he met Ian's eyes. "I'm having this thing," he said. "I guess you'd say it's an affair."

"Is the girl pregnant?"

"God, I hope not. I guess she *could* be. I mean, I didn't use anything. I figured she was taking care of it."

"That kind of assumption often leads to fatherhood."

"She *must've* taken care of it. Why wouldn't she? I mean, she's married. She's gotta know about that sort of stuff."

"She's married? No wonder you're afraid to tell your parents."

"You won't say anything to them, will you?"

"No, not a chance. How long have you been seeing this woman?"

"Not long." He fidgeted and looked down at his hands. "I've known her for a month or so, but we didn't . . . Monday night was the first time we actually *made* it. And then last night. Only twice, so far."

"What about her husband?"

Charles looked up quickly, startled. "What about him?"

"Does he know?"

"Oh, God, I hope not! I mean, he hasn't caught us at it or anything. She tells him she's going to meetings . . . classes and stuff. And we never do it at her *house*."

"I should hope not."

"I've got this camper van. It has beds. That's where we did it. You know, parked like on side streets."

"I guess that's safer than doing it in her house."

"It was her idea. The whole thing's been her idea. I don't even know why she'd want to make it with me. I mean, I'm just a kid."

"That might be reason enough. How old is she?"

"I don't know. Twenty-five or thirty, I guess."

"Do you want out of it?"

"I don't know. Hell, I like it. She's really *hot,* you know? But the whole thing has me scared shitless. Excuse me, that just slipped out."

"I've heard worse."

"She scares me. And I'm *really* scared her husband might find out."

"You should be."

"And hell, Mr. Collins . . . I even scare myself, I get so involved. I don't know what I'm doing. I mean, I *know.* And I know it's wrong. But it's like somebody else is doing it and I'm just watching like some dumb-ass jerk. It's as if I don't have any say in things. I just go *along* with whatever's happening. It's making me nuts."

"What you'd better do is put a stop to it all."

"How do I do that?"

"Quit seeing the woman."

"That wouldn't be easy." He looked down at his folded hands and shook his head as if thinking about impossible odds.

"Where women are involved," Ian said, "nothing is easy." He smiled grimly as he pictured Laura throwing a playful punch at his shoulder for speaking such blasphemy. "Nothing is easy," he muttered.

"What should I do?"

"It's up to you. If *I* wanted out, I'd tell her so. I'd try to be nice about it. You know, tell her how much the relationship has meant to you and how you'll always cherish the memories of it."

He saw a smile creep across Charles's face. "That wouldn't be a lie," the boy said. "I'm sure never gonna forget *her*."

"But don't leave any doubt in her mind that you're finished with the affair."

"I guess I could try that. Maybe . . . God, sometimes things sure get messed up."

"That's why the good Lord gave us mops."

Charles let out a quiet, bitter laugh. "Yeah," he said. "I guess. Anyway, thanks for listening. And for the advice."

"Hope it helps. Let me know how things go, will you?"

"Sure. Will you give me a pass back to study hall?"

Ian wrote out a hall pass.

SIXTEEN

CAREER OPPORTUNITIES

When Janet woke up on Thursday morning, she didn't reach sideways for Dave.

A breeze billowed the curtains overhead and chilled the upturned side of her face. She pulled the covers as high as her ear and curled under their warmth.

It had been nice, yesterday, lying in bed for a long time because there was no big reason to get up. One of life's great luxuries. But today was different. She had to get over to the placement office at U.S.C. You didn't find a job by staying in bed.

Well, some people do.

She laughed softly under the covers.

Prostitutes. And what about housewives? Sure. That's what the libbers wanted you to think anyway. You get married, you're a whore on a one-life stand.

I wouldn't mind that.

She rolled onto her belly. The warm pocket of the pillow felt good against her face.

And how do I find a man who wants the one-life stand? she wondered.

Luck onto him?

Carry a rabbit's foot?

Better get a move on.

She sat on the edge of the bed and shivered. Her sheer nightgown had been fine for summer nights with Dave. It wasn't much good, though, for October mornings alone.

She hurried to the bathroom, pulled off the nightgown and turned on the shower. While she waited for the water to get hot, she looked at herself in the mirror.

Was she gaining weight?

A little, maybe. Not so anyone would notice.

She pushed a few strands of brown hair away from her eyes.

Not bad eyes, she had to admit. But not "dreamy" like the eyes of the guy at the football game.

I'm still thinking about him?

The handsome, mysterious stranger.

Imagining herself with him, Janice grew warm and squirmy inside. The mirror showed a blush spread over her naked body. Her nipples stiffened.

Calm down, she thought. For all I know, he might be a total jerk.

I'd sure like to find out.

"I wonder who he is," she whispered, watching her lips move in the mirror's reflection.

Meg hadn't recognized him, and Meg seemed to know everyone who worked at City College.

He might be a parent.

He hadn't looked old enough, however, to have a kid at City College.

Maybe he's just a football fan.

I should keep going to the games, Janice thought. Maybe I'll see him again.

Wondering about him, she stepped under the shower.

★　★　★

Janet didn't start to get nervous until she was putting on her lipstick.

What's there to be nervous about? she thought. They've either got job openings or they haven't. If they haven't, I'll manage. There's always something.

She picked up her car keys and purse. As she left Meg's house, she looked at her wristwatch. The drive to U.S.C. should take about half an hour—assuming some idiot on the freeway didn't kill her in the meantime.

Always a real possibility. She didn't care much for L.A. freeways.

But what's life if you don't take chances?

Longer, that's what.

"So," Meg said as she poured Burgundy from a gallon bottle, "how'd it go at the placement office? Any hot prospects?"

"For men or jobs?" Janet asked.

"Whichever." With the heel of her hand, Meg slammed the cork home. Then she handed one of the glasses to Janet.

"Well, in the job department, lots of hot prospects if I don't care what I do."

They went into the living room. Janet tossed a stack of newspapers to the floor and sat down on an end of the couch. She took a sip of wine. It was cool and tart and good. "The world would be mine," she said, "if I could only take shorthand."

"Twas ever thus."

"Also, since my driving record is nothing short of extraordinary, I'd be perfectly suited to make deliveries for an Encino pharmaceutical firm. Or Pizza Man."

Meg laughed and made a piggish snort.

"Funny to you," Janet said, "but I hate driving. That still leaves me with a few choice opportunities. For instance, L.A.X. is desperate for x-ray scanners. You know, security? Watching the little screen to make sure nobody tries to board an airliner with a pistol or hand grenade tucked away in his carry-on? That sounded appealing for about two seconds. Then I got to thinking about all that radiation."

"Nix on that."

"Damn right. Junior or no Junior, I'm not eager to get my chromosomes juggled. So I said the hell with that. Especially since I've got this ace in the hole."

"Referring to Junior again?"

Janet stuggled not to laugh with her mouthful of wine. By the time she'd swallowed it, the urge had passed. She said, "No, I don't mean Junior. Just a figure of speech. Ace in the hole. Means . . ."

"You've got the Red Baron up your ass?"

Janet chuckled and shook her head. "You're getting crude. How much have you had to drink?"

"Not enough. Never enough. Anyway, so what *is* this ace you've got up your hole?"

"It's not up *my* hole."

"I see."

"You're trying to confuse the issue."

"I'll be good."

"Thank you." Janet finished her glass of wine and sighed with pleasure. "More?"

"Why not?"

She uncorked the huge bottle and refilled both glasses. "My great asset—my ace in the hole, so to speak—no puns intended so please don't interrupt again—is that I'm an absolute *whizz* on the typewriter."

"You *whizz* on typewriters? That's a filthy habit."

"I'm a very fast and accurate typist."

"Oh! Is *that* what you mean?"

"That's what I mean," Janet assured her. "Did you realize I'm an expert typist?"

"I never even suspected."

"One gets that way after six years of college. All those term papers, the master's thesis . . . I must say, I really became facile at—as we pros call it—tickling the ivories."

"A regular Liberace, huh?"

"Exactly."

"So you won't starve," Meg said, and scratched one of her bushy eyebrows.

"Neither will I teach. Not this year, anyway."

"No openings?"

"Not on their lists. Well, *some* openings. Specialist stuff. Speech therapy, emotionally handicapped, that sort of thing. Nothing for a secondary teacher with an M.A. in English literature."

"And a kid in the oven."

"Oh, that's a well-kept secret."

"So what's the verdict?" Meg asked, grinning strangely as if amused by a private joke.

"The jury's still out," Janet told her, ignoring the grin. "I guess, if nothing else turns up, I'll have to settle for one of the typing jobs. On the brighter side, though, I've got a date for tomorrow night."

"Yeah? Fantastic! Anyone I know?"

"*I* don't even know him. His name's Moses."

"You're pulling my leg."

"Moses Goldstein, but everyone calls him Mosby for some reason I couldn't make out. Something about the Civil War. He's very weird, but he's funny."

"Sounds like it'll be a heavy date."

"You never know."

"So how'd you meet him?"

"He works in the placement office. He said, 'Since you're out of work, you could probably use a good meal. How about tomorrow night?' "

"A mover. What does he look like?"

"A salamander."

When Meg stopped laughing, she asked, "Then why are you going out with him?"

"More to life than good looks."

"Easy for you to say."

"He seems very nice. Besides, I figured it'd be a way to take my mind off Dave and all that."

"Besides," Meg added, "you couldn't think of a pleasant way to turn him down."

Janet shook her head. "That's not it. No problem there. I turn guys down all the time. The self-satisfied asshole types . . . who seem, by the way, to be very much in evidence these days."

"Here here! Which reminds me, I would like to propose a toast."

"A toast? To whom or what?"

"Patience," Meg said. She reached for the bottle.

"I realize patience is supposed to be a virtue, but that's no reason to toast it."

"We're not toasting patience, hon. We're exercising it while I fill the glasses."

"Sit-ups? Push-ups? Jumping jacks?"

"You're getting looped."

"Who, me?" Janet asked.

Meg put the bottle down and said, "Now, this calls for a brief explanation. John Lawrence came into the bookstore today looking for an anniversary card."

"I hope you congratulated him."

"Do you know who John Lawrence is?" Meg asked.

"Can't say I do."

"He's the assistant superintendent of the school district. The headquarters is just across the street from the college, so he comes into the bookstore fairly often. We've gotten to know each other pretty well over the past couple of years. *Anyway*, John's in charge of personnel for the entire district. Well, we had a little chat today. I explained about my dear friend—meaning you—who is as smart as a whip . . ."

"A *bull*whip?"

"*Now* who's interrupting?"

"Sorry."

"Here I am, extolling you, and you're cracking wise."

"Cracking like a *whip!*"

"*Any*way, I told him all about you . . ."

"Not *all*, I hope."

"Only the good stuff."

"How long did *that* take?"

"Quite a few seconds, actually."

"Did you mention I'm smart as a whip?"

Meg took another drink of wine, then said, "Any-waaaaay, the upshot is this: if you drop by John's office at the school district headquarters on Monday morning, he'll put you on the district's substitute list."

"You're kidding!" Janet blurted.

Beaming, Meg shook her head. "Forty-eight bucks a shot."

"Wow!"

"Yup." She raised her glass of wine. "Here's to your future as a substitute teacher."

"Here's to *you!*"

SEVENTEEN

SWEET CHARLENE

Albert woke up in Kansas City, still in the house of Charlene and her parents. The bed was king-sized. Reaching out his arms, he couldn't touch both edges at the same time. What a bed! He wouldn't mind waking up in one like this every morning.

How many mornings did this make?

Three. Three fantastic mornings.

Rolling onto his side, he curled up and snuggled his face against the pillow. A shoulder was exposed to the cool morning air blowing in through the window. He covered his shoulder with the electric blanket.

It was great being so warm and cozy. He could stay here forever, except he had to take a leak.

At the edge of the bed, he reached down and picked up a wadded bathrobe. He threw aside the blankets and started to shiver. The flannel robe helped, but not enough. He ran across the carpeted floor and into the connecting bathroom. With a flick of the switch, a heat light came on overhead. It felt like warm hands on his hair and shoulders as he stood over the toilet.

One of the robe's sleeves had come unrolled. The cuff hung to his knuckles. That Abercrombe had sure been a big guy.

Albert smiled, remembering the ease with which he'd killed the man.

If I can kill a big guy like that, I can kill anyone.

He rolled up the cuff, flushed the toilet, and tied the robe shut. Then he slid open the shower door.

Charlene looked up at him from the tub. Her legs were held upright by clothesline tied to the high shower nozzle. Her bound hands, crossed between her thighs, were fastened by a length of rope to the faucet knobs. A red blanket kept her naked back off the bottom of the tub. A pillow was under her head.

"Good morning," Albert said. "Cold?"

She blinked, but her face was expressionless.

Kneeling on the bath mat, Albert ripped the adhesive tape off her lips.

"Cold?" he asked again.

"No," she muttered, and turned her face away.

"Want a hot shower? That'll warm you up."

"No."

"What? Speak up."

"No!"

"Two were enough, huh?"

Reaching down, he ran a hand up one of her breasts. The skin was cool and rumpled with goose bumps. His fingernail picked at the edge of a bandage. When he realized what he was doing, he stopped. He didn't want her bleeding again. Not just yet.

He cupped his hand over her breast and joggled it.

"Your mom's tits were a lot bigger," he said.

He watched his forefinger follow a threadlike ridge of dried blood down her chest and along her belly to where it disappeared beneath her crossed hands.

Cutting her a little bit at a time had been all right.

But nothing like the turn-on he got when he *really* stuck it in.

Of course, *that* killed them.

He wanted to save Charlene for as long as possible so he could go on enjoying her a little bit at a time—while savoring his anticipation of *the big stab.*

Shove it in all the way.

Maybe today.

"I'm hungry," Albert said. "How about you?"

Charlene said nothing.

"I spoke to you," he said. Reaching behind one of her upraised legs, he gripped the hot-water handle.

"I'm not hungry," she said in a voice barely loud enough to hear.

Albert let go of the handle and slid his fingers down the back of her thigh.

"You oughta be starved. You didn't eat more than two bites of that steak last night." He laughed. "Not that I blame you. It was awfully tough."

She turned her head and looked at him. "You didn't cook it right," she said. For the first time since learning of her mother's death, there was some life in her voice. "You don't cook *anything* right."

He thought about that. "Can you cook?" he asked.

"A lot better than you."

"Do you know how to fry eggs over easy?"

"I've done it."

"Okay."

He spent the next few minutes untying Charlene.

She couldn't move, so he lifted her out of the tub and led her to the toilet.

After relieving herself, she hunched over, head between her knees, auburn hair hanging down, her small breasts pressed flat against her thighs as she rubbed her feet and ankles.

While Albert waited for her to recover, he stroked her back. It was warm. In several places, the skin was stained from cuts that had opened during the night. The deeper cuts were bandaged. Others—from a couple of days ago, he supposed—had already formed scabs, their seams criss-crossing her back. Her muscles went taut as he picked at part of a scab below her right shoulder blade. Blood slowly bloomed out, bright and glistening, to form a droplet. He smeared it with his finger, then licked his finger clean.

"I like the taste of your blood," he said.

She didn't answer.

"Okay," Albert said. "That's long enough." He stepped in front of Charlene, gripped her beneath her arms and lifted her off the toilet. He swung her against the wall. "Don't move," he said.

He let go. She slumped slightly, but stayed on her feet.

He turned away from her, crouched by the tub and snatched out the six-foot length of rope. Kneeling by her feet, he tied one end of the rope around her left ankle.

When the knot was tight, he raised his head. Straight in front of him was Charlene's groin, pale and smooth and hairless—with only a few small nicks from the razor.

I'll shave her again after breakfast, he thought.

Leaning forward, he licked her.

So smooth.

At the touch of his tongue, she flinched. She moaned softly. But she didn't fight him.

A quick learner.

"Yummy yummy," Albert said, and smiled up at her.

She stared straight ahead, her face grim.

"Okay," he said, "let's have breakfast." Keeping the loose end of the rope in his hand, he stood up.

"Can I put my robe on?" Charlene asked. "I'm freezing."

"*I* can warm you up."

"Don't you want breakfast?"

"Yeah. Let's do that first."

Her bright, quilted robe was hanging from a hook on the bathroom door. Albert handed it to her. She put it on, drew its front shut, and slowly fastened its buttons.

"You go ahead of me," he told her.

Holding on to the rope, he followed her out of the bathroom.

Somehow, the robe made her look smaller and more fragile. Her legs, below its hem, looked very cold.

She walked slowly, limping down the hallway, down the stairs and through another hallway toward the kitchen.

Albert enjoyed watching her walk. He had watched many women from behind: women in skirts that blocked his view just as the slanting thighs were about to meet; women in culottes that looked like skirts but cheated with a panel of fabric between the thighs; women in baggy shorts so loose you could probably see everything if you looked up the leg holes; women in tight little short-shorts that hugged their buttocks and showed pale crescents at the bottom; women in loose-fitting corduroys or jeans; others in trousers so tight he could see the outlines of their underwear—or no outline, which was even better. Always the nakedness so obvious underneath. Always the urge to put a hand up the skirt or culottes or down the waist of the trousers. Always the urge, but never the opportunity.

Usually never.

Albert tugged the rope.

Charlene was yanked backward. She grabbed the refrigerator handle to keep from falling.

"Stand still," Albert said.

He let the clothesline fall to the floor, came up close behind her, crouched and reached under the back of her robe. The air felt warmer under there. He slid his hand up the smooth inner side of her left leg.

Charlene didn't move. She seemed to be holding her breath.

Where her thighs slanted close together, Albert felt her warmth on both sides of his hand.

He moved his hand higher.

She stiffened suddenly as if burnt, but she didn't protest or struggle.

"You know better," Albert whispered.

"Huh?"

"Than to fight me."

Keeping his hand between her legs, he stood up and pressed himself against her back.

With his other arm, he reached around in front of her. He opened a button, put his hand inside her robe, and squeezed one of her breasts.

Charlene pressed her face against the refrigerator. "There's nothing left to fight for," she muttered in a tired voice.

"You could fight to get away," Albert suggested. "The door's just over there."

"I can't get away," she said.

"I know."

As both his hands delved and caressed Charlene underneath her robe, he felt the weight of the knife in the pocket of his own robe.

I could do her right now.

But I want to *keep* her. I don't want all this to end. I don't want this *ever* to end.

Anyhow, who'd make my breakfast?

He let go of Charlene, stepped back and picked up the end of the clothesline. Then he went to the breakfast table. He swung out a chair and sat down.

Charlene stood between him and the kitchen door.

The door had four panes of glass in its upper half. Sunlight blazed through them, hurting his eyes when he tried to look at Charlene. He wished he had sunglasses.

"I want my bacon crisp," he said. "Nothing worse than limp bacon."

She raised her head and pulled open the refrigerator door.

"I think you've got to use low heat," he said, squinting as he watched her take out the flat box and shut the refrigerator. She opened the box as she carried it to the counter. There, the sunlight no longer blazed on her.

Much better. He could see her much more clearly now.

She crouched and removed a large skillet from a cupboard. Then she peeled off strips of bacon and arranged them in the skillet.

"If the heat's too high," Albert said, "you'll burn the bacon. It winds up tasting like sawdust. I can't stand burnt bacon. It's better off limp than burnt."

"I'll keep the heat low," Charlene said in her quiet voice. "It'll take longer, though."

"I'm not in any hurry." Scooting down on the chair, he crossed his legs at the ankles. "We'll have plenty of time no matter how long breakfast takes."

"How many slices do you want?"

"How many fit in the skillet?"

"Six. But they shrink up later on." She lifted the skillet and carried it over to the stove. "I could put in a couple more then."

"Do that." Albert flicked his wrist, making the rope leap. A wave seemed to roll down the rope all the way to her ankle. "Six for me, two for you."

"Thanks," she said.

He tugged the rope. It snapped taut, jerking her foot sideways off the floor. She dropped the skillet. It clamored against the burner as she flung up her arms to keep her balance.

Albert slackened the rope. Her heel thumped the linoleum.

"Next time," he said, "don't get smart."

"You're gonna kill me anyway."

"Maybe, maybe not. All depends."

She turned on the burner under the skillet.

"Depends on what?" she asked.

"I don't know. On how you act, I guess."

"I'm trying to be good. I do everything you tell me to, don't I?"

"Pretty much," he admitted.

"I don't try to fight you."

"Not so far." Smiling, he added, "Resistance would be futile, of course."

"I haven't even complained."

"Not very much."

"I've let you do everything, no matter how . . . no matter what. I've gone along with it all, haven't I?"

"Why don't you take off the robe?" Albert said.

She looked over her shoulder at him. "But I'm cold."

"Gosh, that almost sounds like a complaint."

Charlene took a deep breath, then stepped back from the stove and unfastened her buttons. She slid the robe down her arms, caught it with one hand and came toward Albert.

He watched the way her breasts jiggled up and down just slightly as she walked. Her nipples were pointing straight out, pink and stiff like the erasers on brand new pencils.

His gaze roamed down her belly, down to the shaved triangle, down to her hairless cleft.

She thrust the robe at him. "Here."

He took it and tossed it aside.

"Now back to the bacon," he said.

She turned around. On her way back to the stove, Albert stared at her sleek, bare back and the smooth slopes of her buttocks.

He took a deep breath, drawing the scent of bacon into his nostrils.

"Boy," he said, "life doesn't get much better than this."

"Ow!" Charlene blurted, lurching back from the stove.

"Huh?"

"It's spitting!"

"So?"

"It *hurts*."

"You're gonna hurt a lot worse if you let the bacon get burned."

She looked down at herself, shook her head, then frowned at Albert. "Let me wear the robe, okay?"

"Nope."

"An apron?"

"You're fine the way you are."

"It *burns* me."

Albert smiled. "Least you're not *freezing* anymore. Get back to the stove."

She stepped toward it. Flinching and grimacing as specks of hot oil flew against her bare skin, she picked up the spatula. She shoved at the bacon. After a few seconds, she shook her head.

"What's wrong?" Albert asked.

"I can't turn the bacon over with this thing. I need a fork."

"Just use the spatula."

She threw the spatula at the wall, whirled around and stomped her bare foot on the floor. The stomp made both her breasts jump. "It doesn't *work!*" she blurted.

"Okay, okay. Get a fork."

"Thank you."

She hurried across the kitchen, pulled open a drawer beside the sink and took out a long-handled fork. She carried it to the stove. Gripping the handle of the skillet, she started to turn the bacon slices.

"Just don't try any funny stuff with that fork," Albert warned her.

She ignored him and continued to turn the bacon over.

"I've got a knife right here," he said. He reached into the pocket of his robe, took out his switchblade and thumbed its button. The blade snicked out and locked. "Try anything with that fork, and I'll shove this up . . ."

Charlene tipped the skillet. Grease splashed the burner and ignited, flaming the pan.

What the . . . ?

She swung the blazing pan.

"Have your fucking bacon!" Charlene yelled.

Albert jerked the clothesline. It tugged her leg high and threw her backward, but not before the skillet flew from her hands—a fireball splashing flames toward the ceiling, toward the walls, toward him . . .

Eighteen

TRAPPED!

With a cry of alarm, Albert tumbled from his chair. He scurried into the dining room. His robe was wide open. He saw no flames on the naked front of his body. Afraid the robe might've caught fire, however, he threw his knife to the floor and whipped off the robe and swung it up in front of him.

It wasn't on fire, either.

She missed me!

Only then did Albert turn around and look into the blazing kitchen. He saw Charlene through the fire and black smoke.

On her feet.

Looking at him over her shoulder, she clawed at the door to the backyard.

She's gonna get away!

Pain shot through Albert's bowels, nearly doubling him over.

"You bitch!" he cried out.

Only one way to prevent her escape: run straight through the middle of the kitchen.

And burn my ass off? No thanks.

The door swung open and Charlene rushed outside.

Albert wondered about his chances of racing out the front door and catching up to her in the backyard.

Don't try it!

Even if he *could* get his hands on her, the place would soon be alive with firemen and cops.

I gotta get outta here!

Car keys upstairs!

No time!

Albert snatched his switchblade off the floor. He clamped it between his teeth. Pulling his robe on, he dashed to the front door. He threw it open and raced across the front yard toward the neighbor's house.

Too close!

He ran on past the neighbor's house. Trying to hold the robe shut, he sprinted down the block to the corner house. He staggered to a halt on its front stoop.

This'll be far enough, he thought. At least for a while.

As he tied his robe shut with its cloth belt, he realized he still had the knife clamped between his teeth.

Good move.

You make sure your dick's out of sight, but you run all over town with a knife in your fucking mouth!

He hadn't seen anyone, though. Maybe no one had seen him, either.

His jaw ached from biting at the knife.

He took the knife out of his mouth, unlocked the blade and folded it into the handle. Then he slipped the knife into the right-hand pocket of the robe.

After double-checking to make sure his robe was shut, he pounded on the door. "Help!" he shouted. "Fire!"

He waited a few seconds, then pounded some more.

"Fire!" he yelled.

The door swung open. On the other side of the thresh-old stood a gaunt woman in hair curlers and a pink robe. Her eyes looked urgent behind their wire-rimmed glasses.

Before she could speak, Albert lunged forward and took her down. He landed hard on top of her and slapped a hand across her mouth. "Don't scream," he gasped.

Behind her round glasses, her eyes bulged with fright.

"Promise?"

She nodded, her mouth shoving at his hand.

"Okay then." Albert let go of her mouth.

She screamed.

"Stop!"

The scream grated on Albert.

What if someone else is home?

"Shut up!" he warned.

She didn't, so he drove the heel of his hand into her chin. Her mouth slammed shut, teeth crashing together. The scream stopped.

"Thank you," Albert said.

But she started gasping and choking.

Albert climbed off her.

She rolled over, pushed herself up to her hands and knees, then began spitting blood and bits of teeth onto her beige carpet.

"Don't give me any more shit," Albert warned.

She stopped spitting long enough to say, "Creep."

"Shut the fuck up."

"You're a *bum*."

"Any more shit and I'll kill you." Thinking of Char-lene, he muttered, "Fucking bitch."

"Asswipe!"

He swatted the back of her head. A pink curler flew off and rolled across the foyer.

"From now on, do everything I say or I'll kill you. I'll cut the life right out of you. Now, get up."

She didn't make a move to get up. She only turned her head and stared at him.

But not at his face.

The belt of his robe had worked loose and the robe hung open. "Take a good look," he said. "This might be the last one you ever see. Now, get up."

She slowly stood, a hand cupped across her bleeding mouth.

"Let's see the kitchen," Albert said.

She walked ahead of him.

Slowly. Too slowly. Albert shoved her and said, "Get it in gear."

As they entered the kithen, he noticed a wooden rack hanging near the sink. It held five knives of various shapes and sizes. He selected a long, slim-bladed carving knife. "Beautiful," he said.

Much better than the knife in his pocket. The blade of this one was at least twice as long.

He could almost *feel* it sliding in.

Into her?

"Oh m'god," she said into her muffling hand.

"Take it easy," Albert said.

She shook her head. Then she glanced from the knife to his penis and back to the knife, regarding them both with equal horror.

"I'm not gonna hurt you," he said. "Or *fuck* you. Who'd *want* to, you ugly hag."

Her eyes narrowed.

"What's behind there?" Albert asked, pointing the knife at the door behind him. "The garage?"

She nodded.

Not taking his eyes off her, he backed up, reached behind himself and opened the door. Below the hem of his robe, a cool draft blew against his bare calves.

He looked over his shoulder.

A two-car garage, half-empty. The bay door was shut.

The car was an olive green Pontiac, brand new and shiny.

"Keys?" he asked.

She pointed at the kitchen table.

Albert didn't see the keys. He saw a toaster, a coffee pot, a newspaper, a cup with some coffee still in it . . .

Lipstick on the rim of the cup.

Lipstick?

This scrawny old hag didn't seem to be wearing any.

Her forefinger jabbed the air.

Albert followed its aim and saw a key ring partly hidden beneath a corner of the morning newspaper.

He rushed to the table and snatched it up.

And heard distant sirens.

"Let's go. Come on, let's go."

She shook her head, staring down at his penis. "No, please!"

He shoved the handle of the carving knife between his teeth. His right hand free, he grabbed her by the arm and dragged her into the garage.

At the trunk of the Pontiac, he fumbled with the keys and found one that looked as if it might be the one.

"Just come with me," he told the woman. "If anyone drops by here they'll think you went for a drive." He shoved the key into the trunk's lock and gave it a twist. The lid of the trunk sprang up.

"No," the woman said, blood spilling down her chin.

"Yes."

"Please. I don't wanna . . ."

With both hands, Albert jammed the knife into her belly and knocked her backward into the trunk. The whole car shook when she landed.

She lay on her back, legs dangling over the edge. They were skinny and white and veiny. He lifted them, swung them sideways and dropped them into the trunk. Then he slammed down the top.

The shutting trunk blew a quick gust of air against his bare skin.

He looked down at his erection.

Gimme a break, he thought.

Then he realized it wasn't because of *her*. It couldn't *possibly* have been because of her.

It was the stabbing.

Albert smiled with relief, then tied his robe shut and rushed back into the house.

Purse on the kitchen counter.

Maybe grab it on the way out.

He raced upstairs.

Sirens everywhere, hell breaking loose.

Would the cops do a house-to-house search?

Sure. All they've gotta do is hear what Charlene's got to say, they'll be tearing up everything in sight trying to find me.

But that'll take a while, he told himself. Not long, but a while.

At the entrance to the master bedroom, he stopped and gazed in. A huge mirror was fixed to the ceiling over the king-sized bed.

"Fantastic," he muttered.

He stepped into the bedroom. Glimpsing a woman's head, he lurched sideways.

Jesus!

Only a wig form, a plastic head capped with a blond wig.

He slumped and tried to catch his breath.

His stomach lurched at the sudden, tinny sound of an amplified voice.

The fire chief, he realized. Just the goddamn fire chief half a block away, directing his men. Calm down. Calm down and grab some clothes and get out of here.

He rushed to one of the closets and rolled open its door.

Women's clothes.

Wrong closet.

He ran to the other and opened it. More women's clothes.

"Shit!"

Where's the husband's stuff?

On the dresser were two jewelry cases. One was nearly

two feet high, fashioned like a miniature highboy. The bracelets, rings, broaches and earrings inside it were light and elegant. Plenty of diamonds and pearls. Classy stuff.

He sidestepped to the other end of the dresser and opened the plain wooden jewelry box. No diamonds, no pearls. Lots of brass and silver, lots of wood, lots of turquoise. Rustic, Navaho-type stuff.

He opened a drawer. Couched on a stack of bright panties was a cylinder of white plastic nearly a foot long and rounded at one end. He picked it up like a flashlight and flicked the switch. With a quiet buzz, it began to tingle.

He remembered the lipstick on the coffee cup.

Was the "husband" a woman?

Who's got time to worry about it? he thought.

Get outta here! Charlene's probably spilling her story to the cops right now! Telling the whole deal. Describing me!

Male Caucasian, age seventeen, five foot nine . . .

"Whoo!"

It was hard to keep from leaping with joy.

Male? Shit no!

Dropping his robe, Albert rushed across the bedroom toward the blond wig.

NINETEEN

LESTER TRIES HIS LUCK

Each day, Lester had toyed with the idea of returning to the Willow Inn. Each day, when he came to the left-hand turn that would take him there, he kept on driving straight and returned home wondering if Emily Jean Bonner had been there waiting for him.

Today would be different, he told himself as he approached the intersection. Today, he would make that turn.

When he saw the traffic light, he flipped down the arm

of his turn signal. He slowed. The light changed to yellow, then to red. He stopped at the crosswalk.

My God, I'm really going to do it!

What if Emily Jean isn't there?

Maybe I'll drink with someone else. Were other women there last time?

The place had been fairly empty.

Emily Jean'll be there. She has to be.

After buying a margarita at the bar, Lester wandered through the dimly lighted room. The place had more customers than the last time he'd been here. He glanced around, checking the faces at every table.

Emily Jean's wasn't among them.

But he found three possibilities.

Two of the women sat together and the third sat alone. Lester took a table near the lone woman.

She looked sleek and cool. Her blond hair was cut short. Her chiffon blouse, open wide at the throat, lightly draped her breasts and showed the shapes of her erect nipples.

Nice, Lester thought. Real nice.

Too nice. She'll never have anything to do with a guy like me.

He turned his attention to the other two women.

They sat across from each other, both sipping drinks that looked like whiskey sours. From where he sat, he could only see the back of the brunette. Her light-haired friend had a good face, but something annoyed him about it. He watched her talk, watched her listen and respond. Finally, he recognized the problem: she wore a constant sneer.

Forget her. Forget about her friend, too. They're probably both a couple of creeps.

He returned his attention to the lone woman.

She seemed so completely alone—alone with her martini, which she held lightly in her hand even when it rested on the table. Not once while Lester watched did she raise her eyes from the glass.

He wondered if he should try her.

No wedding ring.

But a woman with her looks couldn't possibly be on the make. There had to be a man in the picture, probably a lawyer or doctor or Hollywood producer.

Unless . . . unless a lot of things. She might be recently divorced or widowed. She might be a housewife who likes to dress in her best and grab a quickie from a stranger in the afternoon before her hubby gets home from work. She might be a lesbian. Or a high-priced hooker.

Why not give her a try? Lester thought. The worst she can do is turn me down.

Her glass was empty. She was turning her head, looking for the cocktail waitress.

Heart thundering, Lester stood up and went to her. At the last moment before her eyes met him, he remembered his wedding ring. He quickly pulled it off.

"May I buy you a drink?" he asked.

Her questioning eyes sparkled in the candlelight and she smiled at him. "I'm afraid I'm waiting for a friend to join me. Otherwise, I'd be delighted."

"Well, I just thought I'd ask."

"I'm glad you did. Thank you."

"Well . . . be seeing you."

He backed away, disgusted by the way he'd handled her rejection.

Just thought I'd ask.

Spectacular.

She must think I'm a total loser.

So what? he told himself. Doesn't really matter what she thinks of me. I'll probably never see her again, anyway.

Not returning to his table, he left the Willow Inn.

As he drove toward home, he relived the scene with the woman again and again, each time feeling his skin grow hot with embarrassment.

I shouldn't have tried her, he thought.

He'd *known* it would be a disaster.

Nothing wrong with asking. At least I didn't wimp out.

He suddenly wondered if she really *had* been waiting for a friend to join her. Maybe she'd just said that to get rid of Lester.

I didn't measure up. She said it to blow me off.

It seemed like a strong possibility.

Lester burned with embarrassment.

Then he told himself, If she's a woman who would pull that sort of stunt, I don't *want* to know her.

"Wouldn't mind screwing her, though," he said aloud, and laughed softly.

By the time he reached home, he no longer considered his attempt a failure. Instead, he saw it as a first step, uncertain and awkward, toward a new life.

A life with a woman who might *care* about him.

He would find one sooner or later.

A real woman, not a cold bitch like Helen.

He found Helen napping in the bedroom. She was lying facedown under the sheet. Her shoulders were bare. He could see the shape of her body underneath the sheet.

She's naked under there, he realized.

I could pull the sheet down and roll her over and spread her legs and . . .

Except she's Helen.

TWENTY

ALICIA

Albert liked the woman's Pontiac. It had power and lots of class. Best of all, it had air-conditioning. As far as he could see, its only drawback was the red needle on its gas gauge that kept creeping to the left. Before long, it would point to E.

The mere thought of stopping at a gas station made his insides cramp.

No way could he stop for gas. Not with a corpse in the trunk.

The needle touched E as he drove into Wichita, Kansas. Expecting the engine to die at any moment, he swung into the parking lot behind a Sambo's restaurant and took a space close to the building.

He aimed the rearview mirror at his face.

Not bad, but something looked wrong.

He applied fresh lipstick.

He still looked strange. Then he recognized the trouble: the wig. At close range, anyone could see it was phony. It just didn't fit right.

He pulled it off. His long blond hair was matted flat. He took a brush from the purse and worked at his hair for several minutes, parting it slightly off center and bringing it down his forehead so feathery bangs swept across his right eye.

"Beautiful," he said.

He picked up the purse, climbed out of the car and locked its door. As he walked past Sambo's, the aromas made his stomach churn with hunger. But he kept walking.

He went for blocks. The soles of the sandals burnt his feet. His bra, too tight, pinched his sides.

The bra gave him the look he needed, though. He watched his wavering reflection in store windows. Hard to believe he was actually seeing himself. The girl in the window was slim and long-legged in her turtleneck and skirt. Her short hair gave her a tomboy look.

I wouldn't mind getting her myself, he thought.

Get her alone and . . .

As he imagined slicing her clothes off, the front of her skirt began to bulge.

He walked the next block holding his purse in front.

Don't think about that stuff, he told himself. Think of *bad* stuff.

Like the cops getting me.

That isn't gonna happen, he told himself. Long as I keep

on the move, they'll never lay their hands on me. They'll never even figure out all this stuff was done by the same guy, much less *who*.

By the time Albert reached the corner, the bulge was gone. He sighed heavily and crossed the street.

Just ahead, a movie marquee announced *Fangs of the Wolf* and *Zombie Queen*. Albert stopped beneath it. He stepped in front of the posters: both had photos of screaming, half-naked women.

He went to the ticket window. The chunky, white-haired woman inside busied herself with a crossword puzzle while Albert read the show times. *Zombie Queen* would be starting in twenty minutes.

Speaking with feminine tones he had practiced in the car, he bought a ticket. He stepped into the lobby.

"I'll take yer ticket, honey," called a pimpled man behind the snack counter. He reached out a hand as Albert approached. "Intermission's in ten minutes. Plenty of time to buy yerself a nice snack."

"Maybe later," Albert said.

The air was rich with aromas of perfume and food. Popcorn was popping like softly muffled strings of fire-crackers, the white puffs spilling out over the top of the machine's metal basket. Half a dozen hot dogs rotated slowly on spikes, their brown skins dotted with sweat.

Saliva flooded Albert's mouth.

First things first.

Aware of the man's eyes following him, he took short steps and kept his arms close to his sides, imitating the way he'd seen women walk. He gently pushed open the door marked Ladies and stepped into the restroom.

Nobody at the sinks.

Bending, he peered under the stall doors. No feet.

He quickly locked himself inside the stall at the end. After checking the toilet seat to make sure it was clean, he pulled up his skirt and lowered his panties and sat down.

The toilet seat was cold.

Somebody had chipped "FUCK YOU" into the green paint of the stall door. The only other markings Albert could find were "Angel luvs Blueboy" and "EAT ME" both written in ink above the toilet paper dispenser.

He opened his purse. He took out his knife, thumbed the button to make its blade spring out, then pressed its point to the metal partition and began to scratch letters.

Green paint came off in slim curls.

He wrote, "Albert is a real cut-up."

Grinning, he put the knife away. Then he glanced inside a bin marked Napkin Disposal. Empty.

He flushed the toilet and left the stall. Standing at a sink, he checked himself in a mirror and ran the brush through his hair. Then he returned to the theater lobby.

The man behind the snack counter greeted him with a smile of oddly small teeth and long, pale gums.

"I'll have a hot dog and a Dr. Pepper," Albert said, trying his best to sound like a woman. "Large, please."

That would have to do for starters. It wouldn't look right for a young lady to make a complete hog out of herself.

"Haven't seen you 'round here before," the man said.

"Neither have I," replied Albert.

The man's smile vanished. His eyes darkened as if he wanted to teach Albert manners, but he said nothing. He set the hot dog and Dr. Pepper on the counter. "That's a dollar fifty."

Albert handed him a pair of bills.

"Outta two."

Albert counted the change carefully. Then he took his snacks off the counter.

He was squeezing a stream of mustard onto his bun when the doors opened for intermission. He licked a smear of mustard off the side of his thumb and watched the audience come out.

Except for a couple of old folks and a bearded dirty guy who looked like a wino, the audience was made up of young people. Older than Albert, but young.

There must be a college near here, he thought.

Four of those who came out were girls. One had a pouty scowl that turned her good looks sour. She was followed by a couple walking hand in hand. Both had greasy hair and wore faded dresses that hung shapelessly down their thin bodies. They were decorated with lots of multi-colored beads. The fourth girl, the only good one of the lot, was holding the arm of a young man who had to duck through the doorway.

None of them, Albert thought.

He folded his hot dog into its foil wrapper, entered the auditorium and looked for a seat. He found one he liked near the center, sat down and placed his Dr. Pepper on the floor between his feet.

The hot dog was warm through its wrapper. He took it out. The vinegar smell of mustard made him pucker. He moaned with pleasure as he took it into his mouth: the warm soft bun, the eye-watering mustard, the wiener that sprayed hot juices into his mouth when he broke its skin. He chewed for a long time, savoring it before swallowing.

Then came quiet, distant voices.

He looked over his shoulder. Two women were walking down the aisle.

"Fantastic," he muttered.

One was a blonde at least six feet tall. The head of her friend came up only to her shoulders.

Albert took another bite of his hot dog and watched them. They entered the row in front of him.

The tall one wore faded jeans and a denim jacket. The jacket was open, showing a Woody Woodpecker T-shirt pushed forward by a pair of enormous breasts.

Her friend was a bit chunky, but she looked good in her corduroy trousers and sweatshirt. Wholesome and cute like a puppy. Albert crossed his legs and imagined the feel of a long, smooth thrust into her pudgy stomach.

The theater darkened. He watched the movie, finished his hot dog, drank his Dr. Pepper and daydreamed about what he would like to do to the women sitting in front of him.

At intermission, he bought a buttered popcorn and another Dr. Pepper. When he returned, a man was sitting in his row.

Directly behind the pudgy woman.

For a moment, Albert stood in the aisle wondering whether to look for a new seat.

I like mine.

I was there first.

The man was slouched so that his knees pressed the back of the seat in front of him.

"Excuse me," Albert said.

"I most certainly will." The man sat up straight and turned his legs.

Albert tried to squeeze by without touching, but the backs of his legs brushed against the man's knee.

He stepped past one empty seat, then sank down in the seat he'd been using before intermission. The cushion was still warm.

"What did you think of *Zombie Queen*?"

Albert looked over at the man, forced a smile and said, "It was fine."

Where was this guy during *that* movie? What did he do, change seats so he'd be closer to the two gals?

Or closer to me?

"The pace wasn't quite what it should be," the man said, "but Fung's photography was superb, as usual. Are you a student?"

"No."

"Your popcorn certainly smells good."

Albert almost said, "Then buy some," but the two women could probably hear everything. "Would you like some?" he asked, and started to extend the tub across the vacant seat.

"Thank you. All right if I . . . ?" The man moved into the seat beside Albert, then took a handful of popcorn. "I would've guessed you must be a frosh."

"A what?"

"A freshman. At State. Freshmen have a certain look about them, a certain innocence and intensity that I find quite refreshing."

"I'm just passing through town," Albert told him.

"On your way to . . . ?"

He filled his mouth with popcorn to give himself time to think. After chewing for a while, he said, "Los Angeles. To visit my real father."

"Parents divorced?"

Albert nodded. For a moment, he thought about his mother screaming while he lay hidden under the bed—and how she'd looked when he finally climbed free.

The man put his hand on Albert's knee.

"Don't feel too bad about that," he said. "Were you very old when they split up?"

"It's been a year."

"Terrible thing." The man patted Albert's knee. "I'm afraid that most parents have very little concept of the profound trauma they inflict on their children when . . ."

"Would you take your hand off me, please?"

The man didn't move. Instead, he looked steadily into Albert's eyes and said, "You shouldn't be afraid of the human touch. We all need to touch and be touched. Tactile contact is as necessary to human survival as food, as shelter from the cold. Those who fear it are perhaps in even more desperate need . . ."

Albert gripped the hand that was stroking his thigh.

"Get your goddamn hand off me!" he snapped.

The big blonde in the next row turned her head around. "Knock it off, y'filthy prick, or we'll call an usher." Her eyes moved from the startled man to Albert. "C'mon up here, honey. You can sit with us." Then she glared at the man. "Get the hell outta here, Fred."

Albert hurried down the row.

"Go on," the blonde continued. "Get your trashy ass

outta here. You come in, start hittin' on strangers. Some kinda fuckin' pervert."

As Albert walked up the next row, he saw the man get up and start to leave.

"C'mon and sit right here." The blonde slapped the seat beside her. "Gal can't go anyplace without some prick trying to get a mitt in her drawers. I'm Karen, this is Tess."

The chubby one on the other side of Karen leaned forward, smiling. "Hi," she said.

"Nice to meet you." Albert thought fast. "I'm Alicia." To Karen, he said, "I sure am grateful for your help."

"Fast Freddy oughta be locked in a kennel, the slobberin' degenerate."

"Do you know him?" Albert asked.

Tess leaned forward and said, "Karen calls everyone Fred.

"Only nimble-fingered pussy grabbers like him."

"You'll have to excuse her vocabulary."

"Bullshit," Karen said.

"I don't mind," said Albert as the theater darkened for *Fangs of the Wolf*.

The film began with an eerie howl in the fog. Albert settled back in his seat. He could feel Karen's warmth against his arm. He could smell her perfume.

"My bus doesn't leave till eight," Albert said as he followed Karen and Tess out of the movie theater. "How about if I buy us all some dinner?"

"That sounds real fine, honey. I'd be all for it except I've gotta get home. Steppin' out tonight."

"A bath takes her a long time," Tess said. "There's so much to wash."

"Have you got a date, too?" Albert asked.

Tess shook her head and looked for a moment as if she might cry. "Not tonight."

"Well, maybe the two of us should go somewhere for dinner. I hate to . . . I'm kind of nervous after what happened with that *man*. I'd hate to just sit alone in the bus terminal."

"Over at the depot," Karen said, "there'd be cruds hittin' on you right 'n left."

"I guess we could find a restaurant somewhere," Tess said.

"Instead of that," said Karen, "why don't you c'mon over to *our* place for supper? It'll be cheaper, 'n you won't have to be fightin' off the men."

Tess smiled and nodded. "Good idea. We've got all that lasagna in the freezer."

"You like lasagna, honey?"

"Sure. It's great."

"After we get done eating," Tess said, "I can drive you over to the station in time to catch your bus."

"Great. That's just great. Fantastic."

He walked with them to their car.

TWENTY—ONE

A PRINCE OF A FELLOW

"I hope you won't think I'm rude, but I always like to eat with the TV on." Tess smiled seriously as she turned on the television. "I like to keep up on things."

"It's fine with me," said Albert.

Tess started to set up the TV trays. "I just don't feel right if I'm not up on things, you know?"

A buzzer sounded, startling Albert. He thought it must be the oven timer, but it buzzed again.

"Would somebody-goddamnit get the door?" Karen yelled from the bathroom.

"On my way," Tess called. She placed a tray in front of Albert. "That's probably Steve," she explained as she hurried away.

The television took a moment to warm up. Then the screen fluttered alive and Albert recognized *Gilligan's Island*.

"Hi, Steve. Karen'll be ready in a minute."

Albert turned and saw a stocky, muscular man.

"Alicia, I want you to meet Steve Colvert."

He strutted over to Albert. "Pleased to meet you, Alicia."

"Alicia is on her way to Los Angeles," Tess explained.

"Okay! Gonna make movies, huh? You'll look great on the silver screen. I can see you now. Just don't let yourself get into . . . *Okay! Gilligan's Island!* Hey, this isn't the one where his tooth turns into a radio, is it? Yeah, sure. I'd know it anywhere. I've only seen it five dozen times. One of the best."

"We were planning to watch the news," Tess said, and set up a tray for herself at a chair beside the couch.

"Are you kidding? This is a goddamn classic! You can't turn off a classic to watch the *news*, what's the matter with you? Only violence and corruption, anyway. This is a deathless classic. You can't turn off a deathless classic!"

"I guess we can wait till you leave."

He stood beside Albert's chair, silently watching the television until a commercial came on. Then he said, "Where the hell's Jake tonight?"

"I wouldn't know," Tess said.

"Whadaya mean, you wouldn't know?"

"I don't know where he is. He isn't here. I haven't heard from him."

"You guys have a fight or something?"

"Never mind."

"Okay, okay. Don't get sensitive. Sorry I brought it up. God, you gals always get so goddamn sensitive. You would be good for nothing if it wasn't for your you-know-whats. Am I right, Alicia?"

Albert shook his head, grinning.

A bell rang.

"Excuse me," Tess said. "The oven." She hurried out of the room.

"So, you're on your way to L.A., huh? Traveling alone?"
Albert nodded.

"Aren't you awful young for that?"

"I'm almost twenty."

"No kidding. You look more like sixteen."

"I'm young for my age."

"Uh-oh, it's starting."

"Reckon I'm ready as I'll ever be," Karen announced as she entered the room.

"Shhhh. *Gilligan's Island.*"

"Fuck *Gilligan's Island.* My tail's starting to drag from starvation."

"Looks okay to me," Steve said, not taking his eyes from the television.

"Only okay? Watch I don't trade you in, numb-nuts."

Albert looked over at Karen just as she turned around. Her green dress was tied behind her neck like an apron. It had no back at all until it wrapped around to cling over her buttocks.

"Say!" Steve said when he finally looked.

"Like it?"

"Say!"

She bent down to pick something off the rug—a potato chip crumb?—and the front of her dress drooped toward the floor, showing a pale side of breast.

"Christ!" Steve said.

She turned her head and grinned at him.

She seemed completely unaware of Albert, giving him plenty of time to stare before she finally straightened up.

"We'd better get going," Steve said. "Nice meeting you, Alicia."

"Yeah," said Karen, smiling at Albert. "Have yourself a good trip, honey."

"Thank you." He thought he should stand, but he remained seated because of his erection. "I *love* your dress."

"You oughta get one your own self," said Karen. "Knocks the fellas dead."

"I'm sure it does."

"Let's get going," Steve said.

Tess came in from the kitchen carrying a plate of lasagna in each hand. "You guys leaving now?" she asked.

"We're just about off," Karen told her. "Probably won't see you till Sunday."

"Well, have a nice time."

"Yeah," said Albert. "Enjoy yourselves."

"We will," answered Steve. "We sure will." He put an arm around Karen's back and walked her toward the door. The top of his head was level with her shoulder, which he kissed just before he opened the door.

When they were gone, Albert smiled at Tess and asked, "They're going to spend the weekend together?"

"Oh, sure. They usually do. If they don't have a fight, anyway. I think they'll get engaged one of these days. How about some wine with supper?"

"Great."

He watched Tess go to the kitchen. She still had on the corduroy trousers and sweatshirt she'd worn at the movies, but now she was barefoot. Albert wondered if she was naked under the sweatshirt.

If she isn't, I can sure make her that way fast enough.

She came back with a bottle of Burgundy and two glasses. She set a glass on her tray and brought one to Albert. She poured for him. She smelled of Jean Nate.

"I personally think the guy's a dork," she said, "but Karen's crazy about him."

"He seemed all right to me."

"He's a major dork, take my word for it. *Gilligan's Island*!" She turned to a different channel. A commercial. She glanced at her wristwatch. "The news'll be on in a minute. What time did you say your bus leaves?"

"Eight."

"If we leave here by a quarter past seven, I guess that'll give us enough time." She sat in her stuffed chair beside the couch. "So where are you from?" she asked and started to eat.

"Chicago," Albert said. He took a bite of the lasagna. It was hot and good.

"Chicago? I'm from Milwaukee. We're almost neighbors."

"How'd you end up in Wichita?"

"Oh, some dork that works for Boeing dragged me here against my better judgement. Boy, was that ever the biggest mistake of my life. We no sooner got into town than he dumped me."

"That's terrible."

"Well, he was a jerk. Most guys are."

"I've noticed," Albert said.

"The good ones are few and far between. And mostly they're already taken."

"How come you're still here?"

"Who knows? Hell, I'm halfway done getting my credential from State."

"Credential?"

"So I can be a teacher. Big mistake number two. Boy, if I'd had any idea . . . every guy and his brother, sister, cousin and uncle is in teaching. The chances of getting a job, if I ever *do* get the darned credential, are almost nil."

"That's really . . ."

Albert's voice went dead as he gazed, stunned, at the television screen.

". . . a police artist's sketch of the suspect, who has been tentatively identified as Albert Mason Prince. Prince, a seventeen-year-old male Caucasian, disappeared Saturday night from the North Glen, Illinois home of his father. In addition to the Kansas City slayings, Prince is now being sought by Illinois authorities in connection with the double stabbing deaths of Mrs. Arnold Broxton and . . ."

"Isn't that something?" Tess said. "He looks enough like you to be your bro . . ."

His tray crashed forward as he lunged. He grabbed the wine bottle's neck and swung, smashing the bottle against the back of Tess's head and flinging out an arm in time to stop her face from slamming into her plate.

". . . is considered extremely dangerous. Should you recognize the suspect, please notify your local police at once."

TWENTY—TWO

THE GRAY GHOST

When the doorbell rang, Janet's hand jumped. The lipstick gave her a rakish, one-sided mustache.

"Want me to get it?" Meg called.

"Thanks, would you?" She wiped the mustache off, finished putting on her lipstick, and gave herself a once-over in the bathroom mirror. The polyester blouse was cheerful with red and blue swirls, but it hung against her skin in a way that showed more than she really liked. Especially her bra.

Well, better that than a couple of nipples sticking out. Dave used to be at them constantly when she wore this blouse.

The thought of Dave made her sad and angry.

He's gone, she told herself. He might as well be dead, the bastard.

Except part of him would always be with her.

Forget it. Pretend he's dead. Better for the kid to have no dad at all than a creep like Dave.

She slipped into a pale blue jacket that matched her slacks, flipped a brush through her hair, and left the bathroom.

"Hey-de-*hey!*"

"Hi, Moses."

"*Mosby.* What I lack in speed and brains, I make up in numbers."

"Do you know what he's talking about?" Meg asked.

"Who, me?" Janet looked at Mosby's skinny, grinning face. "Do *you* know what you're talking about?"

"The Gray Ghost. John Singleton Mosby. *General* John Singleton Mosby, a Johnny Reb whose band of guerrillas wrought havoc on the Yanks. My friends started calling me Mosby because . . ."

"You like to monkey around?" Meg suggested.

"Ha! Sharp! Guerrilla, monkey, sharp! You're a character, Meg."

"My friends started calling me Meg because I'm a nut."

"A nut?" For a moment, Mosby looked puzzled. Then his face lit up. "Hey, sure! Nutmeg!" He flapped an elbow sideways toward Janet. "Hope you're as spicy as your roommate."

"We'll see," Janet said and picked up her purse.

"Looks like we're off, Meg. Nice meeting you. Don't wait up."

When they were outside in the cool, foggy night, Mosby put his hand on Janet's shoulder and said, "I'm a sucker for enchiladas, how about you?"

"Fine by me."

He opened the car door for her. She climbed in and leaned across the front seat to open his door.

"Thank you, thank you. My mother thanks you, my father thanks you . . ."

"They're all welcome."

Mosby talked nonstop while he drove. Janet listened and sometimes answered. She smiled and laughed when it seemed appropriate.

After twenty mintues, he pulled into the driveway of *Casa del Toro*. A parking valet in a white jacket opened the car door for Janet.

"Best margaritas in town," Mosby said. He took her hand. "You always go first-class when you travel with the Gray Ghost."

"That's the spirit."

TWENTY—THREE

THE MESS

Tess died with a scream in her eyes.

Albert climbed off her.

He found her gray sweatshirt on the floor beside the bed.

She'd looked so cute and cuddly in it. The bulky thing had made her seem tubbier than she really was.

It had hidden her breasts, too. But they'd been there, all right, when he cut the sweatshirt open. No bra, just bare skin.

She'd been out cold but still in her chair at the time, so her breasts sat on her chest like a couple of small scoops of ice cream. Later, when he put her down on her back, they'd flattened out and almost disappeared. Except for her nipples, which were huge.

Fabulous nipples.

Albert started getting hard again as he remembered how they'd looked—and how large and springy they'd felt in his mouth.

He wished he hadn't killed Tess right away like that. Would've been nice to keep her alive for a couple more days—have some fun with her while he waited for Karen.

"That's the way it goes," he muttered.

He hadn't *meant* to kill her like that. He'd had every intention of enjoying her a little bit at a time, making shallow cuts and bandaging them after he got done, making her last.

That's how he'd handled Charlene and it had been *fabulous*.

Fabulous, right. She got away and I never got to do the best part.

The best part.

So maybe he *had* gotten too excited with Tess, but she wouldn't be escaping from him and he wouldn't be missing out on anything.

He'd gotten to the best part a little sooner than planned, that's all.

Closing his eyes, Albert moaned with pleasure at the memory of those final thrusts.

They were worth it! Shit, you can't always hold back. Sometimes, you just gotta go for it.

But try to do better with Karen, he told himself. Try to take it easy on her so she'll last a while.

Gotta wait till Sunday! How'll I stand it?

Who knows? he thought. Maybe I won't have to wait that long. Tess said they get into fights sometimes and Karen comes home early. Maybe that'll happen this weekend.

Sure hope so.

Just don't show up *now*, he thought. Give me a couple of hours to clean up.

Using Tess's sweatshirt, he wiped some of the blood and semen and feces off his naked body so he wouldn't drip on his way to the bathroom.

He walked backward to see whether he was leaving any mess on the carpet.

It looked fine.

In the bathroom, he shut and locked the door.

Who you trying to keep out, Norman Bates?

He laughed.

But his laughter died as he imagined Tess's gashed body rising off the bed and stumbling toward the bathroom like a zombie from *Night of the Living Dead*.

Like *that's* gonna happen, he thought.

He imagined her pounding on the bathroom door and goose bumps scurried up his back.

"Get real," he muttered, stepping over to the tub. There was no shower curtain. He'd used it to protect the bed before starting in on Tess. Good thing, too. The bed would've been ruined.

He pictured her staggering toward the bathroom door, wearing the shower curtain like a pale, see-through toga.

"Just try it," he said, "and I'll do you again."

Laughing softly, he started the water. When it felt good and hot, he turned on the shower and stepped into the tub.

Water sprayed him *and* the bathroom floor.

Another mess to clean up.

It was only water, though. It would be a cinch compared to the mess in the bedroom. He wished there was a way to avoid cleaning *that* up. But this was only Friday night. No way could he stick around until Sunday without taking care of it.

What if I leave?

It'd sure be safer that way.

And miss out on Karen?

Not a chance, he told himself. No way. He would just have to resign himself to cleaning up all the messes.

He turned off the faucets and climbed out of the tub, done with his first shower of the night.

TWENTY—FOUR

SNEAK ATTACKS

During the first ten minutes of the film, Mosby's hands were busy with popcorn. Once the popcorn was gone, however, he began on Janet's hand. He held it, pressed it, squeezed it, interlaced its fingers with his, and used it to transport his hand up her thigh until she put on the brakes.

Then he moved her hand over to *his* leg. He let it rest near his knee, but soon began to slide it so slowly up his leg that Janet didn't recognize his plan until she felt the hard bulge.

That's when she took back her hand.

And Mosby started on her shoulder.

Janet knew what he was after: her right breast.

Arm stretched across her back, he tried to disguise his intention by holding her right shoulder for a while. Soon, however, he reached around the outside of her arm and went for it.

Too far away.

So he tried for a shortcut by prying into her armpit from behind. This would've taken several inches off the route, giving him a clear shot at her breast.

Janet foiled the attempt by keeping her arm clamped tight against her side.

By the time he quit, her arm was trembling from the effort.

He gave up on the breast only to resume working on her leg. He started at the knee. As the film progressed, so did his hand. It was warm through her slacks. She didn't mind so much, at first. But it steadily crept higher.

Just as she was ready to reach down and stop it, Mosby's hand quickly moved the final distance and pressed against her inseam. She caught her breath.

"Don't," she whispered.

His fingers pressed harder and rubbed.

"Stop it, Mosby."

"It's all right," he whispered.

"Don't," Janet said. "Please." But she didn't try to move his hand away.

It felt good.

She gasped a loud, excited breath.

Heads turned.

She knocked Mosby's hand away and sat up straight, heat pulsing into her face.

A few seconds later, Mosby's hand returned to her knee.

"No," she said.

He began moving it higher, so she picked it up and placed it firmly on his own knee.

"And keep it there!"

During the rest of the film, he kept his hand to himself.

The film ended. The lights came on. "Are we off?" Mosby asked. He grinned as if he were quite pleased with himself.

Janet resisted an urge to make a crack.

They left the theater. The night was chilly. Though Janet was wearing a light jacket, Mosby put his arm across her shoulders. She decided not to complain.

In the vacant Safeway lot where his car was parked, he pulled her against him. He kissed her, and she didn't fight it.

At least we're not in the middle of a crowded movie theater.

Not such a bad kiss, either. It seemed eager, but also tender.

He can't be such a bad guy, she thought, if he kisses like this.

When his tongue touched her lips, she opened her mouth to accept it. She sucked it and tongued it and when she felt his hand gently curl over her breast, she thrust her own tongue into his mouth.

Then his hand moved under her blouse.

She clutched his wrist and took her mouth away. "No you don't," she said.

"Let's go to my place," he said.

"No."

"Come on. Why not?"

"We might end up in bed."

"That's the whole idea. No pun intended."

Janet pushed him away. "Take me home, okay?"

"But Meg's there."

"I know she is. It's her house. You're very nice, Mosby, and I've had a good time tonight, but this is as far as it goes. Seriously. I'm not going to sleep with you."

"Who said anything about sleep?"

"Don't be so lame."

The words seemed to deflate him. "Oh," he muttered. "Okay. Sorry." He smiled a little sadly and opened the car door for her.

On the way to Meg's house, he looked over at Janet and said, "I guess you don't like me much."

"I like you fine." She didn't sound convincing even to herself.

"Then why won't you sleep with me?"

"Don't give me a hard time, Mose."

"No pun intended?"

"You'd be a lot more attractive if you'd stop being so jerky about stuff."

"Jerky?"

"Sorry."

"I'm a *jerk?* God, you must really despise me."

"Nobody despises you."

"You do. Hell, who am I kidding? *Everyone* does. I'm pushy, obnoxious, boring . . ."

"But I think there's a pretty good guy underneath the pushy, obnoxious, boring jerk."

He let out a single, sad laugh and said, "Sure."

"A good guy trying to get out."

"Maybe I don't *want* to let him out," Mosby said. "Maybe if I let him out, he'll get dumped on."

"Everybody gets dumped on," Janet said. "You can't let a thing like that slow you down."

"Easy for you to say."

She looked at him and saw that his face was shiny with tears.

"Life's shit," he said. "You know that? Life's nothing but a stinking pile of shit."

"Hey, Mose, cut it out, okay?" She said it gently and reached out and wiped the tears off his cheek.

He stopped the car in front of Meg's house.

"Why don't you come in and have some coffee?" Janet asked.

Sniffing, he wiped his eyes again. "That isn't necessary."

"Of course not. We'd be a mess if we only did what's necessary. But I'll feel better if we can get you perked up a bit. Okay?"

"Perk up the jerk."

"I'm *not* going to let you drive home crying, pal. Not after a date with *me*. I *never* leave 'em in tears. It's my policy."

He laughed softly.

"Come on," she said. "Let's go in."

She climbed out and waited by the curb until Mosby came around to her side of the car. Then she took his hand and led him to the front door.

It was locked, but Meg had given her a key. She opened the door and let Mosby into the living room.

Meg, in a sheer nightgown, was sitting on the couch. "You're back early," she said. Oddly, her voice was calm. And oddly, her fingers continued to comb through the hair of the man who lay with his head on her lap.

"Fancy meeting you here," Dave said. He yawned and casually stroked Meg's calf. He wore only his briefs.

"Meg? My God, Meg, what's . . . ?"

"He's staying the night."

"*Staying?* Oh. Okay. God, Meg. You're . . . okay, bye. Let's go, Mosby. How about taking me to your place after all?"

"How are you feeling?" Mosby asked.

Janet didn't look up from her coffee cup. "Better. Thanks." She leaned back. Mosby's couch was soft and comfortable.

"I thought you were going to faint," he said.

"So did I."

"Who was he?"

Janet lifted the cup to her mouth and looked at Mosby. "A guy I used to know." She drank some of the coffee. "Former boyfriend."

Mosby sat forward and folded his hands between his knees. "What was he doing at Meg's?"

"I don't know. I don't want to know. Meg always thought he was a creep. She really did despise him."

"Maybe she just *claimed* to despise him."

"No, she really did. I'm sure."

"Then what was she doing with him on the couch?"

Janet shook her head. "I don't know. Except if you're lonely enough, I guess maybe you'll do just about anything. You take what you can get."

He laughed once and said, "That explains it."

Janet set down her coffee cup and frowned at him, puzzled.

"Explains why you went out with *me* tonight."

"You mean I'm desperately lonely?"

"Well?" he asked. "Why else would you go out with someone like me?"

"Hey, Mose, I don't need this. I don't need this at all, I really don't. Maybe you enjoy putting yourself down, but don't use me for it. If I hadn't wanted to go out with you, I would've told you so."

"If you're lonely enough, you take what you can get." He made a crooked smile.

"I said that about Meg, not me. Okay? So lay off."

"I'd rather lay *on*." His smile twitched. "I've got a nice double bed."

"Knock it off."

"I'd rather knock it up."

"*Stop it!* If you want me to leave, just say so. You don't have to drive me off by acting like a shit. Just tell me to go and I will."

He blinked at her, his face crimson.

Please, don't start crying again.

"I don't want you to go," he muttered. "Don't go, please. I'm sorry. It's just that, I don't know, I never should've asked you out in the first place. Big mistake. But I didn't really think you'd say yes. Girls like you *never* go out with guys like me. I figured you'd just tell me to take a flying leap."

"Why would I do that?"

"We're not in the same league." He made a grim smile. "In that great baseball game of life, you're in the majors and I'm in the bush league."

"I don't believe it."

"Believe it. I said it."

"Well, thanks for putting me in the majors, anyway." She shook her head. "The whole idea's full of crap, but thanks. Seems to me, we're all in the same ballpark. We're all trying to hit homers and usually striking out."

"I never even get to first base," Mosby said.

Smiling, Janet reached out her hand. Mosby took it. He helped her up. "Thank you for dinner and the movie," she said. "You made it to third base tonight."

"Only second."

"I'd call it third." She kissed him and stepped back. His hands stayed on her shoulders. "Go off to bed now," she said. "I'll be fine on the couch."

"You'd be fine anywhere." Mosby's voice was shaky. He suddenly pulled Janet forward. His arms wrapped her tightly.

His mouth pressed hard against her lips.

She pushed him away.

"No, Mose."

"Come on." He tried to pull her against him.

Janet kept her hands flat against his chest, holding him back. "No," she said.

His hands felt good stroking her hair. They gently rubbed the sides of her neck. "You're so beautiful," he said.

"I'm not going to sleep with you."

"Why?" He massaged her shoulders. She let her arms fall. "Because . . ."

His palms moved smoothly down the front of her blouse and cupped her breasts.

"Don't, Mosby."

"You don't want me to stop."

"Yes, I do."

"Doesn't it feel good?"

"Sure it does. But stop. Please? I'm not going to sleep with you, Mosby. I mean it."

"You want to," he said. He began to unbutton her blouse.

"No," she murmured.

"When was the last time you had a man?"

"Stop it, Mosby."

He opened her blouse, then slipped his arms underneath it and caressed her back and sides and belly as if his hands were starved for the feel of skin. "You're so beautiful."

"Mosby, don't do this."

"Why not?" He unfastened a hook between the cups of her bra, opened the bra and sank down slightly and kissed her right breast.

She sucked a quick, trembling breath.

"Don't. Please, Mosby."

He flicked the nipple with his tongue.

"Stop it. Please."

"Okay." He stood up straight again and kissed her mouth.

She turned her head away.

As he kissed her cheek, his hand pressed flat against her belly, then slid down inside her pants. His fingers knew just where to go.

"Mosby."

"It feels good. You love it."

"But I don't love *you!*"

"Doesn't matter."

"It *does!*"

"NO!" She dropped to her knees and the hand jerked out, fingers tracing slick wet paths up her belly. Hunching over, she pressed her hands to her face. "Go away," she murmured. "Leave me alone. Just go. Please."

"*That* was third base," Mosby said. He turned away and walked into his bedroom and shut the door.

TWENTY—FIVE

CLEANLINESS

Albert tossed the bloody shower curtain into the bathtub, then stepped into the tub himself, being careful not to tread on Tess. Squatting over her chest, he turned on the faucets. The water rushed out of the tap, straight down onto Tess's face. It pounded her nose, ran over her open eyes and flooded her open mouth.

When the water felt hot enough, he raised the metal knob to start the shower. The spray came out cold. But the cold only lasted a moment.

Albert stood up, lifted the shower curtain and shook it open. The water smacked it with hollow, popping sounds. Holding the curtain overhead, he stared through its frosted plastic and watched the bloody mess slide down its other side.

When it looked clean enough, he stepped over Tess— and on her—and struggled to hang the curtain on the shower rod.

He was nearly done when one of his feet slipped. He sat down hard on her belly.

"Sorry about that, sweetie," he said.

Still sitting on her, he reached for the shampoo. Then he stood up and washed his hair.

"A person can't be *too* clean," he told her. "You know what they say about cleanliness."

When he was done with his hair, he soaped himself all over, then rinsed and climbed from the tub.

He stood dripping on the wet tile floor and stared at Tess through the steam. Her skin looked pale and slippery.

He gazed at the stab wounds.

With hot water still pelting down from the shower noz-zle, he climbed again into the tub.

TWENTY—SIX

RECONCILIATION

Janet sat up, aching from the night on Mosby's couch. Her neck hurt most. She rolled her head to stretch her neck muscles, but it didn't help. In the bathroom, she found a bottle of aspirin. She cupped water from the faucet with her hand and swallowed three tablets.

Then she looked at herself in the mirror. Her hair was tangled. One side of her face was red and creased from the pillow's corduroy fabric. Though she'd buttoned her blouse after Mosby left, she hadn't fastened her bra; its cups hung beneath her armpits like small, wadded handkerchiefs.

"A vision of delight," she muttered.

She opened her blouse, pulled her bra together and fastened it. Buttoning up, she returned to the living room. She stared at the telephone.

Get it over with, she told herself.

Her stomach hurt. Her hand trembled as she picked up the phone and dialed. As she listened to the quiet ringing, she wanted to hang up.

It'll never get any easier, she told herself.

Anyway, maybe there's a logical explanation.

Sure.

Her heart gave a lurch as she heard someone pick up the phone.

"Hello?" Meg's voice.

"Hi. It's me."

"Oh."

"You sound disappointed."

"That isn't disappointment, hon, that's guilt. I feel like shit warmed over. Will you ever forgive me?"

"Hey, it's all right. Not much to forgive."

"Are you kidding? Where are you, at Mosby's?"

"Yeah."

"Come on back here, okay?"

"Dave isn't still there, is he?"

"You've gotta be kidding."

"He isn't, is he?"

"No. Definitely not. It's safe to come back."

"Well, I'm not too sure how to get there, though. I haven't seen my host this morning. For all I know, he might be gone."

"You mean you didn't wake up in his manly arms?"

"Not exactly. I slept on his couch."

"Then check the bathroom. He probably slit his throat."

"Thanks."

"You want me to pick you up?"

"If you don't mind."

"No problem. Where are you?"

Janet glanced at several magazines on the coffee table until she found one with an address sticker. She read the address to Meg. "Do you know where that is?"

"Pretty much. Shouldn't be more than ten minutes from here."

"I'll be waiting out front."

After hanging up, she went to Mosby's bedroom door and knocked. "Mose? Are you awake?"

"I'm awake," he said as if he hated to admit it.

"I'll be leaving in a couple of minutes. Meg's coming over to pick me up."

There was a long silence.

"Aren't you coming out to say good-bye?" Janet asked.

"Good-bye."

"Aw, Mosby, don't . . . Are you decent?"

"You know better than that."

"I'm coming in."

"Why?"

"I want to. Here I come." She opened the door.

Mosby was sitting up in bed. His hair was mussed. His pajama shirt was white with red stripes. Its sleeves were too short.

His clothes from last night were piled on a straight chair. Janet went to the chair, picked them up and tossed them onto the foot of his bed. Then she dragged the chair over to the bed and sat down on it. "I'm sorry about what happened," she said. "Or what *didn't* happen."

"Like what?"

"I'm sorry I couldn't . . . go along with you. And don't say 'better late than never.' It has to be never, Mose. The next time I sleep with a guy, it's going to be for keeps. If that's possible. I shouldn't have let things go as far as they did last night. It wasn't fair to you."

"It was my fault," he said.

"No. No, you just did what most guys would do."

"Guys with the sensitivity of an ape."

"Maybe you're *too* sensitive. After all, you seemed to know I was feeling awfully horny last night. I sure came close to sleeping with you."

"Not close enough."

She smiled. "Anyway, I'm sorry."

"Not half as sorry as I am."

"Don't bet on it."

"Will I ever see you again?" He suddenly looked like a boy fighting off tears.

"Give me a call in a couple of days. We'll have you over for dinner."

"Well," Meg said, and pulled away from the curb. With her index finger, she scratched the side of her nose. "I certainly made a spectacle of myself, didn't I? Like the lens grinder who fell into his machine."

"Don't worry about it," Janet said.

"Do you know what he did? Dave? Do you know what . . . ?" She sniffed and turned toward Janet. Her pouchy lips hung open. Her nostrils were red, her skin blotchy in the sunlight. Janet was thankful for the sun-glasses hiding Meg's eyes. "He . . . I knew he was only us-ing me, using me to get at you, but I didn't care. I really didn't care. Do you want to know something?"

"I don't know," Janet said, and looked out the window. "Probably not."

"He . . . this is really something. He took me from be-hind. Rear entry? That's what they call it in the sex man-uals, rear entry. The way dogs do it." She made a strange squeak that was neither a laugh nor quite a whimper. "The way you do it when the *girl's* a dog."

"For God's sake, Meg."

"He did it that way so he wouldn't have to look at my ugly puss. Isn't that a laugh?"

"No, it's not." Janet's throat felt tight. She swallowed, but it didn't help much.

"You want to hear another laugh?"

"Not really."

Meg's thick lips were trembling. Her cheeks were streaked with tears. "This'll really get you."

"No." Janet found herself starting to cry.

"I loved every second of it. Yeah, I really did. Every damn second. I knew he was only doing it to get at *you*, and I knew he found me repulsive, but I loved it. I really did. Have you got any idea how long it's been since . . . ? Do you know what I do sometimes . . . sometimes when I get tired of lying in bed alone and . . . ?"

"Meg, come on. Don't."

"I go find a scuzzy bar over in Hollywood. There's al-ways some guy so hard-up he doesn't give a rat's ass what a woman looks like, just so she's got a hole in the right place . . ."

"Jeez, Meg, cut it out."

"You have to know. You have to know why I *let* him."

"I get the picture."

"And you have to know I'd let him do it again. Who am I kidding? I'd *beg* him. I really would, hon, I'd beg him on bended knees." She laughed once again. It was more of a snort. "Not that it'll ever happen. He's done with that ploy. A guy like him won't try the same trick twice. More's the pity."

It was a fine afternoon. First, a long sleep in bed, the sheets soft and fresh next to her skin. Then a long, hot bath. Afterward, while she blew her hair dry, she started reading the new William Goldman novel, *Marathon Man*. Wrapped up in the story, she stayed in the bathroom and continued to read it long after she'd shut off the hair drier.

By the time she stopped, it was late afternoon.

She hurried into the guest room, got dressed, then went looking for Meg. She found her on the living room couch, legs tucked under her rump, reading *Cosmopolitan*.

"Hey," Janet said.

Meg looked up at her and smiled. "There you are at last, restored to your natural beauty and shine."

"Like a kitchen floor," Janet said.

"Speaking of kitchens, guess we'd better start thinking about supper."

"How about spaghetti? I'll make it myself."

"Sauce included?"

"You bet. My special tomato sauce with spicy Italian sausage."

"My mouth runneth over," Meg said. "You'll excuse me while I drool?"

"I'd be disappointed if you didn't."

In the kitchen, Janet browned the Italian sausage. She sauteed mushrooms, crushed garlic cloves and took several spices from the cupboard. Finally, she stirred it all into a pot of tomato sauce and left it simmering on the stove.

"I can smell it all the way out here," Meg said, looking up from her magazine.

"Want some wine?"

"Does a moose poop in the woods?"

Janet returned to the kitchen. The bottle of Burgundy

stood on top of the refrigerator. It looked as if nobody had touched it since Thursday when Meg gave her the news about the substituting job. Red wine sloshed its sides as she lifted it down. She found a pair of clean glasses and carried them into the living room.

"Ah, sweet libation," Meg said.

Janet pulled the cork and poured. Then she handed a glass to Meg and sat down with a glass of her own. She lifted it toward her friend. "Cheers," she toasted.

"Cheers. We both need 'em."

They drank.

Meg stared into her glass for a moment, then asked, "Have you got anything cooking tonight?"

"Aside from the spaghetti, not a thing."

"Why don't we take in a movie? There's a good one playing on the mall. The new Clint Eastwood."

"Great. Let's go. What are the show times?"

"Seven-thirty and ten, I think. Just a second, I'll make sure." Meg finished her wine, refilled both glasses, then reached down to the floor and picked up the morning newspaper. "Whew, how about that guy in Kansas City?"

"What guy in Kansas City?"

"Nightmare time. He killed . . ."

"I don't think I want to hear about it."

"Makes you wonder . . . ah, here we go. I was right. Seven-thirty and ten."

Janet glanced at her wristwatch. "Looks like we've got plenty of time to make the seven-thirty."

"Sounds great."

Janet sipped her wine. "You know, I'm feeling pretty good right now, all things considered."

"Me, too. Too bad we're not queer, huh? We could just drink wine and go to the movies and sleep together and have ourselves a fine old time."

"Only a couple of problems, there. Number one, we're not."

"True. Sad, but true."

"Number two, we'd just be trading man-trouble for woman-trouble."

"Your profundity's overwhelming."

"In which case," she continued, "instead of having run-ins with crappy or otherwise unsatisfactory male companions, we'd be beset . . ."

"By shitty females," Meg finished.

"True."

"Sad, but true. And women can be just as shitty as men."

"Shittier, even," said Janet.

"And how many gals do we know with peckers?"

"Very few," Janet admitted. "In fact, I could count them on the fingers of one hand, easily."

"Indeed, an amputee . . ."

The telephone rang.

"I'll get it," Janet said. She hurried into the kitchen. Glancing at the spaghetti sauce, she saw that it was simmering nicely. She picked up the phone. "Hello?"

"Hi there, Janet. Doing anything tonight?"

She hung up.

She walked to the stove and stood over the pot, breathing deeply to get rid of the heavy pounding in her chest. Seconds passed. Then the phone started ringing again.

After the fourth ring, Meg called out, "You going to get it?"

"I've got it." Janet wiped sweat off her upper lip and picked up the phone. "Hello?"

"Hi. Guess we must've been disconnected."

"We were. I hung up."

"You hung up on me?"

"Mother warned me about talking to strangers."

"Oh, that's rich. I see I've found you in rare humor."

"My humor gets very rare when I talk to creeps like you. What do you want, Dave?"

"Guess."

"What do you want?" she repeated.

"I thought we might get together tonight, have dinner

at Henri's, take in a flick, share a bottle of Cabernet and see what develops."

"Sounds wonderful," Janet said. "Try your sister."

She hung up.

TWENTY—SEVEN

LESTER'S NIGHT OUT

"I feel like going to a movie," Lester said.

"Don't let me stop you."

Carrying his supper plate, he followed Helen into the kitchen. "Why don't you come along?"

"Not a chance." She turned on the faucet and started wiping the supper dishes with a soapy sponge.

"I don't *want* to stay home," Lester said. "I mean, it's Saturday night. People are supposed to go out and have *fun* on Saturday nights."

"Go out, then. *Go* to a movie. Whatever you want. It's fine with me. I've got tests to grade and homework for my night class."

"Maybe I *will* go to a movie."

"Go. Have fun."

"Okay. See you later."

Before leaving the house, he picked up Helen's copy of the *Grand Beach Unified School District Personnel Directory*.

At the theater's ticket window, Lester saw that the next show wouldn't begin for nearly half an hour. He bought a ticket and put it into his wallet.

Two doors down from the theater was Harry's Bar. Lester had often seen it, often glanced through its open door at the dark tables, the bar, the television, the men playing pool in smoky light. He had never gone inside. Until now.

"I'd like a margarita," he told the bartender.

The man brought his drink. Not waiting to be asked about a tab, he placed a ten-dollar bill in front of him. Then he drank half of his margarita without setting down the glass and ordered another. When he finished the first drink, he started the second. He took his time with this one.

As he finished it, he looked at his wristwatch. Almost time to head for the movie.

To hell with the movie.

He ordered another drink. When it came, he sipped it slowly. Then he left the bar. At his car, he opened the school district directory.

Bonner, Emily Jean. 4231 37th Street.

Emily Jean Bonner's two-story house was set far back from the road. Lights shone in several of its windows. A Volkswagen bug was parked in the driveway.

Lester tried to make a U-turn, but the road was too narrow.

Instead of backing up to complete his turn, he let his tire ride up over the curb and bounce down.

She must have company, Lester decided as he headed up the walkway.

Maybe not. Maybe that's her VW.

No, she isn't the VW type.

And she wouldn't park in the driveway, would she? Wouldn't she use her garage? She *must* have company.

He muttered, "Shit."

But his disappointment seemed to be mixed with relief.

Just as well, he thought. I'll just drop in, real casual, say I was passing by . . . just a friendly visit.

He climbed the porch steps and pushed the lighted doorbell button. Moments later, he heard footsteps. Then the door opened.

"Why, Mr. Bryant! What a delightful surprise! Won't you please come in?"

She's glad to see me!

Smiling, he said, "Hi, Emily Jean."

She looked wonderful in green slacks and a white turtleneck sweater—better than Lester had ever seen her.

"I just thought I'd drop by and say hello," he said.

"I'm so glad you did." She shut the door and led him into a brightly lighted living room. "Mr. Bryant, I'd like you to meet my daughter, May Beth."

He nodded and smiled at the red-haired young woman sitting on the sofa. "Nice to meet you," he said.

"Very nice to meet you, Mr. Bryant."

"Mr. Bryant is a college librarian, honey."

"Really?" Her smile widened.

My God, she's beautiful!

"I worked in the library at Cal," she said, "when I was an undergraduate."

Blushing, Lester said, "Bet you hated it."

"Not really."

"Student helpers always get stuck with the routine stuff. Bores them stiff."

"I loved it," she said. "I didn't think it was boring at all."

"May I fix you a drink, Mr. Bryant?"

May Beth was holding a long-stemmed glass. Lester saw a similar glass on a lamp table. "That'd be nice," he said. "Whatever you're having would be fine."

"Martinis, of course," said May Beth. "Mother never touches anything but martinis."

"However," said Emily Jean, "I would be delighted to fix you whatever suits your fancy."

I just downed three margaritas, he thought. *I'd better be careful.*

Careful, smareful.

"A martini would be just fine," he said.

"I'll be back in two shakes of a lamb's tail." On her way out of the room, she said over her shoulder, "Do tell Mr. Bryant about your film, honey."

"Oh. Well . . ." May Beth crossed her legs. They were thin like her mother's legs, but gave no suggestion of frailty as they tapered upward into her tight, faded cutoff jeans. "I'm off for Denver tomorrow," she said. "I have a small part in a film being shot on location there." The jeans were low on her hips. Above them, she wore a tank top with a color illustration of a tabby cat. "It'll be my first film," she explained. "I've been on stage until now." The thin fabric clinged to her breasts. Small, round breasts.

"What sort of movie is it?" Lester asked.

"A thriller of sorts. You know, a classy shoot-'em-up. I play the friend of a teenaged girl who gets raped, tortured, the whole nine yards."

Her erect nipples were pushing out the fabric like two fingertips. Lester crossed his legs. "Who's directing it?" he asked.

"Sam Porter."

"Oh? He's not bad, not bad at all. What about the producer?"

"Hal Fisher."

"No kidding? Hey, you're in there with the big boys."

Emily Jean came striding into the room, a glass in her hand. "Here you are, Mr. Bryant." She handed him the martini.

"Thank you."

"Well," May Beth said, "the screenplay is from this really hot best seller, you see. *Some Call it Sleep* by Evan Collier? So it'll probably be a really big picture. I can't believe I've got such a good part in a film like that. Apparently, the producer saw me in *The Glass Menagerie*. He thought I'd be absolutely perfect, so . . ."

The ringing telephone interrupted her.

"I bet that's Jimmy," she said. "Excuse me."

When she left the room, Lester said, "You have a very beautiful daughter, Emily Jean."

"Why, thank you. I most certainly do."

"A spitting image of her mother."

GET UP TO 4 FREE BOOKS!

You can have the best fiction delivered to your door for less than what you'd pay in a bookstore or online—only $4.25 a book! Sign up for our book clubs today, and we'll send you **FREE* BOOKS** just for trying it out...**with no obligation to buy, ever!**

LEISURE HORROR BOOK CLUB

With more award-winning horror authors than any other publisher, it's easy to see why CNN.com says "Leisure Books has been leading the way in paperback horror novels." Your shipments will include authors such as RICHARD LAYMON, DOUGLAS CLEGG, JACK KETCHUM, MARY ANN MITCHELL, and many more.

LEISURE THRILLER BOOK CLUB

If you love fast-paced page-turners, you won't want to miss any of the books in Leisure's thriller line. Filled with gripping tension and edge-of-your-seat excitement, these titles feature everything from psychological suspense to legal thrillers to police procedurals and more!

As a book club member you also receive the following special benefits:

- **30% OFF all orders through our website & telecenter!**
- **Exclusive access to special discounts!**
- **Convenient home delivery and 10 days to return any books you don't want to keep.**

There is no minimum number of books to buy, and you may cancel membership at any time. See back to sign up!

*Please include $2.00 for shipping and handling.

YES! ☐

Sign me up for the Leisure Horror Book Club and send my TWO FREE BOOKS! If I choose to stay in the club, I will pay only $8.50* each month, a savings of $5.48!

YES! ☐

Sign me up for the Leisure Thriller Book Club and send my TWO FREE BOOKS! If I choose to stay in the club, I will pay only $8.50* each month, a savings of $5.48!

NAME: _____

ADDRESS: _____

_____

TELEPHONE: _____

E-MAIL: _____

☐ **I WANT TO PAY BY CREDIT CARD.**

☐ VISA   ☐ MasterCard   ☐ DISCOVER

ACCOUNT #: _____

EXPIRATION DATE: _____

SIGNATURE: _____

Send this card along with $2.00 shipping & handling for each club you wish to join, to:

Horror/Thriller Book Clubs
1 Mechanic Street
Norwalk, CT 06850-3431

Or fax (must include credit card information!) to: 610.995.9274.
You can also sign up online at www.dorchesterpub.com.

*Plus $2.00 for shipping. Offer open to residents of the U.S. and Canada only. Canadian residents please call 1.800.481.9191 for pricing information.

If under 18, a parent or guardian must sign. Terms, prices and conditions subject to change. Subscription subject to acceptance. Dorchester Publishing reserves the right to reject any order or cancel any subscription.

JOIN NOW!

"Well!" She laughed a little nervously. "I shouldn't go so far as that!"

"I should. In fact, I did." He laughed and sipped the martini. It was awful. He never could stand gin. He took another sip. "You must be awfully proud of her, doing so well in her career at such a young age."

"I can't *tell* you how very proud I am, Mr. Bryant. And somewhat envious, I must say. I was an actress myself, you know."

"That doesn't surprise me."

"I played Linda Loman one season. At the Wilshire Theater? I've played many lesser parts in my . . ." She stopped and looked up at her returning daughter.

"That was Jimmy," May Beth said. "He's waiting for me over at his place, so I'd better be on my way. It was very nice to meet you, Mr. Bryant."

"Nice meeting you, May Beth. Good luck on the film. Or should I say, 'Break a leg'?"

"Thanks. Hope to see you again sometime."

"Excuse me, Mr. Bryant. I'll see her to the door."

"Certainly."

Emily Jean walked her daughter out of the room. She returned a few minutes later and sat down on the couch exactly where May Beth had been sitting. She crossed her legs the same way. Her hair was red, but a brighter shade than her daughter's—probably thanks to a beauty parlor.

"You look just like May Beth, sitting there."

"A far older, tireder and uglier version, I'm afraid." She let out a nervous giggle. "Do you suppose 'tireder' is a word? I rather doubt it, don't you?"

"I doubt it," Lester said, smiling.

"I do, too." She picked up a pack of cigarettes. "*More* tired, I'm sure, is the appropriate usage."

"I imagine so." Lester stood up. Taking a book of matches from his shirt pocket, he crossed to the couch. "Let me get that for you," he said and struck a match.

Emily Jean leaned forward with the cigarette in her mouth, held his hand steady and touched the tip of her cigarette to the flame.

Though her cigarette was lighted, she held his hand for a few more moments. Then she let it go and said, "Why, thank you."

"You're quite welcome."

He sat down beside her and wiped his sweaty palms on his trousers. The aroma of her perfume came to him through the smoke's odor.

The same perfume Nikki used to wear.

"That's nice perfume," he said. "My favorite, in fact."

She blew out smoke and watched it rise. "Your visit is certainly an unexpected pleasure, Mr. Bryant."

"Lester, okay?"

"If you prefer," she said. She smiled at him. "I should have thought you would avoid me after my display at the Willow Inn."

"I enjoyed being there with you."

"Why, so did I, Lester."

"I told you some things I've never told anyone before." He took a sip of his martini and grimaced. Then he leaned forward and set it on the table. Looking into Emily Jean's eyes, he said, "I mean, I was in kind of a strange mood. I don't usually go around talking about . . . that kind of thing. Helen and stuff. You know?"

"I believe I understand." She patted his hand. Turning away, she reached out to the lamp table and poked out her cigarette in an ashtray. Then she turned toward Lester and put her arms around him.

Oh my God, here we go!

Trembling, she pressed her mouth against his. Her lips felt cool from her drink, but her mouth was warm inside. She sucked on his tongue.

As they kissed and embraced, they twisted awkwardly until they were lying side by side on the couch.

Lester pulled her sweater up and unhooked her bra

while her hands unfastened his trousers. Her breasts were full and soft and smooth as velvet. He felt his pants go down. Then cool fingers were stroking his penis.

"My, oh my," she said. "What a large and stout . . ."

"MOTHER!"

Emily Jean flinched. Her hand gripped him.

"My God!"

"It's all right, dear."

Lester turned his head and saw May Beth behind the couch, looking down at them. From that vantage point, she could see everything. Her gaze seemed to be fixed on Lester's penis. She blinked a few times, licked her lips, then blurted out, "My car wouldn't start and . . ."

He ejaculated.

"Oh, my GOD!" May Beth cried out and rushed away.

"Oh, dear," Emily Jean murmured. "I'm so sorry, Mr. Bryant. That was certainly unfortunate. I think you'd better be going now."

TWENTY—EIGHT

THE ADVENTURES OF CHARLES

Raskolnikov was about to dispatch the old woman when the doorbell rang through the silence of Ian's house. He jumped, let out a laugh, then shut *Crime and Punishment* and looked across the cluttered study at the wall clock.

Ten past midnight.

The bell rang again.

He set his book on the chair and headed for the front door. The granite floor of the foyer was cold under his bare feet. He flicked a switch to turn on the porch light, then pulled the door wide open.

"He almost got me," Charles Perris muttered. "He almost . . . can I come in?"

"Sure."

Charles was wearing good slacks and a blue sport shirt. The shirt was untucked. Its front looked damp. The sour smell of vomit followed him into the house.

"I threw up," he explained.

"Nothing to be ashamed of."

"You ever throw up? From drinking?"

"Sure I have."

"Yeah?"

"More times than I care to remember."

"No kidding?"

"I never kid about drinking, Charles. It's a trifling sin and a major solace." Those words sounded familiar. He wondered where he'd picked them up. "Have a seat. Could you use some coffee?"

"Great."

In the kitchen, Ian took two mugs out of the cupboard. He touched the side of the percolator to make sure the coffee was still hot enough. Then he filled them. "Cream and sugar?" he called.

"Yes, please."

He added the cream but decided to let Charles handle the sugar. "There you go," he said, setting the coffee cup and sugar bowl in front of the boy.

"Thanks. I can really use this. I just woke up. I passed out after I threw up."

"How did you manage to find my house? I thought it was a well-kept secret?"

"The faculty directory."

"How'd you get your hands on that?"

"He brought it home with him. I was hiding in the utility closet. I saw him drop it by the phone as he came in. That's what gave me the idea. I couldn't go home . . . not shit-faced like this. So I grabbed it and left."

"Left where? *Who* came home?"

"Mr. Bryant."

"*Lester* Bryant?"

Charles nodded. He dumped a spoonful of sugar into his coffee. Another.

"You're . . . ?" For a moment, Ian felt as if reality were dissolving. He watched Charles empty a third spoonful of sugar into the coffee. Then a fourth. He saw the spoon dip into the tan liquid and stir. Finally, he muttered, "Man, oh man. The woman you were telling me about the other day—the married one—is Helen Bryant?"

"She thinks I'm a wonderful poet," he said as if that explained it.

"Oh, man." Ian took a drink of his coffee. It tasted bitter. Maybe Charles had the right idea with all that sugar. "How did it happen?"

"What?"

"The whole thing. How did you happen to end up in the sack with one of your teachers?"

It'd make a lot more sense, he thought, if the teacher was someone like Mary Goodwin. Mary wasn't that much older than the kids. Plus she was beautiful, stacked, and wild. But *Helen Bryant?* How could a good-looking kid like Charles fall for *that* piece of work? The ice queen.

She's not even pretty!

Must be those sexy outfits she wears, Ian thought.

"She liked me," Charles said.

"You're good with understatement."

"She said my poetry shows sensitivity and loneliness. We talked about it one day after school. Last Friday? She asked me to read some of it to her, and when I did she started to cry. My God, she actually cried about my poetry and said it was lovely . . . and then she kissed me."

"In her *classroom?*"

"Yeah. But it was after three and nobody was around."

"What did you think when she kissed you?"

"It sort of scared me at first. I mean, she's not just a woman, she's a teacher, you know? But then . . . I guess I liked it."

"Did anything else happen?"

"Yeah. She . . . we kind of felt each other up. We didn't take off any clothes—nothing like that—but, you know. And then she asked if I'd like to see her sometime, see her at night. By that time I was feeling really . . . you know, excited? So I said, 'Sure,' and we decided we'd see each other Monday night."

"That's when you had intercourse in the van?" Ian asked.

"Yeah. And then the next night, too. You know the funny thing? I've got her for second-period English, you know? Well, she used to treat me special. Like the teacher's pet. But now she ignores me. She acts like I'm not even in the classroom. Funny, isn't it?"

"Understandable. She's just being careful. What happened tonight?"

"I didn't think I'd be seeing her. We hadn't been out since Tuesday, you know. I figured she wasn't interested anymore, so I made plans to go to a movie with a couple of the guys. But she called me at home."

"Who answered the phone?"

"Me. Good thing, huh? What if Mom or Dad had picked it up?"

"Knowing Helen, she probably had a story ready."

"God, that woman's crazy."

Mighty good likelihood, Ian thought.

"What did she say on the phone?" he asked.

"That her husband had gone to the movies without her. The way she sounded, it was like he'd deserted her or something. Anyway, she wanted to see me. So I phoned my friends and told them I couldn't make the movie. Then I drove over to Helen's. I parked at the end of the block, just in case. I mean, I was awfully nervous about actually going to her house. I'd never done that before. It was like, I don't know, going into enemy territory or something."

"The enemy being her husband?"

"I guess so. I mean, if he caught me making it with his wife, it'd be my ass, you know? So I was really scared shitless about the whole thing."

"If you were so frightened, why did you go?"

"I was thinking about what you said, Mr. Collins. About wanting out? So I figured this'd be a good chance to break up with her. I thought I'd be really nice about it and tell her how she's such a cool woman and everything, but how it was really messing with my head and I'd better stop seeing her. And I thought I might ask about transferring out of her class. But the minute she opened the door, she threw her arms around me and kissed me. I mean, this was a *real* kiss, too. And she was rubbing herself against me." He shook his head and sighed. "That went on for a long time," he said. "Then she got me a drink."

"Did you *ever* get around to breaking off the relationship?" Ian asked.

"I was planning to. I kept waiting for the right time, you know? And we kept drinking. Then she went to fill our glasses for, I don't know, the fourth or fifth time, I guess. She took a little longer than usual. When she came back, she had the drinks, all right. But she was wearing this black nightgown."

"Holy smoke," Ian muttered.

"God, it hardly covered anything. I mean, you could see right through it. I could see *everything*. I nearly . . ." Charles shook his head.

"The next thing I knew," he continued, "we were in her bedroom. Right on the same bed where she sleeps with her husband. And we were *doing* it. I don't know how long we were at it. Seemed like a long time. An hour or so. Then we heard the garage door open and she said, 'That's Lester.' So I just grabbed my clothes and ran. I should've run out the front, I guess. Or out to the patio. But I didn't know which end was up. I mean, I was scared shitless and half-smashed, so I just ran for the kitchen— which was the way Mr. Bryant was coming in."

"But he didn't see you?"

"I hid in the utility closet with the clothes washer. I mean, the goddamn door was opening right in front of my nose! But I ducked into the closet just in time. I didn't get the door shut all the way, so I looked out and that's when I saw him put down the faculty directory. Then he left. Went to bed, I guess. I didn't hear anything from the bedroom. Helen must've pretended to be asleep or something."

"You didn't vomit while you were at their place, did you?"

"No. Man, that would've really . . . I didn't puke till I was driving over here. There were some stale cigarette butts in the ashtray, and . . . I guess the smell of them . . ." He suddenly looked as if talking about the odor might bring back his nausea.

After a few seconds, he went on. "I pulled over and hung my head out the door and barfed my guts out."

"An auspicious way to end your adventure," Ian said. "How are you feeling now?"

"Not very drunk, anyway. The sleeping must've . . ." He trailed off and stared at his empty coffee mug.

"Why don't you take a shower?" Ian suggested.

"Here?"

"Yeah. Right here, right now. While you're at it, I'll throw your shirt in the washing machine. By the time you're ready to go home, nobody'll be the wiser."

"Just me," Charles said.

"We can hope for that."

TWENTY—NINE

KAREN'S HOMECOMING

Albert spent Sunday the same way he'd spent Saturday: sleeping, eating food from the well-stocked kitchen, watching television, never leaving the apartment.

Twice each day, he'd dumped four trays of ice cubes into the bathtub water. The technique seemed to be working; Tess's body hardly smelled at all by the time on Sunday night when he heard footsteps in the hallway.

He hurried into the bathroom and waited behind the closed door.

"Tess must've gone to bed early," he heard Karen say. "How's about one for the road?"

"Can't get enough of me, can you?"

"Shhh, she'll hear you."

"Okay, okay. Mmmm."

"Stop that. Wait a minute and I'll make sure her door's shut."

Albert held his breath as Karen walked past the bathroom and down the hall. He heard a door bump quietly shut. "It's okay," she said on her way back.

"Okay!"

"Not so loud!"

"Sorry, sorry."

Albert heard nothing for a few seconds. Then, "Mmmm, what's this?"

"You oughta know, Tiger."

"Mmmmm. Aw, shit. Time out, okay?"

"The beer again," Karen said. "Can I give you a hand?"

"Wait'll I get back."

"I don't know, honey. You could probably use a little help in there. Your aim's so piss-poor."

"I can handle this myself."

"Won't be half the fun."

Albert heard quick footsteps. He pressed himself against the bathroom wall, shivering. The light came on. The door shut. Heart thudding wildly, Albert stared at Steve's back.

If he turns around . . . ?

Albert clamped a hand across Steve's mouth, lurched against him and rammed the knife into his back.

The point hardly went in at all.

Hit his spine?

Steve grunted and went up on tiptoes.

Albert tried again, this time stabbing to the right. The blade punched in deep. Jerking and shuddering, Steve sank to his knees.

Albert grabbed him by the hair, tugged his head back and cut his throat.

He held him up for a while, letting him bleed out.

When Steve seemed to be unconsious or dead, Albert eased him down to the floor.

He stepped over the body, being careful not to slip on the bloody tiles, and flushed the toilet. His robe was bloody. He took it off and wiped the butcher knife on a towel. Then he turned off the bathroom light. He waited, naked and shaking.

Soon, he heard the quiet thumping of feet. Karen must've taken off her shoes.

He pressed his ear to the door and wondered what else she might've taken off. Maybe everything.

No, that's not what I want.

He liked the green dress she'd been wearing Friday night.

That's what she oughta be wearing.

The footsteps stopped. Albert shifted the knife to his left hand and stepped far to the side.

She knocked on the bathroom door. "You gonna take all night?"

Albert reached out and knocked twice on the door. Then he crouched.

Karen opened the door.

Albert sprang, his shoulder catching her in the belly, driving her backward through the doorway and across the hall. She slammed the wall hard. His fist got her five times in the belly before he let her drop to the floor.

He moved back and looked down at her.

She was curled on her side, clutching her belly, loudly sucking air. She still wore the backless green dress.

All right!

Reaching down, Albert sliced the strap behind her

neck. Then he jerked the dress front down. Karen hugged her loose breasts.

"Move your arms," he said, and slashed one.

She yelped and moved her arms.

"Fantastic," Albert said. "God, what knockers. Fantastic, fantastic."

Now be careful with this one, he told himself. Don't get carried away. Make her last.

He did his best.

She spent the next five hours tied to her bed with panty hose, a pair of underwear stuffed in her mouth.

After she died, Albert returned to the bathroom and hauled Tess out of the tub. He put her on the bed with Karen. Then he took a long shower.

He slept, that night, on the living room couch.

THIRTY

THE FIX-UP

"Now," Janet said after supper Monday night, "if somebody'll just oblige me by getting sick, I'll be in the chips." She finished drying a plate and picked up another.

"Colds should start knocking them down pretty soon," Meg said.

"I sure hope so."

"They can't escape it. Not a chance. With at least a hundred and fifty students breathing germs on them, they're sitting ducks. Before you know it, they'll be dropping like flies."

"You're mixing your metaphors."

"There! You *already* sound like a teacher. Just a matter of time." Meg rinsed a glass and set it on the drain board.

"What do you think my chances are of working into a full-time position?"

"A hell of a lot better than they were," Meg said. "Thing is, you are now an official employee of the district and they like to hire from within their ranks. Trouble is, not many teachers are leaving. A few years ago, they'd replace maybe seventy or eighty teachers every fall. Last year, it was down to only sixteen."

"That's not very encouraging. And this fork's not very clean." She handed back a fork with egg yellow crusted between its tines.

"You've got to know the right people," Meg explained. "Having a guy like John Lawrence in your corner's a major step in the right direction. So how did you get along with him this morning?"

"I don't know. He seemed very impressed by the fact that you recommended me."

"Ah, but of course."

"You must carry a lot of weight."

"Unfortunately, it's mostly in my ass."

"I wish you'd stop putting yourself down like that. You're as bad as Mosby."

"Does Mosby do that?"

"All the time. You two could get together and have a regular marathon of self-abuse." Even before Meg could grin, Janet realized what she'd said.

"Hell! If he'll cooperate, we could forget the *self*-abuse and do it to each other."

"I'll phone him right now," Janet said.

"You wouldn't dare."

"Sure! You fixed me up with a job. The least I can do is fix you up with a man."

"Oh, no you don't!"

"We'll ask him over for supper tomorrow night so the two of you can get better acquainted."

"No. Now really . . ." She was shaking her head, but smiling.

"We'll have your special flank-steak recipe. And French

fries. He'll go berserk. Absolutely berserk, just wait and see. After dinner, I'll scoot on outta here and you'll have him all to yourself. He'll be all *over* you, I guarantee it."

"You're out of your tree."

"Hang on a second. I've got his phone number in my purse." She draped the dish towel over an open drawer and started across the kitchen.

"Wait," Meg said. "If you're serious about going through with this, we'd better make it for Wednesday. Tomorrow's too soon. We'll have to buy the food and I'll want to get my hair done and . . ."

"Wednesday's fine."

Janet went into the living room and found her purse on a chair. Mosby's phone number was tucked into the wallet. She took it out and returned to the kitchen.

Meg had turned off the faucet. She was drying her hands and watching Janet. Her face was red. "I don't know about this," she said.

"What's the problem?"

"What if he doesn't like me?"

"What's not to like?"

"My face, for starters. Moving on down from there . . ."

"You look fine," Janet told her.

"Oh, sure."

"But if you don't want me to call him, I won't. We can just forget about it."

Meg grimaced, showing her pink gums. "Not to mention, he saw me in that *nightgown*. How embarrassing is *that?*"

"I didn't hear him complaining. Knowing Mosby, he probably *loved* it. He's one very horny guy."

Meg snorted. "Get him over here."

Janet grinned. "Are you sure?"

"What've I got to lose but my virginity . . . if that?"

Janet dialed the number. After a couple of rings, she heard someone pick up.

"Hello?"

"Hi, Mosby." She winked at Meg.

"Janet?"

"Yeah. How've you been?"

For a moment, the phone was silent. Then Mosby said, "Okay, and you?"

"Just fine. Say, Meg and I thought you might like to come over here for supper. How about Wednesday night?"

"This Wednesday?"

"Right. Day after tomorrow."

"Gee, I don't know."

"What's not to know?"

"I'd like to, but . . . I don't know, it's pretty short notice and . . ."

"You can get your hair done tomorrow."

"What?"

"Just a little joke, Mose. Hey, are you okay? How come you're not overwhelming me with your wit and charm?"

"I don't know."

"Is something the matter?"

"No. Everything's fine."

"You sure?"

"Everything's hunky-dory. I'm tired, is all. Work was a drag today and I stayed up till about three o'clock last night watching *Casablanca*."

"Did Rick get her this time?"

"Huh?"

"He didn't send her off with Lazlo again, did he?"

"Yeah. What do you think, it *changes?*"

"I keep hoping."

Mosby huffed out a laugh. "You're nuts."

"So, you'll be coming, won't you? We're having steak, French fries and booze. Just the three of us: you, me and Meg."

"What time?"

"What time's good for you?"

"I don't care."

"How's seven?"

"Fine, but . . ."

"See you then?"

"I don't know. I *shouldn't*, but I guess I will. How can I pass up an invitation like that, huh?"

"You can't. It's impossible. See you Wednesday."

"See you."

She hung up and turned to Meg. "He's coming."

"Sounded like you had to twist his arm."

"Something seemed to be bothering him. He's probably embarrassed about seeing us again after what happened last time."

"Can't imagine why."

THIRTY—ONE

HOUSE CALL

The house across the dark lawn looked fine. Nothing special about it. Albert only picked it because it was the smallest one on the block. Probably not more than a couple of bedrooms.

He didn't feel much like taking on a crowd tonight.

Outside the car, he was cold. Especially his bare legs.

He hurried toward the house.

All along the street, windows were dark. The chances were good that nobody would see him.

He climbed steps to the front door. Standing in the shadows, he took the switchblade out of his purse.

He lifted the hem of his skirt and cut through it. Knife clenched in his teeth, he ripped. The skirt made a dry rasp as it tore upward almost to his hip. He put his leg through the slit. It looked slender and pale gray.

Because of the darkness, shaving it had probably been a waste of time.

But fun.

He'd ended up shaving off all his hair from the neck down, not only to improve his masquerade as a girl, but also because he enjoyed lathering himself with the foam and gliding the razor blade over his skin.

Life is just full of little pleasures, he thought.

He jerked open his blouse. Its buttons popped away. Gazing down, he spread the blouse wide open so both cups of his bra showed. The bra was a black, lacy number he'd found in Karen's dresser.

It had real breasts inside.

Karen's.

The cauterized areas felt a little funny against Albert's chest. Sort of crisp and greasy like grilled steaks. But they looked good in the bra. In decent light, you could see her nipples through the lace.

But in decent light, you could also see the fried edges pressing against his chest.

Just as well that the porch light was off.

Holding the knife behind his back, Albert pressed the doorbell button. He pushed it again and again and again very quickly.

At last, he heard footsteps.

A man's voice. "Yeah? Who's there?"

"I need help!" Albert gasped. "Please, I just got raped. The man's still after me! I got away but . . . Help! Please! Oh, God! Let me in! Please!"

The guard chain rattled and the door was swung open by a man in pajama bottoms, his hair mussed. He looked half-asleep and confused. "You better get in here," he said.

He took a moment to look into the darkness after Albert was inside.

As he took the moment, Albert stepped in close behind him, clutched his mouth and jammed the knife into his back.

He now had a house in Denver.

THIRTY—TWO

LESTER ALONE

Another Tuesday night alone. The bitch.

Lester needed her like he needed a hole in the head.

Off to a goddamn school-board meeting, this time.

So who needs her?

If she wasn't off to a meeting or some class at U.C.L.A., she'd just be shut away into the back room hammering away at lesson plans or some such crap.

The bitch.

With difficulty, Lester swallowed a final mouthful of re-fried beans. They were barely warm. He folded the empty aluminum tray into a triangle. He carried it into the kitchen, bounced it off a wall and into the wastebasket. It left a brown smudge on the wall.

THIRTY—THREE

FOREWARNED

Ian dropped the drumstick bone into the Pioneer Chicken box. He continued to read his paperback copy of *Crime and Punishment*, holding it with one hand while nibbling the gluey crumbs off his thumb. When he finished the chapter, he set down the book, brushed bits of chicken crust off the front of his work shirt, and got up from the couch.

He carried the box of bones into the kitchen. He stuffed it into the grocery bag he used for a wastebasket, then washed his hands with hot water and soap. As he washed, he considered doing a few of the dishes that cluttered the top of his counter.

Later.

For now, he only needed a mug. He found one. It had a puddle of coffee in the bottom. Tan coffee. The mug that Charles had used Friday night.

Poor guy. Messed up with Helen Bryant.

What's the matter with that woman, anyway? Doesn't she know you don't fuck your students?

Half a dozen tiny blue islands of mold were floating in the remains of the coffee.

Ian rinsed the mug, washed it with a soapy sponge, and poured fresh coffee into it. In the study, he cleared off space for it on his desk.

Occasionally taking sips of his coffee, he started to read the five pages he had written the night before, making corrections as he went along, changing words with his red pen, several times scratching out entire sentences.

Then the telephone rang.

He reached down to the floor, where the phone was resting next to his dictionary.

"Hello?"

"Mr. Collins?"

"Yes."

"This is Charles. I hope I'm not disturbing you." The nervous tremor of his voice worried Ian.

"No, it's all right. What's going on?"

"I don't know. I mean, I had a date all set up with Helen for tonight. I was supposed to meet her in the parking lot of the May Company, but I stayed home."

"That's *one* way to end an affair."

"Yeah. Well, the thing is, she phoned me from the store. God, she was pissed! Anyway, I guess it sort of slipped out about you."

"You guess *what* slipped out about me?"

"That you know."

"Ah." He felt a quick squirm of fear in his belly.

"She wanted your address."

"Did you give it to her?"

"Well, it's *her* directory. I'm sorry. I probably shouldn't have, but . . ."

"It's fine, Charles. Don't worry about it. She could've gotten my address easily enough, anyway. I suppose she must be planning to pay me a visit."

"I guess so. I just called to let you know, warn you."

"Thanks, Charles."

"I'm sorry."

"Don't worry about it."

They hung up.

Ian picked up his mug. It was still half-full. The coffee was still hot, and tasted good. After taking a couple of sips, he put down the mug. He picked up the pages of his novel and tried to resume reading, but his mind was full of Helen. He let the pages flop onto his desk.

"A brave night to cool a courtezan," he muttered, and finished his coffee.

THIRTY—FOUR

THE VISITOR

Intending to take a shower, Lester was heading for the bathroom when the doorbell rang. His heart lurched. It pounded rapidly as he went to the door. For a moment, he thought about leaving the guard chain hooked until he could see who was there. But that would be embarrassing. He didn't want to look yellow. So he flipped the chain loose and opened up.

"Good evening, Lester."

"Emily Jean!" He gaped at her.

"Aren't you going to ask me in?" she drawled. Her smile tried to look cheerful, but came off self-conscious, uncertain, hopeful.

"Sure. Come in. Sorry . . . I'm just so surprised to see you. And *glad* to see you."

She stepped inside and Lester quickly shut the door.

"How've you been?" he asked.

Weird. Like talking to a stranger.

She *is* a stranger, he thought. Almost, anyway.

"I've been just fine," she said. "And what about yourself?"

"Well, okay. Not bad, I guess. Would you like a seat? Some coffee? I wouldn't mind a cup of coffee, how about you?"

"To be quite honest, Lester, I would prefer a kiss."

The request stunned him. He wanted to shrink away. He wished to God he had never opened the door, because this was too strange and frightening.

But he stepped closer to Emily Jean and kissed her on the mouth.

Weird. Really weird.

A married man in his own house kissing a woman he hardly knew.

So why the hell not?

She's so old.

But she wants me!

From the feel of her breasts against him, Emily Jean wasn't wearing a bra tonight. Her mouth was fierce. Her arms clutched him tightly, frantically, as if to keep him from escaping.

He pulled his head back and pushed her gently away. Her eyes looked questioning, hurt.

"Do I frighten you, Lester?"

"No, I'm not frightened."

"I shouldn't blame you if you were. Sometimes, you know, I frighten myself." She laughed nervously. "I've given myself a terrible turn, visiting you like this. I'm astonished that I could behave in such an outrageous fashion."

"So am I. But I'm glad."

"Are you?"

"Sure," he said, and knew he didn't sound very convincing. "I'm just nervous, that's all."

"I'm a bundle of nerves, myself."

"Why don't we sit down?" He headed for his easy chair.

Don't be ridiculous! This is my chance!

He veered away from the chair and sat on the sofa.

Emily Jean sat beside him, close but not touching.

"I guess you know about Helen and the board meeting," he said.

"Oh, I had no idea where she was going. It's a terrible thing to admit, but I parked across the street and watched the house. I was simply delighted to see her drive off. But frightened. You have no idea. I sat in my car for half an hour before I gathered enough courage to climb out." She laughed. This time, her laughter sounded more relaxed than before.

"I'm glad you did," Lester said.

"I hope I'm not interrupting anything."

"Not a chance." His fear, too, was subsiding. "You're just the person I hoped would drop by." He stroked the back of her hand and told himself that he wasn't bothered by its branching blue veins. "How did things go with May Beth?"

She took a deep breath and sighed, shaking her head. "The poor dear. We had ourselves a long, heart-to-heart talk, and I'm sure it did us both a world of good. Really, though, for a girl to see her mother with a man that way . . ." She shook her head again.

"Must've been an awful shock."

"Oh, I'm certain of that. May Beth is a strong girl, though. She said to me over and over, 'Everything's cool, Mom. Don't worry, everything's cool.' She even went so far as to claim she was relieved to find I didn't entirely abandon sex after Robert ran off. Robert, my ex-husband."

"How long has he been gone?"

"Six years last June. We were married at seventeen, divorced at forty-six. I've heard it's a common occurrence, but I must say I was hardly prepared . . ."

"I guess we're never prepared for crap to hit us."

Emily Jean turned over her hand and interlaced her fingers with his.

"Have you had many men since your divorce?"

"Such an improper question, Mr. Bryant! Lester." She smiled. "And so ambiguous. How many, for instance, is 'many'? And what, for gracious sake, do you mean by 'had'?"

His heart thudded. "I'd be happy to demonstrate."

"I'd be more than eager to witness such a demonstration."

"Would you care to participate?"

"Why, I most certainly would."

"Shall we go to the bedroom?"

"That's a fine suggestion."

He led her into the bedroom. Plenty of light came in from the bright hallway, so he didn't turn on any lamps.

He took her into his arms.

Her mouth was just as hungry as before. Her fingers pressed and clawed. She gasped through her slippery mouth as her pelvis pushed against him.

He put a hand up the back of her sweater, slid it to the front and started working on one of her breasts.

Her hands under his shirt were cool and dry. One wedged under his belt. The fingernails raked his buttocks.

He moved a hand down the side of her leg, under her skirt, and up.

No hose or panty hose or anything!

A moan escaped Emily Jean as his fingers slid and delved into her.

She tugged his belt open, undid the button at his waist and pulled down his zipper. Then her hand went in.

That oughta get the damn thing up.

It didn't.

"This would be a great time," he whispered, "for Helen to walk in."

"She won't."

"Unless she got a flat tire or something."

"My, but you are a worrier."

"Things like that happen."

"Indeed they do. But I do believe we've already *had* our bad luck in that department."

His pants went down. His shirt came off.

"I'd just hate for Helen to walk in on us like this," he said.

"I'm confident she won't."

As Lester watched, she stripped off her sweater and skirt. Tall and slim, she bent over the bed, threw back the covers and slipped between the sheets.

Lester joined her.

She moaned quietly as he embraced her.

Her hand went down again to his penis. She gently pressed, stroked, jiggled. It stayed limp.

She worked at it for a long time.

Lester took his mouth off her breast. "I don't know what's wrong, but . . ."

"Don't worry, honey. Try turning around."

"What?"

"You know, so we're vice versa."

"Oh, okay." He straddled her face, eased himself down, and began licking the slippery cleft between her legs.

Emily Jean writhed under him. She groaned, gasped. He could feel her mouth, all right: the wetness, the lips, the teeth. The sucking felt good, but not good enough.

What the fuck's the matter with me?

He climbed off her.

"I'm sorry," he said, turning and lying down beside her. "I don't know . . . This has never happened before."

She didn't look at him. She lay on her back, gazing at the ceiling. "It's my fault," she muttered.

"No! No, it's not. You're a hell of an exciting woman."

"I'm so much older than you."

"You're fine."

Beneath the sheet, he felt a finger lift the head of his penis and let it flop. But the hand didn't go away. It cupped him warmly and stayed.

"It's not your fault," Lester said. "It's just me. I don't know what's wrong. Must be the circumstances. Nerves. Hell, I was fine Saturday night, wasn't I?"

"I should certainly say so." She still gazed at the ceiling, but the trace of a smile lifted a corner of her mouth. "*Excessively* fine, considering the mess you made on my sofa."

He blushed fiercely. "I can't *believe* I did that in front of your daughter. I mean, she *saw* it."

"She shouldn't have come barging back into the house that way."

"She had no idea we might be . . ."

"She should have at least considered the possibility. Why, I've always been *so* careful not to interrupt May Beth when *she* has a man in her room, and she does this to me."

"You shouldn't blame her," Lester said.

Emily Jean turned her face and looked at him oddly. "She's a beautiful young lady, isn't she, Lester?"

"Takes after you."

"She's *far* more beautiful than me. And she has such a *splendid* figure . . . the most *exquisite* breasts. They're so high and firm! Mine were that way when I was her age. However, I never *dressed* in such an immodest fashion."

"It's just the way kids like to dress these days. You must see a lot of it, being a teacher."

"I see rather more than I care to. I don't approve at *all* of those—what are they called—tank tops? They're so awfully revealing, especially when a girl doesn't wear a brassiere. And May Beth *never* wears a brassiere."

Lester suddenly realized he was aroused.

"Why, Saturday night, for all her tank top hid, May Beth might as well have been naked." Emily Jean's encircling fingers moved slowly up the length of his shaft.

"What are you . . . ?"

She found his hand and placed it on her breast. Her nipple was stiff and jutting.

"And those jeans, those cutoffs? They were *so* immodest. I could see the crotch of her panties, couldn't you? Why, if she'd had no panties on . . ."

"You shouldn't be saying this stuff. She's your daughter."

"Close your eyes, darling."

He shut them. His hand was lifted and carried to the warm, damp hair between her legs.

"Wouldn't you love to have her under you, hot and naked?"

"This is crazy . . ."

"It's fine, darling."

At her urging, he silently crawled on top of her.

"Now she's under you, darling, open and eager for your throbbing manhood."

"Emily!"

"May Beth," she corrected. "Call me May Beth."

He slid into her, moaning the name "May Beth" and damn near believing it as he rode her to a furious climax.

THIRTY—FIVE

HELEN DROPS IN

"You don't look very surprised."

"I was forewarned," Ian said. "Would you like to come in?"

Helen stepped into the foyer. Her eyes darted.

"Don't worry, we're alone."

"Did Charles call?" she asked.

"He said you might be dropping by. May I take your jacket?"

"I'll keep it, thank you. I don't plan to stay long. I just

thought we'd better . . . talk." She hurried to a rocker and sat down, her back rigid. The chair tipped backward. Gasping, she grabbed its arms. She shifted her weight forward to stop it.

Ian sat on his couch. He crossed his legs. "I've been planning to speak with you about this, Helen."

"How long have you known?"

"Since Friday night."

She stared down at her folded hands. "Who have you told?"

"So far, no one."

"But you plan to tell Harrison?"

Ian nodded. "Unless we can work something out."

She smiled. A cold, vain smile. "I can get you a thousand dollars in cash tomorrow afternoon."

"That's not . . ."

"Five thousand, then. And if that isn't enough, I can make monthly installments of . . . say, a hundred. No more than a hundred at a time, or Lester might catch on. He never looks at my accounts, but more than a hundred would . . ."

"Helen, I'm not interested in your money."

At first, she seemed frightened. Then confused. Then amazed. She smiled and licked a corner of her mouth. "Well *well*, Mr. Collins."

"Not that, either. I want you to leave the school, leave teaching. When your contract comes up for renewal in the spring, don't sign it."

"Just quietly fade away, is that it?"

"Tell Harrison that you're tired of the merry-go-round, or something. Nobody will ever have to know about you and Charles."

"What if I tell you to shove it?"

"I'll take Charles into Harrison's office and you'll be lucky to last out the week."

"You wouldn't do that," she muttered. "You're too fucking *gallant*."

"If it's gallantry you're counting on, you're out of luck. I love to see the bad guys fall, and you're a bad guy."

"Get fucked, Collins."

"All in good time. Right now, I've got other things to do. So good night, and let me know your decision within the next few days."

"Suppose I dig up some dirt on you?"

"I've never seduced a student, Helen."

"You make it sound so dirty."

"It is dirty."

"Suppose I find someone who says you did?"

"It'd be a lie."

"Suppose it's a good lie?"

"In that case, I'd be forced to make this recording public." He reached under the couch and pulled out a cassette recorder. It was purring quietly.

"This is blackmail, you know."

"Good night, Helen."

THIRTY—SIX

LUST IN THE AFTERNOON

Just before 3:30 on Wednesday afternoon, Lester parked a block away from Emily Jean's house and headed down the shaded sidewalk. He loosened his necktie. He opened the top button of his shirt. The warm breeze felt good against his neck. He felt great, free. He headed up the walkway to her front door and rang the bell.

The door opened. "Good afternoon, Mr. Bryant."

He gaped at her, his heart suddenly pounding fast. He took a deep, trembling breath.

"Such a pleasant surprise, you dropping by like this. Won't you please come in?"

He stepped inside and shut the door.

"You look . . ." He shook his head. Smiling, he reached for her. He put a hand on her pale, freckled shoulder and fingered the strap of her bright yellow tank top.

"Outasight, huh?" She hooked her thumbs into the belt loops of her cutoff jeans and threw her hips sideways.

"Amazing."

She put her long, thin arms around him.

"Would you care for a drink?" she asked.

"No, thanks. I just want you."

As they kissed, he put a hand up the back of her shirt. Her skin was smooth and bare all the way up. He moved his other hand to her breast. She moaned and her teeth gripped his upper lip. Her hand pressed the front of his slacks. "Outasight," she said again.

"Not for long."

She smiled, took hold of his belt buckle, and led him upstairs to a bedroom. The late afternoon sunlight slanted onto the bed. A single bed, neatly made.

A lean, sweaty rock star gazed down at it from a poster on the opposite wall.

Emily Jean stepped against Lester. As she kissed him, she pulled out his shirttail and pushed her hand down the front of his trousers. Her hand was cool inside his underwear. And then it was gone.

She crossed the room and turned on a stereo. John Denver began singing of his home in the Rockies. "Do you like John Denver?" she asked.

Lester nodded.

Emily Jean crossed her arms, reached down to her waist, then pulled the tank top over her head. She tossed it onto a chair. She walked to the bed, naked except for the cutoffs slung low on her hips. Slowly, she helped Lester undress.

He embraced her, enjoying the smooth warmth of her skin and the rough touch of her jeans.

When the jeans were off, she was all smoothness.

They moved to the bed.

"May Beth," she said, "always insists on sleeping in the raw."

"It feels better that way," Lester said.

"I think she pretends to be with a man. The one on the poster there, perhaps. Or perhaps you. That you're on top of her, and your weight is crushing her. Perhaps you're gently biting the side of her neck."

Emily Jean squirmed as Lester's teeth nibbled her flesh. "It gives her goose bumps," she said.

Her fingernails scraped down Lester's back, chilling him.

"May Beth groans as you take her breast in your mouth, as you ever so gently lick it. And . . . as you suck it." Emily Jean groaned as Lester continued to follow her directions. "And then she feels you go into her. Yes. You push in deep and deeper and . . . ahhh . . . All the way. There. Yes. All the way in."

They lay exhausted beside each other, Emily Jean's head resting on Lester's chest. He shut his eyes.

So nice. A woman who appreciates me. So nice.

When he opened his eyes again, the room was dusky. He ran a hand through Emily Jean's hair.

"You make a very handsome pillow, Mr. Bryant," she said, her voice low and languid. He felt her head turn. She kissed his chest.

"What time is it?" he asked.

"Six-ish, I should imagine. Will Helen be missing you?"

"Hardly. She may wonder why I'm late, but she certainly won't *miss* me."

"I am so sorry."

"Don't be."

"It's always sad, what life does to people."

"Not always. It's not sad, being with you. I find it uplifting."

She laughed softly. "With me or with May Beth?"

"With you," Lester said. "It bothers you, doesn't it?"

"What's that?"

"That . . . well . . . doing this May Beth thing? Pretending."

Emily Jean rolled onto her back, stretched her arms up, cupped her hands behind her head and frowned thoughtfully at the ceiling. "I'm sure it must trouble me. After all, a woman prefers to think she has the power to arouse a gentleman without relying on . . . the power of association?" Her voice lifted as if the statement were a question and she looked sideways at Lester.

He rolled onto his side, propped himself up on an elbow, and looked at her. The sheet was down at her waist. She had nice breasts for a woman her age.

A woman her age?

How the hell do *I* know what the breasts of a fifty-year-old woman should be like?

Fifty-two, he corrected himself.

He moved a hand up one of the soft, shadowy slopes.

"It's only an ego thing, I'm sure," she said. "But of course, what isn't? A woman does, after all, like to think she's . . . sexy."

"You're sexy."

"I am, at any rate, a fair actress. I'm able to create a reasonable illusion of May Beth."

"A damn fine illusion."

The dark skin of her nipple seemed to crawl under Lester's fingertip, rumpling and thickening.

"Fine enough for our purposes," she said.

"Uh-huh." A column of flesh was there in the center now, firm and high and blunt. It grew even more as Lester's fingertip encircled it. "Does it make you jealous?" he asked.

"Of May Beth? Heaven's no."

He rolled the column between his thumb and forefinger. She moaned.

"After all, Mr. Bryant, *I'm* the one you've been sleeping with."

"That's right. It *is* you, not May Beth. It's my own darling Emily Jean."

He climbed onto her.

"Again?" She grinned, but her eyes glistened with tears.

"Again."

"Heavens, Mr. Bryant!"

THIRTY—SEVEN

MOSBY COMES TO DINNER

"What *happened* to you?" Meg's voice sounded strained and urgent.

Shaking out the match she was using to light candles on the table, Janet hurried into the living room.

"Would you believe I walked into a door?" Mosby asked.

"No."

"A door walked into me?"

From the look of it, the damage to his face was several days old. The scrapes on his chin and cheekbone were scabbed over, the bruises gray. A bandage covered one eyebrow. The eyelid beneath it was dark and pufffy.

"What happened really?" Janet asked.

"Really?" He shook his head. "Hell, it was nothing."

"Looks like you were in a fight," Meg said.

"You might call it that. On the other hand, you might call it a massacre." He laughed. "Did I hear someone mention booze? On the phone, I think it was."

"Sure," Janet said. "You two sit down and I'll get you something. What would you like?"

"Beer would be great if you have it."

"Plenty of beer," she said. Listening to the conversation, she went into the kitchen, removed three cans of Budweiser from the refrigerator and poured them into three mugs.

"So," Meg said, "did you emerge victorious?"

"Well, I'd have knocked the guy from here to January but he had me at a disadvantage."

"What was that?"

"He was quicker and stronger."

Janet heard laughter and snorts.

"I still could've beaten him, but my gun was in the other room."

More laughter from Mosby, more snorts from Meg.

Janet wasn't smiling as she carried the mugs into the living room. "Where did it happen?" she asked.

"In my face."

"At home, or . . . ?"

Nodding, he said, "In my apartment."

"Was it somebody you knew?"

He nodded. As he took one of the beers, his eyes met Janet's and quickly turned away.

"Oh no," she muttered.

Meg frowned. "What?"

"It was Dave," Janet said. To Mosby, she said, "It was, wasn't it? The truth. *Dave* beat you up, didn't he."

Looking guilty, Mosby nodded. "I knew I shouldn't have come over here."

Meg moved closer to Mosby on the couch and put her hand on his knee. "Tell us about it," she said.

"Well, he started with his right hand and worked his way to his left."

"Knock off the jokes, okay?" Janet asked.

"Yeah, okay. Well . . . I answered my door on Sunday night and there he was. He pushed me and started punching." Mosby's voice cracked. He stopped. He drank more beer. He sniffed. Then he waited a few more seconds. "I didn't fight back," he finally said. "There wasn't any point in that. I mean, why should I want to hurt him?" He glanced from Janet to Meg. "You know what I mean? I didn't have any reason to hurt him." Mosby laughed once.

A nervous, embarrassed laugh. "Besides, if I'd fought back, it might've made him mad."

"Why did he *do* it?" Meg asked.

"To pay me back."

Janet groaned. "For taking me out."

"And to warn me not to do it again."

"That does it," Janet said. She jumped to her feet, breathing heavily. "That really does it. See you guys later."

"Janet?"

"I'm gonna pay a visit to that . . ." She searched her mind for a term foul enough, but gave up and rushed to the bedroom for her coat and purse. When she came out, Meg was blocking the hallway. Mosby stood behind her, looking confused.

"Hey, hon, you can't . . ."

"Excuse me."

Meg offered no resistance, stepping aside when Janet reached her. Mosby also let her by.

"I knew I shouldn't have come here tonight," he mumbled.

Janet hurried outside, pulling her coat on as the foggy night air seeped like water through her blouse. The handle of the car door was cold and wet. When she had trouble climbing into her Maverick, she wished she'd changed out of her ankle-length skirt. She wiped her hands dry on her coat, then started the engine.

As she began pulling away from the curb, dim head-lights appeared in her side mirror. She hit her brakes. A municipal transit bus lunged by.

"Holy . . . ?"

She rolled down her window, put out her head and looked down the street. The intersection was only a few car lengths behind her, but she couldn't make out a trace of the traffic lights. The nearest street lamp was a high, eerie ball of pale fog.

"Worth a gal's life," she muttered. "And *yours*," she added, glancing down toward her belly.

She stepped on the gas. Her car swung away from the curb and climbed to forty. No headlights in the mirror.

The driving kept her nervous all the way and she thought very little about Dave. When she parked in front of his apartment house, the tension of driving went away and she realized with a sudden cramping chill that she was probably about to face him. She leaned forward against the steering wheel.

Calm down, she told herself. There's no need for this. He's a rotten fucking bastard, and I was an idiot to ever love him.

Which I don't anymore.

The Dave I loved is dead.

Maybe the Dave she'd loved had never really existed at all. Maybe he'd been an illusion.

Created in my own image, she thought. My own image of how a man *should* be. A figment of my imagination because I couldn't find the real thing.

"A cheap imitation," she muttered.

The sickening cramp had subsided. She got out of the car and headed for the fog-bound entrance of the apartment house. The foyer was warm. She opened her coat and climbed the stairs.

The upstairs floor gave slightly under each footstep like thin ice on a lake and she wondered, as she had so often wondered when living here, whether one of her feet would break through.

The door to 230 stood open. From inside came the windy whine of a vacuum cleaner. She walked in.

The living room was bare.

Tim Harris, the landlord, smiled at her and turned off the vacuum.

"How you doin', Janet?" He wiped his hands on the front of his T-shirt as if to spruce himself up for her.

"I'm okay. Where's Dave?"

"Moved out. Three, four days back. Left a note for you, though. I got it right . . ." He grimaced as he shoved a hand into a tight rear pocket of his jeans. "Here y'go." He pulled out a folded, wrinkled envelope and handed it to her.

She ripped open the envelope. The note inside was scribbled in red ink.

Dear Janet,

I knew you would have a change of heart and come back to me. My new place makes this look primitive. It does, however, require a woman's touch. So do I. Phone 520-9862. With eager anticipation, I am

Yours,

Dave

"Does the phone work?" Janet asked.

"Disconnected."

"Okay. Thanks."

She hurried down to her car and drove four blocks to the Safeway market. There were pay phones beside the entrance. She parked, jumped out of her car and hurried to the nearest phone. She snatched up its handset. The plastic was cold in her hand. She dropped coins down the slot. Careful not to let the earpiece touch her, she listened for a dial tone. It came. She dialed the number from Dave's note and heard the phone ring twice.

"Hello?" Dave asked.

"It's me."

"Ah! You got the message I left with Harris."

"Yeah. I also got the message you left with Mosby, you miserable bastard."

"Such language!"

"What do you *mean*, hurting Mosby that way?"

"Doing what?"

"You heard me. I don't know why the hell he didn't have you arrested, but if you ever touch him again, I'll go to the police so fast your head'll spin."

"You *are* out of sorts tonight. Here I thought you'd phoned to patch things up."

"Things are beyond patching."

"They could get worse, you know."

"Could they really?"

"Let's get together," he said. "How about Friday night?"

"How about never?"

"If you don't see me Friday, maybe Meg will. Think she might? We had such a good ol' time together *last* Friday. She's not quite my type, being ugly as shit, but she does have all the right equipment."

"You filthy pig."

"Got a pencil? Here's my new address. Ready?"

"I'm not coming over."

"Up to you, sweety. But I'd better give you the address just in case. You never know when you might get the urge for some sweet lovin'."

In her purse, she found a ballpoint pen and a business card from Val's Beauty Salon. "Okay, give it to me." She copied the address on the back of the card. Then the phone number.

"If you're not here by seven o'clock Friday night," Dave said, "I'll have to pay a visit to Meg."

She hung up and stared down at the walkway. The concrete was wet from the fog. A passing shopper stepped on a white wrapper from a Three Musketeers bar, flattening it. When the foot went away, the wrapper opened again nearly to the same shape as before, but wet and dirty. Janet picked it up. She dropped it into a trash can near the door. And wanted to kick the metal can.

No, that's Dave's way. Kicking things.

To win, she thought, I've gotta be better than him.

THIRTY—EIGHT

THE SHOOT

Driving to a doughnut shop in Denver that night, Albert hit the brakes.

What the hell's going on?

He wondered if he should turn around and go the other way. In spite of all the activity, however, the street looked clear. He could probably drive right on by the commotion without any trouble.

His stomach lurched as he saw a cop.

The cop was looking at him, waving him ahead.

Okay.

Slowly, Albert drove toward the parked trucks, the crowd, the brightly lighted apartment house, the cop. He wished he were still in women's clothes, but the cop only seemed interested in keeping the street clear.

For what? This looked like the scene of a fire or accident or crime, but where were the fire trucks, the ambulances?

And what were those big trucks for? Those motor homes?

Albert had never seen a scene quite like this before. It was strange and vaguely frightening.

He wanted to get past it all, get to a store for doughnuts and return to the safety of the house.

Until he saw the cameras.

They're shooting a movie here?

That must be it, he realized, feeling a mixture of relief and curiosity.

It's gotta be a movie or a TV show. Unless it's just some lousy commercial.

He wondered how safe it would be to stop and watch for a while. There were at least a couple of cops. But even if the cops *did* pay attention to him, his hair was now cut so short that he barely resembled the police drawing or the photos his father must've provided to the authorities. The chances of being recognized were slim—and he really wanted to watch the filming.

Maybe I'll get to see a star.

At the intersection, he turned right. He parked at the first empty stretch of curb and climbed out.

The clothes of Willard P. Andricci, Management Consultant, were much too large for Albert. But he rather liked the loose, comfortable way they felt.

As he walked toward the crowd, he began to worry about someone noticing their poor fit.

Well, the coat should hide most of it.

Tomorrow, maybe he would go shopping. Buy some boots, some jeans, a shirt or two. And maybe something to disguise himself: a hat, hair dye, glasses if he could get some that wouldn't give him a headache the way Willard's did. He'd only been able to wear Willard's glasses for a few minutes before they'd started to make his head pound.

I really oughta get myself some good ones, he thought. *Nobody'd* recognize me if I had glasses on.

But nobody seemed to be looking at him, anyway, as he entered the crowd of spectators. Moving slowly, pressing between bodies, he worked his way closer to the front.

Closer to where he might glimpse the familiar face of a star.

"Quiet on the set," someone said. A firm voice. "Everybody, quiet on the set."

Sudden silence. Albert could hear the wind shaking leaves in the nearby trees. A man held a slate board in front of a camera, but Albert was too far away to read the writing on it.

"Action."

Suddenly, a man was running, pistol in hand, toward the apartment-house door. He wore black clothing and a ski mask. The apartment door opened. A camera moved toward it on a dolly. A sound boom swung above it. Two men walked out, both in business suits. Albert recognized the one on the left: someone from *Mannix*. He tried to remember the man's name as he watched the mouths move. He couldn't hear what the actors were saying, but he heard someone say, "Cut, cut." One of the actors at the door shook his head. The other began to laugh. The man in the ski mask shifted the pistol to his left hand where he held it by the barrel.

"Do you know what they're shooting?" a man asked Albert.

"I don't know."

A girl turned around. "It's *Some Call it Sleep* from the Evan Collier book."

Albert stared at the girl. She was beautiful, slender and only a bit older than him. Maybe twenty? She wore a plaid jacket like a lumberjack. The wind blew strands of hair across her face and whipped steam off the surface of her coffee. She pursed her lips, sipped the coffee and turned away.

"Are you an Evan Collier fan?" Albert asked.

She smiled over her shoulder. "Me? I think he's terrific. I've read most of his books."

"Me, too," Albert said. He'd never heard of Evan Collier, much less read any of the man's books.

"*Some Call it Sleep* is probably his best, and it's a good script. Pretty faithful to the novel. Collier didn't write the screenplay, though. Max Radow did that."

"You've read the screenplay?" Albert asked.

Smiling, she nodded. Wind blew wisps of red hair across her face. "I have a part in the movie."

"No kidding?"

"Oh, I'm not the lead. Nothing like that. But it's a speaking part. I've got two scenes."

"That's fantastic!"

"Well, it's a start. Nothing spectacular, but . . ."

"Can I have your autograph?"

She laughed. "You don't really want it, do you?"

"I sure *do!* I'm a *big* movie fan." Albert searched his coat pockets. In the left pocket, he touched paper. He pulled it out and held it up to the light. A Master Charge receipt.

"That'll do fine," she said.

"I don't seem to have a pen."

"Here, I've got one." She took a pen from her purse. Then she glanced at both sides of the receipt. "You aren't Willard, are you?"

"Sure," he said.

Something's wrong, he thought, his stomach going tight.

"I've never heard of a guy your age with a Master Charge."

"Oh, that. I'm Willard junior. It's really my father's account."

She nodded and said, "Ahhh." Using her purse for backing, she scribbled on the receipt. "There you are, Willard."

Albert lifted the paper into the light and read aloud, "To Willard, my very first autograph as a film actress. All my best wishes forever, May Beth Bonner."

"That's nice," he said. "Thank you."

"You ought to put it someplace safe," she told him, smiling oddly so that he couldn't be sure how serious she was. "One of these days when I'm famous, it'll be worth some big bucks."

"Oh, I'd never sell it."

"You're sweet, you know that?"

"Quiet on the set."

May Beth turned her back to Albert. He stepped forward and stood beside her to watch the action.

After the scream of a siren interrupted the take, Albert asked, "How long does all this go on?"

"Until they get it right," May Beth said. "This is the last scene for tonight, but they need to get it perfect before they call it quits."

The final scene.

Albert's pulse quickened and his stomach began to feel sick with excitement.

"Quiet on the set."

Albert wiped his sweaty palms on his trousers.

The last scene!

He had to think of something fast. He couldn't let this babe get away, he just couldn't. She was far more beautiful than any of the others.

"Well, that's that," she said, turning to him.

Over already. So fast.

"Do you want to go somewhere?" Albert blurted.

"What?"

"Let's go somewhere. Together. I'll buy you something to eat. Are you hungry?"

"Not especially."

"How about a drink?"

"A drink drink? I could go for that, but . . . no way are you going to pass for twenty-one."

"We've got all sorts of stuff at home," he explained. "My parents are gone, so we'd have the place to ourselves."

"This is starting to sound serious." Though she smiled, her eyes seemed to be sizing him up. "Let's go over here," she said and led him out of the crowd. When nobody was nearby, she asked, "What do you have in mind?"

"A drink. I thought we might have a drink together, that's all. I've never known a movie star."

"Sure, but I bet you want to do a little more than have a *drink* with me."

"We could like talk, get to know each other."

"Fuck," she said.

"Huh?"

What did she say? Albert wondered. She didn't really say *fuck*, did she?

Sure sounded like it.

"That's what you *really* want to do, isn't it, Willard?" Smiling, she reached out and squeezed his arm through the sleeve of his coat. "Come on, admit it."

"Admit what?"

"You want to fuck me."

It *is* what she said.

For a moment, Albert suspected he might be asleep and dreaming. He'd sometimes *had* dreams similar to this, in which he encounters an amazingly beautiful girl and against all laws of human nature she *wants* him, she comes to him naked and he is just about to take her into his arms when he wakes up.

This seemed very much like the start of a dream like that.

But Albert felt as if he were awake.

This is happening, man!

"You *do* want to fuck me, don't you?" May Beth asked.

"Well . . . Sure, I guess so."

"Of course you do. That's all *any* guy wants to do. The nature of the beast."

Albert shrugged.

This is real!

"How much money have you got?" she asked.

His heart sank.

Money?

He suddenly remembered Betty, half-naked in his car, her breasts smooth against his face.

Such a long time ago.

What if I'd had the twenty bucks to pay Betty that night? he thought. No trip to the Broxtons. None of this.

"You want money?" Albert asked.

"Guys like to fuck. *I* like to buy stuff. How much will you pay me?"

"You a hooker?"

"No, of course not. A hooker? Give me a break. I'm an actress."

"But you want money."

"Hey, a guy takes a gal out on a date, buys her an expensive dinner, maybe takes her to a show. He spends all that money on her, then she's supposed to fuck him. That's how it *usually* works. I'm just taking the payment in *cash* instead of food and entertainment. You see? No big difference."

"Guess not," Albert said, though he suspected there might be a flaw in her reasoning. "So, okay. How about twenty bucks?"

"Do you know what I'll do for twenty bucks? I'll drive back to my motel and watch Johnny Carson. Alone. You want *me*, you'll have to do a lot better than that."

"How about forty?"

"Let's see it."

He opened his billfold. It was thick with cash.

"Make it a hundred," she said, "and I'll stay all night."

"That's a *lot*."

She looked him in the eyes. "You've probably never even *talked* to a gal as pretty as me, much less fucked one."

His legs felt weak.

"Okay," he said. "I'll give you a hundred."

"Then we've got a deal." She held out her hand.

Albert shook it.

Smirking, May Beth pulled her hand back and said, "The *money*, Willard. The *money*."

"You want it *now?*"

"That's the idea."

"I don't know. What if I give it to you and you split?"

"Where's your house?" May Beth asked.

"It's a few miles from here."

"I'll follow you in my bug. It's just over there." She pointed down the road, and Albert saw a yellow Volkswagen parked at the curb. "If you're afraid I'll run away with your money, you can keep an eye on me in your rearview mirror."

"I've got a better idea," Albert said. "Let's leave your car where it is and I'll drive you in mine. Then I'll bring you back here when we're done in the morning."

She stared at her car for a while. "Do you think it'll be all right there?"

"It'll be fine. This is a really safe neighborhood."

"Is it?"

Who knows?

"Are you from around here?" Albert asked.

She shook her head. "I live in California."

"Well," he said, "there's hardly any crime *anywhere* in Denver."

She turned to him and nodded. "Okay, I guess we can go in your car. Soon as you've paid up." She held out her hand again.

This time, Albert filled it with three twenties, three tens, a five and five ones.

May Beth folded the money and stuffed it into her purse. Then she took hold of Albert's hand. "You've got yourself a date," she said.

THIRTY—NINE

RED HOT

Albert touched a control button on the dashboard and the garage door began to rise.

"Those things are really cool," May Beth said. "I've been trying to talk my mother into getting one for our place."

"You live with your mother?"

"Something wrong with that?"

"No. I'm just curious. No reason *not* to live with your mother. Not if you get along with her okay."

"We get along fine," May Beth said.

She didn't sound as if she meant it.

"In California, right?"

"Right. Grand Beach. That's west of L.A., over near Santa Monica. It's a pretty nice area."

Albert pulled the car into the garage and stopped it beside a red Buick.

"Are you sure nobody's home?" May Beth asked.

"Oh, this other car?" He shrugged. The Buick was registered to Karen Winters. Its trunk contained the body of Willard P. Andricci, owner of this house, tightly wrapped in plastic garbage bags. "I drove Mom and Dad to the airport," Albert said, "so they wouldn't have to pay for parking."

"Yeah, those airport parking fees are ridiculous."

"I don't have to pick them up till Sunday." He climbed out of the car. Over by the door to the kitchen, he pressed the remote button. The garage door began rumbling down. As May Beth came toward him, he unlocked the kitchen door and opened it.

They stepped inside.

May Beth took off her jacket and draped it over a kitchen chair. She had on a white T-shirt and no bra. The dark tint of her nipples showed through the fabric.

Albert took off his coat and draped it beside hers.

"How about those drinks you were mentioning?" May Beth asked.

"You get a hundred bucks *and* drinks?"

Smiling, she raised her red eyebrows. "I could use a martini, Willard. Do you have a problem with that?"

"Guess not."

"I'll bet you could use a nice drink, yourself." Reaching out, she rubbed the side of his neck.

"I'm not too sure how to make a martini."

"I'll show you." She brought a hand up between his legs and gently squeezed him through his trousers.

He moaned. Her hand stayed there as she said, "I'll need glasses, a shaker, ice, gin, dry vermouth, and olives if you have any."

"Oh, okay," he muttered.

She took her hand away.

Feeling disoriented, Albert started to gather the ingredients.

What's going on? he wondered.

This sort of thing had never happened to him before.

Well, Betty had been something like this. She had touched and teased him and made him hard. It was exciting but . . . difficult.

A knife would make it easy again.

He searched the refrigerator for olives.

The knife can always come later, he thought.

He might as well let May Beth run things for a while. After all, he'd paid her. He was the boss.

"Here they are," he said.

She laughed. "You *do* have a lot to learn, Willard. Nobody uses black olives in a martini."

"Oh, you want green olives?"

She nodded, grinning at him as if he were an idiot.

She wouldn't be acting this way, Albert thought, if I had a knife in her belly.

He shut the refrigerator door. "I guess there aren't any green ones."

"Well then, we'll have to do without."

After Albert had gathered everything she needed, May Beth poured the ingredients over ice inside a silver shaker. She twirled a spoon through the mixture, then filled the two glasses.

"Let's go someplace comfortable," she said, handing one of the martinis to Albert.

He saw that the ice cubes were still inside the shaker. He took out two and put them into his glass. "Want ice?" he asked.

She gave him a patient look. "No thanks."

"Why not?"

"It melts and ruins the drink. Let's go in the living room."

"Okay," he muttered.

As they left the kitchen, Albert felt weak and vulnerable.

It doesn't have to be this way, he told himself. I can take control any time. All I've gotta do is get out my switchblade.

But this isn't so bad, he thought. This is okay for now.

He followed May Beth into the living room. They sat close together on the sofa.

"Is this your first time?" she asked, and took a sip of her drink.

"First time I've paid for it."

"If it's *not* your first time, I can assure you that you *have* paid for it. In other ways. It never comes free."

Does when you have a knife.

"Maybe not," Albert said. "Anyway, you're sure right about one thing—I've never done *anything* with a girl as pretty as you."

She finished her martini in several quick swallows and shuddered. "Oooo, that *was* delicious." She leaned forward and set her glass on the coffee table. "We'll have another later," she said. Then she turned to Albert and kissed him. For a moment, her lips were cool from the drink.

Albert still held his glass. He reached out blindly behind him and set it on the arm of the sofa. Then he embraced May Beth. His hands roamed over her back. He wanted to touch one of her breasts, but was afraid to try.

I'd better get my knife.

Before he could go for it, she was above him, straddling him, pulling off her T-shirt. Reaching down, she took both his hands. She lifted them to her breasts. The firm tips of her nipples prodded Albert's palms. She moved his hands in slow circles.

For a while, she seemed to be in a trance, concentrating only on the feel of his hands against her breasts. Then she pulled his hands away, leaned low over him and touched a nipple to his lips. He stuck out his tongue and licked it.

Just as he was about to suck it, the breast went away from his mouth. Lips took its place. Her tongue slid in.

The kiss went on for a long time, Albert fondling her breasts and squirming under her.

When her mouth went away, she eased herself down on top of him. She licked and kissed each of his nipples and pulled at them gently with her teeth.

Kneeling over him, she unfastened his trousers. She tugged them down to his ankles, then hunched over him. As her cool fingers encircled him, he moaned and shut his eyes. Then he felt her tongue. Then her lips. The tight, slick ring of her lips slid down him, then up.

Then they went away.

Albert opened his eyes.

May Beth was off the sofa, standing, taking off her jeans. Her face was strange: vacant but intense. Though she saw him staring, her expression didn't change. She stepped out of her panties and dropped them to the floor.

Albert stared at her thatch of curly red pubic hair.

I'll shave that off . . .

She came back to the sofa. Bending over, she removed Albert's shoes, his socks. She pulled the trousers off his ankles and tossed them to the floor.

"Here?" Albert asked. His throat was tight, his mouth parched.

May Beth didn't answer. She climbed onto the sofa and knelt over him. Her fingertips took hold of him. They pulled gently, guiding him to a wet place between soft and yielding folds.

"No!" he gasped. Rolling sideways, he threw her to the floor. His glass fell, splashing her face. An ice cube hit her forehead and slid off.

"Jesus!" May Beth cried out. "What's the matter with you!" Her eyes were wide with shock. She started to get up but Albert dropped onto her. He pinned her arms. "What's going on? Did I hurt you? What's wrong?"

"You."

"Get off! Let me up!"

"Not till I've fucked you!" he shouted and smashed his fist against her temple. He struck her again and again until she went limp. Then he climbed off and crawled over to his trousers. He grabbed them by the belt, picked them up and shoved a hand down the right front pocket.

Car keys.

Where's my knife?

He tried the left pocket. A hanky. A comb.

His switchblade must've fallen out, maybe when May Beth pulled the trousers off him. He tossed them out of the way and looked around on the carpet.

Where is it?

He dropped low and peered under the coffee table.

Not there, either.

Shit!

He glanced back at May Beth. Still down.

So he ran into the kitchen. He slipped a knife out of the rack. It was a carving knife with a serrated, nine-inch blade. Though he'd never touched it before, the sleek wooden handle felt familiar to his grip. He rushed into the living room.

Now May Beth was on her hands and knees, struggling to get up. She saw the knife in his hand. A low moan escaped from her. She swayed to her feet.

Something in her hand.

An empty martini glass. She hurled it at Albert. It glanced off his shoulder and broke against the wall behind him.

Her pale, sweaty belly heaved as she gasped for air. He would put it in right there, just below her navel, where she was smooth and flat and shiny.

She grabbed a lamp, yanked its cord so the plug leaped from the wall socket, and threw it with both hands. Albert tried to dodge it, but the lamp caught his shins. As he yelped with pain, May Beth dodged to the left.

Raced for a window.

But the window was shut.

She didn't seem to care. She made a running dive. Her fists broke through the glass and the rest of her naked body followed. Albert glimpsed her pale buttocks, the backs of her legs, the bottoms of her feet. Then she disappeared into the night.

He ran to the window. Hands on the sill, he leaned out. He expected to see her sprawled motionless on the grass.

But she was on her feet.

Blood streamed down her back and legs, but she was running. Running across the backyard and screaming, screaming her head off.

Another Charlene.

Another goddamn Charlene!

How come the best ones always get away?

Oh, my God! I've gotta get outta here!

He started putting on his clothes.

Where'll I go? he wondered.

Anywhere. Doesn't matter. Just get out of here fast.

She knows my car. I won't get five miles.

Maybe drive it one mile, take another house and stash it in the garage?

Hurrying through the kitchen, he saw May Beth's purse on the table. He grabbed it, rushed through the door to the garage and tossed it onto the car seat.

As it hit, something inside made a metallic tinkle.

Her keys?

Albert jerked open the purse and saw a big brass ring. He pulled it out. Half a dozen keys hung from it. Two of them looked like car keys.

Volkswagen keys.

I'll use *her* car for the getaway?

It was several miles away, over where they'd been shooting the film.

I'll drive over and switch. She'll think her stupid little bug is still safe and sound where she left it. Might be hours before she finds out it's gone.

FORTY

AFTERNOON DELIGHT

Parked at the curb across the street from Emily Jean's house, Lester watched a car pull into her driveway. It stopped and Emily Jean climbed out. She raised the garage door, then returned to her car and drove into the garage. After she pulled the door shut, Lester waited for two minutes before climbing from his own car. He walked to the front door and rang the bell.

Quick footsteps. The door opened.

"Why, Mr. Bryant! How nice of you to drop by. You certainly arrived early."

"I couldn't think of a good excuse to leave work early, so I took the whole day off."

She pressed her face against his chest. "I do wish I'd known. I would've phoned in sick, myself, and we might've spent the entire day together. Wouldn't that have been lovely?"

He felt the loss like a sharp pain. "It occurred to me," he said, "but I thought you might have qualms about missing work."

"Heavens, no. I make it a point, every year, to be absent several days whether I'm ill or not. I see it as a reward for my hard labors and dedication. Besides, substitutes too must eat."

"Why don't we pick a day next week and both call in sick?"

"Do you dare?"

"Sure. I'll say it's a relapse. It'll be fine. Today's my first absence in six months."

"Well, then, shall we plan on next Tuesday?"

"What's wrong with Monday?" Lester asked.

"Monday illnesses arouse too much suspicion."

"Okay then, Tuesday it is." He kissed the side of her neck. The mild scent of perfume excited him.

"Would you care for a drink?" she asked.

"Why not?"

"No reason. I'll just whip up a batch of margaritas."

"Great. Don't you drink martinis, though?"

"I'll be quite happy with margaritas, I'm sure." With a lazy, contented smile, she hugged him and they kissed again. "I shall return in two shakes of a lamb's tail."

"Okay. Oh, and don't bother salting the rim of my glass, okay? It's too much trouble and I don't go much for all that salt."

"As you like it. My, wouldn't that make a clever title for something?"

"As you like it? It does have a nice ring to it."

"Alas, it has probably been used. There is nothing new under the sun, Mr. Bryant."

"Aren't we?"

"New?" She frowned as if thinking very hard. "We're certainly rather new to each other, aren't we?"

"New and improved," Lester said.

"Indeed we are," she said, then went into the kitchen.

Lester wandered around the living room, waiting. He glanced into the fireplace. Three split logs were stacked on the grate with kindling and paper wads underneath, waiting for a chilly night. On the mantle, a pewter ashtray held a single, mashed cigarette. There was lipstick on the filter.

"I do hope you like Camembert," Emily Jean said, coming from the kitchen with a tray of cheese and crackers. The margaritas were balanced precariously.

"Once inside my mouth, it's great. The trick is to get it there without smelling it."

"Why, you *must* smell it or you'll miss half the flavor." She set the tray on the table in front of the couch. "Do sit down."

He sat, and then Emily Jean was sitting beside him, against him, and he put his arm around her and squeezed her shoulder.

"A toast would be appropriate, don't you think?"

"I guess so," Lester agreed.

"To all brave hearts and lovers."

They gently clinked their glasses and drank. "That was a nice toast," Lester said.

Emily Jean smiled. "It did have a nice ring to it."

"Like 'as you like it,'" he said, and sipped the cloudy drink.

"Exactly."

"Or 'all's well that ends well.'"

"I don't care much for the ring of that one," said Emily Jean. "It may sound a trifle pessimistic to you, but I suspect that nothing ends well. Not a thing."

Lester's stomach tightened. He took a long drink and a deep breath. "That's an awful way to look at things."

"Awful, perhaps. But accurate, I'm afraid. Things always start out so dazzling bright and full of promise. Like the first snowfall of the year. Have you ever lived where it snows?"

"I grew up in Chicago."

"Then you know. It falls so lovely white and melts on your eyelashes and covers the lawns and roofs and the tops of cars and it's simply beautiful. Then young men have heart attacks shoveling it and cars skid into each other and trees. And after the snow has been on the ground for a short time, it's gray and ugly."

"If you break the surface," Lester said, "it's still white underneath. As white as the day it came down."

"Such a pleasant thought. And do you know something? You're absolutely right!" She looked at him with solemn respect as if he were a stranger with remarkable insight. "I've done that myself. Why, I recall a summer several years ago. I was hiking in the Sierra. It was August, I believe. Late August or early September. At any rate, it was toward the end of summer and the first snow hadn't come yet, but I found a gray, crusty old patch of snow. It had lasted since winter because it was sheltered from the sun all day long beneath an overhang. Well, the water in my canteen was lukewarm and cool refreshment sounded mighty welcome. So I kicked through the dirty crust and the snow underneath was so white it nearly blinded me. I scooped it up and ate it from my hand. Biting it. I still recall the way it tasted, and the way it squeaked against my teeth. Have you ever eaten snow?"

"Many times," he said. "But not since I was a kid."

She shook her head sadly. "We did so many marvelous things when we were children. I used to lie in the grass and watch the shapes the clouds made. Did you do that?"

"Sure."

"There was always a high percentage of bearded men and sheep."

Lester laughed.

"I'm perfectly serious. I also used to walk through puddles in my galoshes, stamping down hard to make big splashes."

"I did that, too. *I* was very big on throwing things."

"Rocks?"

"Rocks, bricks."

"Snowballs?"

"And spitballs and paper airplanes."

"And chunks of dirt that exploded into a million bits!"

"And once, when I was very lucky, my older brother— over my shoulder with judo."

Emily Jean laughed. "All for the sheer joy of throwing," she said, and hurled her empty glass at the fireplace. As it struck the grate and smashed, Lester threw his. It glanced off the bark of a log and exploded against the bricks.

They both were laughing and then they were in each other's arms. The laughter stopped. They lay down on the couch and held each other for a long time. They said nothing. They hardly moved. They simply held each other close.

Then they moved their faces apart. Lester's cheek was hot from pressing against hers. She looked in his eyes and he smiled and she kissed him. "Shall we move into the bedroom?" she suggested.

She led him upstairs and entered the room with the blue bedspread and the sweaty rock star writhing on the poster.

"Let's go to your room," Lester said.

She looked at him solemnly.

"If we're going to make love, Emily Jean, I want to do it on your bed—not on your daughter's. With you. No more pretending you're her."

"We tried that before, darling. It didn't work."

"It'll work now."

She began to cry. Lester held her. He led her quietly through the hallway to a bedroom with blowing curtains and two swirling landscapes of Van Gogh above the bed.

And it worked.

They were asleep when the telephone rang. Lester opened his eyes. The room was dark.

He felt a rush of alarm.

How late is it?

The phone rang again.

Must be at least six o'clock, he thought, or the sun wouldn't be down.

What if that's Helen on the phone?

It rang again.

She doesn't know I'm here.

The hell with Helen, he thought, and smiled. So poetic: the hell with Helen.

Emily Jean reached an arm through the darkness and picked up the phone. Her voice sounded sleepy and pleasant as she said, "Hello?" She listened for a moment. "Yes, this is she." Seconds passed. Suddenly, she blurted, "No! How badly?"

Lester climbed out of bed.

"I see."

He started putting on his clothes.

"Yes, yes, I understand."

He tried not to listen. He felt out of place and wondered if he should leave the room.

"No, not that I know of."

He stepped into the hallway, buttoning his shirt, and didn't return until he heard Emily Jean hang up.

"It's May Beth," she said softly as if dazed. "Somehow . . . she's been hurt. She was taken to the hospital . . . in Denver. County General . . . all cut up . . . last night."

"How bad is she?"

"Critical. The doctor said, 'critical.' She was unconscious until . . . half an hour ago." Emily Jean shook her head. "I have to go to her."

"I'll drive you to the airport," Lester said.

She sat up in bed. "Oh, thank you. But you can't do that, Lester. Helen . . ."

"The hell with Helen," he said. "Let's get going." He sat beside Emily Jean and put his hand on her warm, fragile shoulder.

She was already dressed and dialing the phone in the living room when the doorbell rang.

"Could you get it for me?" she asked.

What if it's Helen?

The idea made Lester feel squirmy and sick.

"Sure," he said.

I hope it *is* Helen.

He hurried to the front door and swung it open.

"Trick or treat!" shouted a trio of little kids: a ghost, a vampire and a Yoda.

Isn't Halloween tomorrow?

No, this is Thursday. *This* is Halloween.

Here are the trick-or-treaters to prove it.

Lester wondered if Emily Jean had candy stashed away somewhere.

She was still on the phone to the substitute office. He could hear her speaking slowly and clearly, the way people do when talking to a tape recorder.

Lester reached into a pocket of his trousers. He felt some coins down there, and scooped them out.

"Here you go, kids."

They held out their bags.

"Happy Halloween," Lester said, and dropped a quarter into each bag.

FORTY—ONE

TRAVELER'S FRIEND

Butler Avenue. Butler would do fine.

Who done it? The Butler, of course.

If I had a Butler, he would tuck me into bed . . .

Albert shook his head sharply, trying to clear it. He flicked on the Volkswagen's right-hand turn signal, moved over a lane, and exited Interstate 40.

Welcome to Flagstaff, he thought.

Staff of life. Sleep. Or is it bread? Staff of life?

Who knows? Who cares?

He hadn't slept since when? Pueblo, Arizona. That quiet dark street in Pueblo where he parked and slept until dawn broke through his windshield. But that was . . . thirteen hours ago? No, fourteen. Something like that.

So much driving. Endless. Putting miles between . . .

This is it. End of the road. Till tomorrow.

He saw a big neon sign.

TRAVELER'S FRIEND

The small flashing green sign below it read VACANCY.

Albert pulled into the driveway of the motel and climbed out. The air was cold and helped to clear his head. The desk clerk was a smiling, blond woman. Mrs. Friend or Mrs. Traveler?

He signed the registration card as Arnold Price.

He paid with a twenty-dollar bill. One of those he'd given the girl last night . . . the one that got away.

Got away like Charlene.

Win a few, lose a few, he thought.

But I keep losing the best of the bunch.

"I can give you room fourteen," said the woman.

"Good. Thank you."

Key in hand, Albert returned to his car. He found a space in front of room fourteen. Got out. Opened the door of the room. Shut it. Bolted it. Pulled off his clothes. Turned back the covers. Climbed naked between the cool smooth white sheets.

Sleep was at the bottom of a dark hole, waiting for him. He fell toward it, spinning.

FORTY—TWO

CONFESSION

"I hope you enjoyed yourself," Helen said. She glanced at him from the couch, then returned her eyes to the ceiling as if its pebbled surface were a far better companion that Lester.

"I had a fine time."

"Do you know what time it is?"

"Yes, I know what time it is. I don't know why you

should care, though. It's no later than the time you usually get home from your goddamn classes and board meetings and shit."

"I didn't *have* any classes or board meetings. This is Halloween. What I *had* were gangs of rug rats ringing the doorbell. I ran out of candy at about six o'clock and had to stop answering the door."

"Sorry," Lester said. "I thought Halloween was *tomorrow* night like the faculty party."

"Where were you?"

He thought about the airport and the three-hour wait for Emily Jean's flight to Denver. They had eaten supper there. She had cut her sirloin steak into dainty bites, but couldn't eat them because she was sick with worry about May Beth. Later, she'd declined his offer to take her into the bar, so they had waited on plastic chairs at the departure gate.

She left holding out her boarding pass like a ticket to a violent game she was afraid to see. Lester watched her and found himself crying.

"Well, where were you?" Helen asked again.

"I went to the airport."

"You were at the airport until eleven o'clock?" Her voice was mocking. "I hope you enjoyed yourself."

"I did. I got a big thrill out of watching all those people fly away."

"You probably wished you were one of them."

"Sure did."

"Well, why the fuck didn't you go! You think I want you around here all the time acting like some kind of goddamn baby?" She turned her head and looked at him. Her eyes and nose were red, just as Emily Jean's had been red at the airport when she had spoken quietly of May Beth. "I don't need you. You're nothing but a goddamn baby. What the hell happened to you, anyway? I used to think you were a man."

"You happened to me."

"Sure, lay the blame on me. That's just like you."

"Of course it is. I'm going to bed."

"Sure. Now you're gonna run off to bed like a bad little boy."

"Why should I stand here and take all this crap from you? You're supposed to be my loving wife, but you've been treating me like shit for years. What the hell is the matter with you, anyway?"

"I'll tell you what's the matter. Do you really want to know? Are you *sure* you want to know?" With the sleeve of her sweater, she wiped tears from her face. Then she glared at him, dared him with mocking eyes.

"Go ahead," he said.

"After I ran out of candy for the little bastards and you *still* weren't home, I went over to a friend's house. And you know what we did?"

Lester seemed to shrink inside. "Bob for apples?" he suggested.

"We screwed our brains out."

The strength drained from his legs. He dropped onto a chair.

"It wasn't just tonight, either." She sat up on the couch and leaned forward, elbows on knees. Her voice quickened. "I've been seeing him for weeks. For *weeks*, Lester. All those nights when you thought I was in class or at a meeting, I was in his bed—*fucking!* Because he's a real man and you're nothing but a worthless loser!"

He held tightly to the arms of the chair. The lights of the room looked dim and hazy. Helen's eyes, far away, were fierce as she laughed.

"How does it feel?" she asked. The words had a hollow ringing echo. "How do you like the idea of your wife in another man's bed? Another *man?*" Her laugh washed over him like a breaker, engulfing him, drowning him. "You're no man. *He's* the man. You're nothing. You're a cipher. You're a dickless wonder—that's what *he* calls you.

He laughs at you. We both do. You're so fucking pathetic it's sad."

"Who is he?" Lester heard himself ask, and wondered why he'd asked.

Doesn't matter who the bastard is.

Nothing seemed to matter except the warm darkness that was quickly overtaking him.

"Ian Collins, of course. Who do you think? He's the only real man I . . ."

The floor slammed into Lester's face, jarring him with a blast of pain, and he began to vomit. He thought he would never stop, never cleanse his guts of the filth that seemed to be clotted there.

But finally he did stop. He pushed himself away from the mess and got to his knees. He wiped his mouth and runny nose. Blinking tears from his eyes, he saw Helen's contempt.

"You fucking whore," he said.

Helen grinned. "Why don't we go to the Halloween party tomorrow night as a pair? I'll be the slut and you be the cuckold."

"Fuck you."

"Better still," she said, "you'd better just stay home. Ian says he's gonna kick your ass the next time he sees you." With a laugh, Helen got up from the couch. "Don't forget to clean up your puke before you come to bed."

"Who says I'm coming to bed?"

"Wouldn't you like a chance to outperform Ian? I'll let you give it a try . . . if you don't mind putting it into some leftover Ian." Helen chuckled and walked away.

Lester heard the bedroom door shut.

"G'bye," he muttered.

With a trembling hand, he reached into his pocket and pulled out a handful of change. And a single key.

The key to Emily Jean's house.

"G'bye, whore," he muttered.

FORTY—THREE

THE CALL

The ringing became part of Janet's dream.

Excuse me while I get the phone, she said to the man in her dream.

Not until we're done, he said, and selected a long-bladed scalpel from a tray beside the operating table.

No! Janet cried out. You *can't* take my baby out yet. It's not nine months and by then the phone won't be ringing anymore.

If you don't want me to take it out, he said, how about if I stick this *in?*

NO!!!

Janet suddenly woke up, gasping and drenched with sweat, and found herself in bed. Though the window curtains were open, the room was gloomy with gray light.

The phone jangled, making her flinch.

My God, Janet thought, it *is* ringing!

She rolled onto her side. As she reached out, her hand knocked a drinking glass off the nightstand.

"Hello?" she asked.

"Is this Janet Arthur?"

"Yes." She suddenly felt alert, excited.

"I'm Hazel Green from the Grand Beach Unified School District offices. Will you be available for substituting today?"

"I sure will!"

Sitting up, Janet turned on the lamp. She took a note pad from the table.

"The classes we'd like you to take will be Mrs. Bonner's eleventh- and twelfth-grade English."

"Fine."

"Do you know how to get to the high school?"

"Yes. I've driven past it. I know right where it is."

"Very good. You'll need to report to the high school's main office before eight o'clock this morning to pick up your schedule and lesson plans."

"I'll be there."

"They'll be expecting you. Good-bye, now."

"Good-bye," she said. "Thank you for calling."

She hung up the phone, leaped off the bed, clapped her hands together once so hard they hurt, and yelled, "A-WWW-RIGHT, LET'S HEAR IT FOR BIG JANET!!! *WHOO-EEE!!! YESSSS!!!*"

Then she remembered Dave. Tonight, she had to see him. Otherwise, he would probably cause more trouble—maybe put the make on Meg again . . .

She sank back down on the edge of the bed and muttered, "Terrific."

Suddenly, she had an urge to crawl back into bed, pull the covers over her head and stay there.

Can't do that, she told herself. Gotta get cleaned up and ready to go.

My first substituting job!

High school, eleventh- and twelfth-grade English.

They might be reading someone really good.

Feeling better, she climbed out of bed and headed for the bathroom.

FORTY—FOUR

ALBERT PLANS AHEAD

There was a pool of warmth in the middle of the bed. Albert curled inside it. Whenever he moved, his body touched its cold shore. Trying to stay inside the warmth started to make him feel cramped, however, so he finally gave up. He rolled through a plain of cold sheets and got out of bed.

He rushed to the bathroom, leaned over the tub and turned on the hot-water faucet. The water came out cold. While he waited for it to warm up, he urinated.

When the water was hot, he stoppered the drain. He stepped into the tub, adjusted the heat and stood as the water climbed his ankles. Then he stretched. The muscles of his legs and back and shoulders and neck were stiff and it was a luxury to stretch them. When he was finished, he sat in the hot water. He let it rise higher and higher. Then he turned off the faucets.

He lay back until only his knees and head remained above the surface. The heat of the water seemed to penetrate his skin, softening his muscles until he felt that he would never be able to move again.

But he would have to move. And soon.

He had taken a big chance, coming to a motel like this. What if the gal at the front desk had recognized him from the news drawings or photos?

Well, she hadn't done that or the cops would've grabbed him by now.

But he'd better not try this again. From now on, he should only stay at houses. Taking houses seemed to work fine.

Even *that's* risky, he reminded himself.

He'd been lucky back at Charlene's place that nobody from her school or from her father's store . . . or even from her mother's bridge group . . . had gotten too curious. Three people can't just drop out of their lives for very long without someone noticing.

Especially not on *weekdays*, Albert thought. Too much goes on during the week.

Next time, he should take over a house on a Friday night. That way, he could spend a couple of days without having to worry about anyone being missed from a job or school.

Today's Friday!

And Albert knew exactly which house to hit.

He even had a key.

May Beth had talked about living with her mother. Maybe the mother would be there. If she looked half as good as May Beth, he might end up having a pretty good time with her.

Albert unwrapped a slim bar of soap and began to wash his face.

FORTY—FIVE

GOING HOME

"Blessed Virgin College. May I help you?"

"Rhonda, this is Lester."

"You still under the weather?" Her voice sounded sympathetic.

"I'm afraid so."

"Well, I'll give Sister Martha a ring when she arrives, and let her know."

"Good. Thank you."

"You take care of yourself and get well, Lester."

"Okay. Thanks again. Good-bye."

He looked at the alarm clock beside Emily Jean's bed. Almost seven-thirty. Too early to leave.

So he went down the hall to the bathroom and took a shower. He stayed under the hot spray for a long time. When he was done, he got dressed and went downstairs. He made coffee. While it percolated, he fried bacon and eggs. He ate in the living room, watching a cartoon show on the television.

Shortly before nine, he went out to his car.

A cramp began twisting his bowels as he drove toward home.

What if Helen's there?

She won't be.

Before entering his house, he checked the garage. Empty. Some of the pain went away, but not all of it.

Fairly certain that Helen was at school, he entered the house. He took two large suitcases from a storage closet. They should hold enough to keep him going for a week or two until he could find an apartment.

Maybe he wouldn't *need* an apartment.

Maybe he could stay on at Emily Jean's house.

Would she let me?

Maybe. He suspected that she had fallen in love with him.

One gal's trash is another gal's treasure.

He carried the suitcases into the bedroom. Instead of starting to pack them, he dropped them to the floor and sat on the edge of the bed.

Staring at the wall, he wondered whether he really wanted to live with Emily Jean.

Even if she *does* love me, I'd be stuck with someone who's twice my age . . . and a little weird.

Very weird, that stuff about pretending to be May Beth.

May Beth!

If I *do* stay at their house, May Beth will probably be there, too.

If she lives.

If she lives, she'll come back and live at home. It'll be the three of us . . .

Lester imagined himself stretched out on a bed with both of them, the mother and daughter, both naked and slim and eager, both kissing him, stroking him, sucking him, but one so much younger and prettier and firmer and smoother, the other so much more desperate and strange.

It'll never happen.

When May Beth comes home, he thought, I'll get tossed out.

Emily Jean isn't about to let me live in the same house with her main *rival*.

Only way I get to stay on with Emily Jean is if the girl doesn't make it.

I sure don't want that to happen, he told himself. It'd be so devastating to Emily . . .

And I'd lose any chance of . . .

WHAT'S WRONG WITH ME? I don't even know the girl. She probably wouldn't even LIKE me, much less . . .

If she dies, Lester thought, maybe I won't even *want* Emily Jean anymore.

What's *that* all about?

He didn't want to think about it.

He suddenly wanted to flop on the bed and not get up. Not get up at all.

But he would *have* to get up sooner or later. If he stayed till mid-afternoon, Helen would probably come home.

He didn't want to face her.

He didn't want to face anyone.

I ought to do everyone a favor and blow my brains out, he thought.

Helen hates my guts. Emily Jean's a pathetic loser. I don't stand a chance with May Beth. I'll never stand a chance with *any* woman that *I* want.

Was it Groucho?

I wouldn't want to be in any club that'll take me as a member.

Something like that, Lester thought.

Story of my life.

In the second drawer of his dresser, he found his Ruger .22-caliber revolver. He unsnapped the guard strap and slid it free of its holster.

FORTY—SIX

THE LOUNGE

Janet dropped a dime into the vending machine in the faculty lounge. Stepping back, she watched a cardboard cup drop into place. When the machine stopped its loud humming, she bent down and lifted out the cup. The coffee inside was muddy brown. She wrinkled her nose.

"I wouldn't drink that if I were you," said a slim, striking woman who was sitting on the couch.

"It does look sort of disgusting."

"The hot chocolate is much better," the woman told her. "It's five cents more than the coffee, but worth every penny."

"What've I got to lose?" Janet dumped her coffee into the sink, found three nickles in her purse, and turned the machine's selection knob to Hot Chocolate. She inserted her nickles and waited.

"Is this your first time at Grand Beach High?" the woman asked.

"It's my first time anywhere."

"Must be quite an adventure for you, then. You have Emily Jean's classes, don't you?"

She picked up the cup. The hot chocolate looked fine. "Is that Mrs. Bonner?"

The woman nodded and fit a cigarette into the end of a long, silver holder. "She and I are usually the only ones in here now. Everyone else with fourth-period preparation makes a beeline for the mixed lounge, which is an absolute madhouse." She lit her cigarette.

"Mixed lounge?" Janet asked and sat in an armchair.

"We have a grand total of three faculty lounges at this establishment. The men's lounge, which is the lair of the male chauvinist contingent. Venture in there at your own risk. Abandon all hope. Then there's the mixed lounge, where chaos reigns. Finally, the women's lounge, as blissful as the eye of a hurricane. That's us." She blew out a stream of smoke and squinted as if inspecting it. "By the way, I'm Dale."

"I'm Janet."

"Is English your field, or have they placed you in an alien subject? They seem to have a preference for that, you know."

"I'm an English major." Janet decided not to mention

her master's degree. She tasted the hot chocolate. "Mmm. You were right about this."

"Good, isn't it?"

"It's great."

"I'd have one with you, but I can't afford the calories."

Janet stared at her chocolate. If Dale, as slinky as a *Vogue* model, couldn't afford the calories, then Janet shouldn't. She took another sip, anyway.

"As it is," Dale said, "I'll be a rather plump Ophelia."

"A plump what?"

"Oh, I'm dressing up as Ophelia for the faculty Halloween party tonight. Ophelia of *Hamlet*? My husband, who's much more literary than I am, insisted on dressing as the ghost of *King* Hamlet. He gave me a choice of Ophelia or Yorick."

"I think I knew him."

"Didn't everyone? At any rate, I opted for Ophelia."

"Are you going mad or sane?"

"Oh, mad, of course. Mad as a hatter."

"A wise decision," Janet said, nodding sagely and smiling. "Sounds like fun."

"Oh, we generally do have memorable parties. Jim Harrison—the principal—came to last year's party as a geek. You wouldn't believe the uproar he caused. He had a plastic garbage bag containing several plucked chickens. Deceased chickens."

"Oh, dear."

"At intervals throughout the night, he would pull a chicken out of the bag and bite off its head."

"My God."

"It was really quite zany. And ghastly. All the men, of course, thought this was the greatest thing ever. Actually bit their heads right off! Jim's a lovable man, but coarse . . . terribly coarse." Dale puffed her cigarette and shook her head. "Poor Emily Jean was so repulsed by his act that she tossed her cookies—retched into Ian's swimming pool. She was mortified, though Ian took it remarkably well. Nothing fazes Ian." She gazed at her smoke and grinned with one side of her mouth. "I suppose Emily Jean won't be making it to tonight's festivities."

"Suppose not," Janet said.

"In fact, now that I think about it, maybe she called in sick today as an excuse *not* to attend tonight's party. She was miserably embarrassed about last year's fiasco. On second thought, she *is* on the social committee. We had a planning party a couple of weeks ago and she seemed *very* enthusiastic about attending. So I suppose she *must* be indisposed. Otherwise, she wouldn't miss it. She hasn't missed a faculty party in years. They *are* fabulous parties."

"They do sound memorable," Janet said.

They sound *awful*, she thought.

"The great trick is to avoid being the person remembered."

"I should think so."

"If you don't have any plans for tonight, why don't you come to this one?"

"Oh, I don't know."

"Do you have a boyfriend?"

"Not at the moment."

"Well, then, you definitely shouldn't pass up this opportunity. We have several men on the faculty who would be delighted to meet you."

"I'm not sure I want to meet *them*."

"Oh, they're not *all* chauvinists, geeks and cretins. Several of them are quite delightful."

"I'm afraid I already have some other plans for tonight, but . . ."

But I don't want to see Dave!

But if I don't show up, he'll go after Meg again.

"I don't know," she said. "I think I'd feel out of place, just being a substitute and not knowing anyone and . . ."

"No problem. Everyone loves to see a new face, especially a pretty one. You'd be welcomed with open arms—

at the very least." She twisted her cigarette out of its holder and mashed it into a wobbly ashtray that looked as if it had been made by a student in metal-craft class. "What do you say?"

"Well, maybe. I suppose I could cancel my other plans . . ."

"Wonderful! The social committee provides soft drinks, ice and an assortment of edible goodies. But if you prefer the hard stuff—as most of us do, it's B.Y.O.B. The party starts at eight at my place. Hang on a second and I'll find you a copy of my map. You'll have a marvelous time, just wait and see."

"Is it a costume party?" Janet asked.

"Costumes are optional. But it's always fun to dress up, isn't it? And wonderful to be someone else if only for a night."

FORTY—SEVEN

INJUN JANET

Exhausted but happy after her day of teaching, Janet returned to Meg's house. She took a long bath, then stretched out on her bed in the guest room.

When she woke up, she felt good. The room was gray.

She looked at the clock: 5:10.

Morning or afternoon? she wondered.

Then she remembered that this was Friday afternoon, that she'd been up since dawn and spent the day subbing at the high school. It had been great. Mrs. Bonner's lesson plans had been flexible, so—this being the day after Halloween— Janet had devoted every class period to masters of the macabre. All the kids were familiar with Poe, so she'd taught about lesser known writers such as M.R. James, Algernon Blackwood, H.P. Lovecraft and William Hope Hodgson. A lot of the kids had seemed *really* interested.

Maybe that's why they behaved so well, she thought.

A few of the kids had been rats, but most had been fine.

Best of all, she'd been asked back. By the end of the school day, the people in the main office had apparently found out that Mrs. Bonner would be continuing her absence for at least another week, so they'd asked Janet to fill in for her.

Somebody over there must've put in a good word for me.

But who? She'd been so busy in her classroom that she hadn't met anyone except the principal, the office secretaries and the teacher in the faculty lounge who'd invited her to the faculty Halloween party.

Maybe I'd better go to that, after all.

Earlier, she had pretty much decided against it. She wasn't crazy about parties in the first place, this sounded like a rowdy bunch and they would mostly be strangers. Who needs it?

But the situation was different now that she'd been asked to sub at the high school for a full week.

She might as well get to know some of the people so she wouldn't be spending the week among strangers. Besides, from a practical standpoint, she'd heard that teachers are encouraged to *recommend* which subs they want.

If they get to like me, they'll ask for me. I might end up subbing every day.

Might even end up with a full-time position.

Right, she thought. An exciting idea, but she couldn't exactly hope for a full-time job. Not with a baby on the way.

How will I even go on subbing?

Starting to feel scared, she quickly climbed out of bed.

"Let's just take this a day at a time," she muttered. "So far we're doing just fine, thank you very much." She smiled down at her flat belly. "Aren't we, honey? Yes, we are. So tonight we go to the faculty Halloween party . . . but as what?"

Janet had no idea.

She wished Meg would get home from work. Meg might have some costume ideas.

But no telling when she might return. Her job at the college bookstore lasted until six, but she sometimes went out afterwards for drinks, sometimes for dinner as well.

This being Friday—T.G.I.F.—she probably *would* go out after work.

I'm on my own, Janet thought.

Since the party wasn't supposed to start until eight o'clock, she had plenty of time to visit a mall and buy a costume.

I'm not going to *buy* a costume, she told herself. Only people with no imagination *buy* Halloween costumes.

So use your imagination.

Janet looked at herself in the closet mirror.

How about going as Lady Godiva? Stark naked . . . with a box of chocolates in each hand.

That'd be a hit, she thought.

She put on fresh white panties and a white bra.

A good start, she told herself. Now what?

She swung open the closet door, pulled a string to turn on its light, and stared at the hanging garments.

Has to be something simple. I obviously can't go as a kangaroo.

She flipped through the hangers, glancing at each outfit.

Too bad I was never a cheerleader.

Yeah, right.

It came as no surprise, but she found no costumes or uniforms of any sort. She owned just an ordinary array of old and new clothes. They allowed for certain possibilities: hobo, pirate, cowgirl, gypsy, hippie . . . If she dared to wear a certain slinky, low-cut evening gown, she could go to the party as a lounge singer.

Or high-class call girl.

She chuckled and shook her head and muttered, "Don't think so."

On the last hanger, she came upon a white doeskin shirt

that she'd only kept because it had been a present from her parents. They'd given it to her as a souvenir after a trip to Arizona.

What the hell were they thinking?

Smiling, she shook her head.

Dad obviously thought I'd look cute in it.

And I do, she thought.

She'd only worn it once—to a Merle Haggard concert with her parents. But she'd looked *real* cute.

I could wear *this* to the Halloween party, she thought.

Would never want to wear it anywhere *else* . . . unless I get invited to the Grand Ole Opry . . .

She lifted its hanger off the bar, pulled it out of the closet and held it out for inspection. Though the shirt was several years old, its white buckskin looked clean and new. So did its colorful beadwork. Its fringe swayed all over the place.

"Never seen so much fringe in my life," Janet muttered. It dangled off the shoulders, ran all the way down both sleeves, crossed the back at shoulder-blade level, and circled the entire hemline.

Get me a coonskin hat, she thought, and I can go as Davy Crockett.

In white doeskin? I don't think so.

Maybe Calamity Jane.

It's all a moot point if the thing doesn't fit, she thought.

So she removed it from the hanger and pulled it on over her head.

It felt loose enough to wear. It also felt wonderfully smooth and soft against her skin—though the fringe tickled her thighs.

Jeans will take care of the tickling.

She stepped back from the closet, swung its door shut and looked at herself in the mirror.

"Not bad," she muttered.

Who am I kidding? I look terrific.

The V-neck, cross-hatched with leather laces, almost plunged low enough to show her bra. But not quite.

Though her bra didn't show, plenty of leg did.

I'll wow them all, she thought, if I don't wear jeans with this.

Wouldn't dare.

Why not? she thought. I used to wear miniskirts just as short.

Raising her arms, she watched the shirt rise. Through the swaying fringe below its hem, she could see the white crotch of her panties.

That *also* happened with miniskirts, she reminded herself.

In one of her dresser drawers, she found a black leather belt. She put it on, drawing the shirt in snugly around her waist, and fastened the buckle.

Davy Crocket my ass, she thought. I look like a sexy Indian maiden.

Moccasins!

She pulled a pair out of the closet and slipped her feet into them.

Back at her dresser, she opened a drawer and took out a red bandana. She rolled it into a band, then tied it around her head.

Now all I need is a feather.

Where do I find a feather? she wondered.

At a dime store, that's where. Maybe over at the Woolworth's on the Third Street Mall.

Forget it. I'm not going out like this, and I'm not going to change.

I'll have to go featherless.

Unless Meg has one.

Thinking of Meg suddenly reminded her of Dave.

She picked up his red-inked note, took it down the hallway to the kitchen and picked up the phone. Her hand was shaking. On the first try, she misdialed.

He probably isn't home, anyway.

She tried again. As the phone started to ring, she took a deep breath that made her feel sick.

Please don't let him be home.

It rang seven times. Then she hung up.

She breathed deeply again and the sickness was gone, replaced by a weariness as if picking up the phone and dialing it had used up all her strength.

She went into the living room. Sitting on the couch, she felt her shirt's fringe and the couch's rough upholstery through the seat of her panties.

This shirt *is* awfully short, she thought. I'd better wear jeans.

If I go.

I really *should* go.

But what'll Dave do?

He won't do anything, she thought, because I'll be at the party and he won't know where to find me. And he won't do anything to *Meg* because I'll warn her and she can go to a movie or something.

Janet suddenly heard footsteps outside. A key slid into the lock and the knob turned. The door swung open.

"Hey there, hon! Whatcha up to?"

"Not much."

Meg pulled her key out of the lock and elbowed the door shut. "Guess what I'm . . ." Her voice stopped. She gaped at Janet and a big smile spread across her face. "Let me guess. It's either a pow-wow, *Let's Make a Deal*, or an orgy."

"That bad?"

"Hell, that good. You look great. What're you dressed up for? Trick or treats was yesterday."

"Long story."

"Give me the brief version."

"I subbed at the high school today . . ."

"They called you *already?*"

"Yep. And while I was there, I got invited to the faculty Halloween party. Which is tonight. Since I'll be subbing at the school all next week, I figured I'd better go to the party. So I needed a costume. So this is it, unless you can come up with something better."

Meg slung her purse onto the rocker. "Stand up and let's have a look."

Janet stood up. "Charming, huh? Do you think it's too . . . revealing?"

"It is a bit skimpy, hon. But if I had your figure, you'd never get a *stitch* on me."

"I don't want them to think I'm . . ."

"A brazen hussy?"

"Something like that."

"Shit, you look as cute as a butterfly's butt. You'll charm their pants off."

"Hmm. Don't wanta do that." She started for the hallway.

"What're you doing?"

"Going for my jeans."

"Don't!"

"Yep. You convinced me."

"Hey, I was kidding. You look great. For heaven's sake, don't hide your assets."

In the bedroom, Janet put on her faded blue jeans. Then she checked herself in a mirror. Much better. She felt relieved as if she'd just backed out of a bet she couldn't afford to lose.

Meg came into the room, pressed her thick lips together and shook her head in exaggerated despair. "You've blown the entire effect."

"I feel better now."

"Well, just remember, you can always shuck the jeans if the mood strikes."

"Thanks for the tip. Have you got a feather?" She touched her headband. "I could really use a feather."

"Sorry. Haven't got one of those. But how about war paint? We used to use lipstick when I was a kid."

"Did the Indian women go in for war paint?"

"Only when they were fighting off men. You'll probably be doing a lot of that tonight. With or without the jeans."

"I'd be doing *more* of that if I stayed home."

"Me *no sabe*."

"I'm breaking a date with Dave."

"Uh-oh."

"Wednesday night when I phoned him, he . . . *we* decided to see each other once more. Tonight."

"You agreed to it?"

"I thought it'd be a chance to finish things."

"It'd finish things, all right. He'd probably rape you and . . . God only knows. You saw what he did to Mosby. The guy isn't stable."

"Oh, I think he's stable. He's just an asshole."

Meg shook her head. "He could hurt you, Janet. He really could."

"Well, anyway, I'm *not* seeing him tonight."

"Thank God for that."

"But I haven't been able to get in touch with him. I don't know how he'll take it and I'm afraid he might come over here looking for me. If I'm not here, he might take it out on you."

Meg's sallow complexion flushed. Then she forced out a husky laugh. "So happens, hon, I'll be at a party myself tonight. At Mosby's place. Just the two of us. Candlelight and fondue."

"Really?"

"Really."

"Wow! You and Mose?"

"Righto. We sort of hit it off the other night while you were out chasing Dave."

"That's great! Is it serious?"

"With me, it's *always* serious."

"I'm speechless."

"Nothing to be speechless about—we aren't married yet." But the corners of Meg's eyes were crinkled with happiness. "Anyway, I won't be coming back tonight, so you don't have to worry about Dave messing with me . . . *plus*, you'll have the place all to yourself in case you meet someone fabulous at the party."

"I don't work as fast as you."

"Hell, you don't *need* to work. Let's put on that war paint, okay? It'll give you back some of the zip you lost by putting on the jeans."

"Ah, I don't think so. Let's forget the war paint. I don't want them thinking I'm wacko."

FORTY—EIGHT

COWBOY LESTER

Lester shut the door of Emily Jean's bedroom and stepped in front of her full-length mirror. He tilted his Stetson forward, buttoned the collar of his white shirt, and adjusted the slide of his bolo tie.

Helen had always hated the bolo tie. "Makes you look like a hick," she'd told him when he bought it in Phoenix. But he liked the casual way it looked and he liked the polished umber of the petrified wood on its slide, so he'd bought it in spite of Helen's protests. "It'll be a cold day in hell," she'd said, "before I'll be seen with you when you've got that monstrosity on."

In the mirror, Lester saw himself sneer at her. "A cold *night* in hell," he muttered, and laughed once.

Then he walked slowly backward, hunched over just a bit, arms poised near his sides the way gunfighters always held them in the movies. He inspected his stance in the mirror, then straightened slightly.

Better.

Suddenly, he went for his revolver.

As it cleared his holster, his left hand cut through the air, palm slamming the hammer back to full cock. He squeezed the trigger.

The hammer clacked down.

His thumb drew back the hammer again as he extended his arm and aimed carefully at the face in the mirror.

He squeezed the trigger again.

Then he cocked the pistol again and squeezed the trigger again.

Cocked again, squeezed again.

Cocked, squeezed.

FORTY—NINE

IAN THE MISANTHROPE

Too early to leave. If Ian left now, he would probably be the first to arrive at the party. He used to have a reputation for arriving first and being among the last to leave, but that was several years ago when he still enjoyed the faculty parties.

He leaned back on the chair and folded his hands behind his head.

Either the parties had changed, or he had. Somehow, he'd stopped looking forward to them, stopped enjoying the company of the other faculty members.

That's it right there. He'd stopped enjoying the teachers. Some of them, he disliked. Some, he pitied. Others meant nothing to him at all. He tried to think of a teacher he really liked.

Emily Jean Bonner. But she was really no more than a casual acquaintance. She wasn't really a friend.

He remembered quoting Thoreau to Laura once, saying, "I've found few companions so companionable as solitude."

"That's because you're a misanthrope," she'd explained.

"Nope. Because I'm particular."

"I'm honored that you count me worthy," she'd said, grinning.

He looked at his wristwatch. He could probably leave now, and not be first to arrive at Dale and Ronald's house.

Why go at all? he wondered.

Because you don't want to turn into a complete recluse. And because sometimes you get good material.

He smiled, remembering how he'd turned Harrison's geek performance into a short story that he'd sold to *Playboy* for a tidy $2,700.

Apparently, none of the teachers ever did read the story; his cover remained intact.

He picked up his mask and headed for the garage.

FIFTY

PARTY TIME

Cars lined both sides of the street.

"Somebody must be having a party," Janet muttered. "Hope we can find a place to park."

If I *can't*, she thought, maybe I'd better go on to Dave's place.

Oh, sure. Like this?

Forget it, she told herself.

She slowed down, darted her eyes to a lighted porch and read the big numbers of the address. This was the house.

At the end of the block, she turned right and soon found a parking place. She killed the engine, the lights.

"Here goes nothing," she said.

Gripping the top of the sack that held her wine bottle, she pushed open her door. She dragged the sack across the front seat, stood up and swung the sack out of the car and into her arms.

As she walked, her ankles were cold.

Good thing I wore the jeans, she thought, or I'd be freezing my butt.

And maybe some guys at the party would end up grabbing it.
She felt crawly with fear.

Calm down, she told herself. This might be a rowdy bunch, but there's nothing to be afraid of. Nobody's going to *attack* me, for Pete's sake. It's a party full of *teachers*.

And Dale did say there'll be some available men.

Maybe some assholes, but maybe some decent guys.

Anyway, she thought, I can always leave if things get too hairy.

And go to Dave's?

Thanks, but no thanks.

She headed up the walkway to the front porch. Ahead of her, an older couple stood waiting to be let in. The man was dressed in white coveralls and a cap like a house painter. The woman was encased in a cardboard box covered with contact paper. Paper made to look like red bricks. Maybe she was supposed to be a fireplace chimney.

Janet was wondering about their costumes when Dale opened the door and began to greet the couple.

Her Ophelia costume consisted of a purple velvet gown with puffy shoulders and a plunging neckline. She must've spent an hour attaching foliage to the gown so she would appear to be tangled in water lillies. Her mussed hair was littered with stems and leaves.

Who would want to put that in their hair? Janet wondered.

Maybe the stuff's fake.

Spotting Janet, Dale called, "You made it!" and beckoned her forward. "Janet, I'd like you to meet Phil and Susan Parsons. Susan is our media specialist." To the Parsonses, she said, "Janet subbed for Emily Jean today and I thought she might enjoy seeing teachers at play."

"Well," Phil said, "this is a good place for it. I'm sure you'll enjoy yourself."

Chuckling, Susan added, "Sometimes we enjoy ourselves *too* much."

"Hardly possible," Dale said. "One can't enjoy oneself *too* much."

"Don't know if *that's* true," Phil said.

"There are pipers to pay," added Susan, smiling pleasantly at Janet.

"People are bound to be ralphing before the night is out," Phil said. The chubby, bespectacled man demonstrated by hunching over slightly, throwing open his mouth and yelling "*Rallllph, rallllph!*" at the porch floor.

Susan gave his arm a playful slap. "Stop that, dear. You're embarrassing."

Janet laughed.

This isn't gonna be so bad, she thought.

"Why don't we all come in out of the cold," Dale suggested.

Janet followed them into the house. "I was curious about your costumes," she told Susan.

"Phil! Janet is curious about our costumes."

Phil, beaming with delight, pulled a trowel out of his coveralls pocket.

"I'm bricks," Susan explained.

"And I'm . . . ?" Phil raised his thick gray eyebrows, grinning and waving his trowel.

"Oh, no!" Janet started laughing. "You're the *bricklayer!*"

"At your service." Phil bowed.

Susan punched him softly on the arm. "Not at *her* service, at *mine*. Never forget that, old man."

"You never *let* me forget it."

Susan took hold of his sleeve and started pulling him away. "It was a pleasure to meet you, Janet. I'm sure we'll be seeing more of you around."

"See you later."

As they worked their way into the crowd, Dale stepped close to Janet.

"They seem really nice," Janet said.

"Oh, they're dears, they truly are. If you'd like to shed your purse, you can put it in the bedroom." She pointed in the general direction.

"Thanks. Maybe I'll drop it off later."

"The bar is out on the patio. And so are a fair number of men." She winked, said, "Enjoy," then hurried away to answer the ringing doorbell.

Janet walked through the crowded living room, smiling briefly at unfamiliar faces that turned her way. Most of the people seemed to be in costume. She spotted a vampire, a clown, a pirate . . .

"Janet!"

She turned her head and met the lively, mischievous eyes of the principal.

"Hi, Mr. Harrison."

"Welcome to the party."

"Thanks."

He looked her over.

She looked him over.

He held a drink in one hand and wore an old leather flying cap with the ear flaps up, goggles across his forehead. He also wore a long white scarf around his neck. That seemed to be the extent of his costume. Below the neck, he was dressed in a long-sleeved shirt, slacks and loafers.

"Snoopy?" Janet asked him.

He let out a joyous laugh. "Bite your tongue, squaw girl! I'm Charles Lindbergh!"

"Ah."

He brought his other hand out from behind his back. A plastic doll, naked and smeared with blood, dangled by one tiny foot. "And here's the baby."

"That's *horrible!*"

Harrison beamed. "I know, I know. Halloween, you know. *Gotta* be horrible on Halloween. Anyway, I'm glad you could make it to the party. Dale told me that she'd invited you. Janet, I want you to meet Steve and Cathie Lindstrom."

They'd come as a matching set of hobos, in bowler hats, old checkered shirts with patches, and ragged jeans.

"I love your outfit," Cathie said.

"Thanks. How're things on the freights?"

"Windy," Steve said, grinning.

"Steve," Harrison said, "is one of our ace science teachers and Cathie is his ace wife." To the Lindstroms, he said, "Janet was Emily Jean Bonner today. I hear she did a fine job. In fact, she'll be with us all next week. Maybe longer."

"Welcome aboard," Steve told her.

"Thank you."

Cathie looked concerned. "I hope it's nothing terribly serious about Emily Jean."

Frowning, Harrison shook his head. "She's fine. Her *daughter* was seriously injured yesterday, so Emily Jean went to be with her."

"A car accident?" Cathie asked.

"She was assaulted. Out in Denver."

"How *awful!*" Cathie said.

"Apparently, she barely escaped with her life."

"Good God," Cathie said.

Harrison nodded, happened to glance down at the bloody infant doll in his hand, then grimaced and put it behind his back.

"Is she going to be all right?" Cathie asked.

Harrison nodded. "I talked to Emily Jean on the phone today. The girl should be fine."

"Thank God for that," Cathie said.

"We're all grateful," Harrison said. "Emily Jean thinks the world of her." He suddenly seemed to cheer up. "*But* every cloud has its silver lining, and we get the pleasure of having Janet in our midst for the next week or so." He raised his glass as if toasting her, and took a drink.

"Thanks," Janet said. "Well, I'd better put some of this stuff down. Nice to meet you both."

"Our pleasure," Steve said.

"See you later," said Cathie.

She smiled at Harrison, then turned away.

She made it into the cool, fresh air of the patio before meeting anyone else.

"I don't believe we've met." The young man's smile was too friendly, the front of his shirt too open, his chest adorned with too many heavy gold chains. "I'm Brian Baker, and you are?"

"Janet."

"Hello, Janet." He warmly shook her hand. "It's such a pleasure to meet you." Keeping her hand, he eyed the open neck of her doeskin shirt. "Or should I call you Pocahontas?"

"Janet's fine."

"I chose not to come in costume," he said, still holding her hand. "I don't believe in such silliness."

Silliness? Thanks a bunch, fella.

"Open shirt, gold chains," Janet said, "I thought you were dressed up as a sleazy movie producer."

He let out a harsh laugh.

Janet pulled her hand away from him and took her wine bottle out of the sack. "Are you a teacher?" she asked.

"I've often thought I might have a fling at teaching someday. It might be amusing to shape those young minds. May I help you with that?"

"Thanks, but I opened it at home."

"You look stunning."

"Thank you."

"May I call you Stunning Fox?"

A real charmer.

She pulled a plastic glass out of a stack. "How about Janet?" she suggested. As she poured her Burgundy, she asked, "Are you here *with* a teacher?"

"I came with a dear friend, Eve Tunis. She's off gallivanting. There's nothing between us, of course. She only asked me to escort her because we're such dear friends and she abhors being seen alone."

"*Are* you in show business?" Janet asked.

"I plead guilty. I'm an *actor*."

Surprise, surprise.

He put his arm across Janet's shoulders. "Tell me . . ." His mouth was too close. She could feel his breath on her lips. It smelled of onions. "Did you come alone?"

Hearing a commotion behind her, Janet turned. A man dressed in chain mail and armor like a medieval knight was moving across the living room. The visor of his helmet was down. Dale walked beside him, holding his arm, flora dangling from her hair and gown.

"Make way!" the knight called in a deep, powerful voice. "Make way for the ghost of good King Hamlet, untimely slain. Make way, make way!" He pushed through the crowd, leaving laughter and wisecracks in his wake. "Step aside, fair lady. Good King Hamlet has a rendezvous. Make way, make way!"

In the patio, he raised his visor. He had a remarkably handsome face.

Rock Hudson as King Hamlet.

"Janet," said Dale, "I'd like you to meet my husband Ronald."

"Hello," Janet said. "Nice to meet you."

"Janet and I were just discussing theater. My name is Brian. Brian Baker, and you are . . . ?"

"Ronald Harvey. This is my wife, Dale."

"It's such a pleasure to meet you both," Baker said.

"Didn't I see you in a commercial last week?" asked Dale.

His eyes filled with astonishment. "Why, perhaps."

"For an underarm deodorant, wasn't it?"

"Why, yes! You *did* see my commercial!"

"And your marvelous physique. But it's chilly out here. Why don't we step inside and you can tell me all about it?"

"Wonderful." He looked at Janet. "Coming?"

"I think I'll stay out here in the fresh air."

"We'd be so much more comfortable inside."

"No, you go on ahead."

"I'll be with you later."

When he was gone, Ronald said, "Dale's very good at rescues."

"Sure is. What a relief." Janet shook her head, then drank some wine.

"You've got quite a costume there," Ronald said. "Did Pocahontas really wear jeans?"

Pocahontas again. Terrific.

"Oh, yes. It's a historical fact verified in the journals of John Smith."

"Do you suppose she was prompted by the weather or by modesty?"

"Probably a little of both."

"More than likely," Ronald agreed. "How do you suppose she'd have gotten along with Hamlet?"

"The king or the prince?"

"Why, the king. The prince was nothing but a whelp, wet behind the ears."

"The king was married, though."

"To *Gertrude*. Awful. Can you imagine what it'd be like to live with *Gertrude?*"

"Not very easily."

"Neither can I. Must've been tough on the guy. What he really needed, perhaps, was a Pocahontas."

Beautiful.

"Is that so?" Janet asked. She couldn't keep a bit of sharpness out of her voice.

"Oh, I'm sorry. Just joshing. I didn't mean to put you on the defensive. You'll think I'm as bad as that Baker character. Forgive me?"

"Nothing to forgive. We were talking about Pocahontas and Hamlet, not us. Right?"

"Of course we were."

She looked him in the eye. "Pocahontas doesn't mess around with married men."

"I understand completely."

FIFTY—ONE

NEW ARRIVALS

Ian watched a woman climb out of her gray Mercedes like a bride, but she wore no veil. Instead of shoes, she had slippers on.

The flowing white was no wedding gown at all, Ian realized as he approached her from across the street. It was a nightgown.

"Hello, Mary," he called.

She stopped and turned. The breeze, gentle as it was, molded the light gown to her legs and held it there. "Ian?"

"Right."

"I'm glad I heard your voice before I saw you. You look dreadful."

"Thank you. And you look lovely."

"Thank *you*, Ian."

As he stepped over the curb, he swept his eyes down from Mary's face. The front of her gown dipped so low it covered very little of her breasts, which bulged out of the top of her strapless black bra as if ready to pop out. Her forearms and hands were stained red. Her brief, black panties were clearly visible through the gown's wispy fabric.

"Lady MacBeth, I presume."

"Bravo."

"I thought maybe Cinderella till I saw the blood."

"The damn spots," Mary said.

"May I take your bag?"

"Thank you."

Bottles clinked inside the sack as she handed it to Ian. Her breath smelled sweet with liquor. "Quite an outfit," he said.

"I thought something literary would be nice."

"You've got literary, sexy *and* violent," Ian said. "The perfect Halloween costume."

"Gotta give the fellas something to think about."

"You'll be the life of the party."

"What're *you* supposed to be?" she asked.

"Just ghastly."

"Well, you succeeded."

"Thank you."

Mary frowned at the lighted house. "Is this it?"

"I believe this is it," said Ian.

The walkway to the porch was narrow, so Ian allowed Mary to take the lead. Her nightgown, penetrated by the porch light, was almost completely transparent. Ian watched her through it. Then, ashamed of his voyeurism, he looked away.

I'm sure to get a story tonight, he thought. Just keep an eye on Mary.

Where Mary goes, trouble follows.

She stepped onto the porch, rang the bell, and glanced over her shoulder at Ian. The way she smiled, she seemed to know the effect of her appearance.

Ian shook his head, amazed at her. He wondered how much she'd had to drink.

The door opened.

For a moment, Dale looked stunned. Then she found her smile. "How nice to see you, Mary. And so *much* of you, at that."

Mary smiled as if pleased by the compliment, then curtsied. She stepped through the doorway.

Dale glanced at Ian with poorly concealed distaste. Then she said to Mary, "Won't you introduce me to your date?"

Ian grinned beneath his mask.

"Oh! I'm sorry! Such a faux pas! Dale, I want you to meet the newest man in my life." Without the slightest pause, she came up with a name for him. "Oscar Wade."

Oscar? Thanks a bunch, Mary.

"Nice to meet you, Oscar." Politely, Dale offered her hand.

Ian took it gently. "The pleasure is mine," he said, raising the pitch of his voice so she wouldn't recognize it.

Now I've done it.

Might be fun, he thought.

"The bar is out back on the patio," Dale told him. "You can put your drinks out there."

He started through the crowd, through the jumble of familiar faces that looked at him without recognition. He was a stranger. Mary's date.

The eyes of many men were envious. The eyes of several men and women held suspicion and dislike. After giving him a quick perusal, they all turned to inspect Mary, who followed close behind him.

Harrison suddenly whistled and shouted, "*Whoooeee! Get a loada Mary!*"

FIFTY—TWO

THE FUSS

Out on the patio, Janet heard a sudden explosion of cheers, whistles and shouts from inside the house. "Sounds like the place is coming apart," she said.

"Let's see what the fuss is all about." Ronald took hold of her arm and walked her toward the open door.

She wished he would let go. His touch seemed too possessive, too intimate.

Guess he didn't get the message.

But she thought it would be rude to simply pull out of

his grip, so she let him continue clinging to her arm even after they entered the house.

The center of attention was a beautiful young woman with thick, flowing black hair and an amazing figure.

Stacked, as Meg might say.

Not only stacked, but she was wearing a nightgown that showed most of what she had. The tops of her breasts were bare as if being shoved out of the gown by the strapless black bra beneath them. The color of her skin showed through the gown's wispy fabric. And so did her skimpy black panties.

No wonder all hell had broken loose.

Ronald's hand tightened.

Looking directly at Ronald and Janet, the woman climbed onto a coffee table near the center of the room. She held up her arms for silence. They were reddishbrown, the color of dried blood.

She stared at the hand that held Janet's arm, then glared into Janet's eyes.

As the crowd settled down for whatever show was about to take place, she cried out, "Yet *here's* a spot! Out, damned spot! *Out*, I say!"

The partygoers cheered, clapped and shouted, "Bravo!" Others yelled, "Go for it, Mary!"

A couple of guys yelled, "Take it off!"

Mary nodded and smiled, but seemed agitated. Her face was red. So was her chest. So were the tops of her heaving breasts. Eyes wild, she pointed a finger at Ronald and cried out, "Unhand the strumpet, foul toad!"

Laughing softly, Ronald let go of Janet's arm. "She must be plowed," he whispered.

Pointing her finger at Janet, she yelled, "Get thee to a nunnery, squaw!"

FIFTY—THREE

HOUSE HUNTING

Albert left the Santa Monica Freeway at Grand Beach Boulevard. A fog had rolled in. In spite of its gray blur, however, he was able to read the street signs.

He passed 14th Street. Then Vista, then 12th.

Wrong direction.

At 11th, he turned right. He went around the block and turned onto Grand Beach. Now, the street numbers grew higher. Some had names instead of numbers, but he ignored those and continued eastward until he found 37th Street.

He turned left and found himself on a quiet, residential street. No cars were approaching from either direction, so he stopped at the curb and took May Beth's driver's license out of his shirt pocket.

4231

Squinting through the fog at the house to his right, he found the address on a wooden plaque beside the door.

3950

Three more blocks.

He stretched his stiff back and rubbed his neck.

It would be so great to get out of the car.

No more driving. Not for a while. Not for a long while, if he could help it.

When I wear out my welcome with May Beth's mother, he thought, I'll just find me another place to stay. Should be no problem at all.

The Los Angeles area was enormous. One city after another. Millions of people. In a place like this, he could disappear forever.

Forever. House after house, girl after girl.

Striking and vanishing.

Fantastic!

Albert rolled his head to work the kinks out of his neck, then pulled away from the curb. Driving slowly, he watched house fronts and caught another number.

3990

He waited at a stop sign, though no cars were approaching.

At the end of the next block, there was no stop sign. Then he came to another one. He stopped. As a car crossed in front of him, he looked again at the girl's license.

4231

The house should be near the start of the next block, the second or third on the left.

Not bothering to look for it, he turned left and parked close to the corner.

He climbed out of the car. It felt great to stand. He stretched his muscles and filled his lungs with the cool, moist air. He thought he could taste the fog.

A fantastic night!

Nobody drove the street. Nobody walked the sidewalk. Only Albert. The soles of his sneakers were almost silent on the pavement.

The two-story house at 4231 looked big and old. The windows of its upper floor were dark, but a light shone in the main window at ground level. The driveway was empty.

Albert crossed the front yard at an angle, tracing a path through the wet grass. When he saw his footprints on the concrete stoop, he wished he'd taken the walkway. But the footsteps would dry by morning and probably leave no trace at all.

He held a knife in his right hand, so he pressed the doorbell button with his left.

FIFTY—FOUR

MARY, MARY

Cheers and whistles.

"You tell 'em, Mary!"

"Get thee to a *nunnery!*" she shouted again at the girl with Ronald.

Poor kid, Ian thought. She really looked flustered.

"Get *thee* to a clothes store!" Dale yelled at Mary.

"Up *thine!*" Mary shouted at her.

A lot of people laughed. But not the girl in the white leather shirt.

Where'd she come from? Ian wondered. Could she be a student teacher he hadn't noticed before? That didn't seem likely. Maybe she was here as someone's date.

"Take the *rest* off!" advised vice-principal Reiser.

"Yeah!" shouted Jim Green, one of the social studies teachers. "Come on, Mary! Show us what you've got!"

"Take it off!" Reiser chanted. "Take it *all* off!"

"You guys knock it off," Harrison said. "This has gone far enough."

The girl looked relieved.

She's not *Ronald's* date, Ian thought. That's for sure. But he'd probably latched onto her, anyway. Though the guy had been married to Dale for years, he made a habit of seeking out the best-looking gal at any gathering and flirting with her.

He'd obviously done it again. And Mary didn't like it, not one bit.

So what's between Mary and Ronald? Why should she be this upset? Have they been seeing each other?

"Mary," Harrison said, "get down off the table before you fall and break your neck."

"*Then* get thee to Alcoholics Anonymous!" Dale suggested.

"Fuck thee!" Mary shouted back at her, then let out a wild laugh, jumped off the coffee table and made a deep bow that must've given everyone nearby a wonderful view down her cleavage.

More cheers, applause, whistles, shouts of "Bravo!" and "Atta gal, Mary!"

She smiled and waved at some of the guys, then hurried over to Ian and clutched his arm.

"Quite a performance," he said.

"Thank you very much, sir."

They made slow progress across the room as Mary took compliments from all sides. Almost entirely from men. The women obviously appreciated neither her costume nor her antics. Some ignored her. Others eyed her with disdain, loathing or pity.

Helen Bryant dead ahead.

She wore the same "fifties girl" costume as last year: a pink scarf around her neck, a tight white cashmere sweater, a long gray skirt decorated with a poodle patch, white socks and saddle shoes.

As they approached her, she cast a narrow glance at Mary, looked at Ian without interest and kept on walking.

Doesn't recognize me.

This is very convenient, he thought. I'll have to wear a mask more often.

Then he saw the girl in the white leather shirt. She was standing with Ronald in front of the open patio door, glancing in Ian's direction and looking slightly nervous.

Ian felt a strange surge of anger and disappointment when he noticed Ronald Harvey's hand on her arm.

Jealousy?

Good God, I can't be jealous. I don't even know her.

He wanted to know her, though. He wanted badly to know her. Something about the way she looked . . .

Doesn't make sense, he told himself. Sure, she's a great-looking young woman, but that's no reason for my heart to be flip-flopping.

"Hello, Ronald," he said.

"I don't place your face, but the voice rings a bell."

"Ian."

Ronald laughed. "That's quite a mask, fellow. Positively ghoulish."

"Hello, Ron." The intimate sound of Mary's voice surprised Ian. "When are you planning to introduce me to your new friend?"

The new friend looked more confused and vulnerable than ever.

"Mary, this is Janet. She's a substitute teacher. She was Emily Jean today."

Emily Jean absent? Ian hadn't noticed. Of course, he rarely saw much of her during school hours. She always spent the nutrition break in the women's faculty lounge, off limits to the guys. And Ian usually ate lunch in his classroom so he could spend the time writing.

"Doesn't she have a last name?" Mary asked.

"It's Arthur," Janet said in a strong voice.

"Well, Janet Arthur, I hope you have better luck with Ron than I did."

She gave Mary a blank look and said, "Oh."

"When he's done with you, he'll toss you away like a used rubber."

Blushing deep red, Janet walked away quickly.

Ian watched her.

What if she leaves the whole party?

"That takes care of that," Mary said. "Who *is* the little slut, anyway?"

Ronald shrugged, his chain-mail shirt shimmering. "I barely know the young lady. We only met tonight."

"Oh, sure."

"Honestly, Mary . . ."

Ian stopped listening.

Midway across the living room, Janet stopped beside Dale.

Without a word, Ian stepped around Ronald. He set the bags of liquor on the patio table, then hurried back into the house. Janet was still standing with Dale.

Heart pounding, he walked toward her.

FIFTY—FIVE

THE FRIENDLY STRANGER

"I wonder what *he* wants," Dale muttered.

Janet watched the tall, slim man approach. He was dressed in a black silk shirt, black trousers and black boots. A frightful mask covered his entire head. The skin of the mask had a sick, yellow hue. One bloodshot eye bulged grotesquely. The mouth was a twisted wreck full of crooked brown teeth. Ugly. But worse than ugly. Somehow, the mask was unnerving.

"He was with that Mary," Janet said.

"Indeed he was. I noticed. Shows what good taste he has, whoever he might be."

"Excuse me, ladies," he said. He did have a nice voice.

But that godawful mask!

Dale suddenly smiled. "You cad!"

"Incognito can be fun, but it can also get a guy into trouble."

"Well, you're certainly not in trouble with me. You fiend! Where *did* you get that terrible mask?"

"A gift from a friend. She works in films . . . a special-effects makeup artist."

"And a *good* one, obviously. I'm so relieved it's *you* under there. Not some creepy boyfriend of Mary's. *And* I was starting to think you weren't going to show up."

"Been here all along."

"Janet," Dale said, "I want you to meet this beastly excuse for a friend, Ian Collins."

"Very nice to meet you," Janet said. Smiling, she tried to see his eyes but the mask sent shivers up her spine so she looked at his chest instead.

"It's very nice to meet *you*," he said. "I'd like to apologize for the way Mary acted. It was inexcuseable. I have no idea what made her say those things."

"She's half-stewed," Dale suggested.

"Probably," Ian said.

"It wasn't your fault," Janet told him.

"Oh, I know. This is in the nature of a group apology. It shouldn't have happened. Is there some way I can make it up to you?"

"You already have."

"You seem to be out of wine. I'd be glad to get you a refill."

"Okay. Thanks. I brought a bottle of Almaden Burgundy. It's in a bag under the table."

When he took her glass, his hand touched hers. The touch seemed intentional, but she found that she liked it.

She watched him walk away. He moved with the control of an athlete, stepping around clusters of people without breaking his smooth forward motion.

"Ian teaches English," Dale told her. "He keeps pretty much to himself, but he's . . . quite a fellow."

"He seems very nice. Is he married?"

"Widowed. I've known him quite a while. He seems to be a very straight-arrow guy. Very intelligent, sweet. But I've *never* seen him with a date."

"What does he look like under the mask?"

"He's breathtaking."

"Maybe I'll get to find out for myself before the night is out."

"Wouldn't surprise me at all, Janet. Just a guess, but he seems to be somewhat *taken* with you."

"He does?" Janet felt the heat of a blush on her skin.

"You could do a lot worse than . . ." The doorbell rang. "Excuse me for a moment while I get that."

As Dale left her, Janet looked toward the patio door. She couldn't see Ian. But Mary was there in her see-through nightgown, nodding her head in response to something Ronald was telling her. She looked terribly angry.

"Alone at last." The smooth voice of Brian Baker.

Janet turned around to face him. "Do you know where the bathroom is?" she asked.

"Allow me to show you the way."

"Just tell me. That'll be fine."

"Certainly." He put a hand on her back and spoke softly. "There are two restrooms, actually. One is halfway down that hall." He pointed. "The first door on your right. If it should be occupied, there's one in the master bedroom at the end of the hall."

"Thank you."

"Do hurry back, now."

As she walked away from Baker, she glanced toward the patio. Still no sign of Ian. She hurried to the hall, hoping he would take a long time at the bar, maybe get distracted for a couple of minutes by someone out there; she didn't want him to return too quickly and think she'd run off.

The door of the first bathroom was shut, so she continued down the hall to the master bedroom. A lamp was on. The king-sized bed was littered with purses and coats. The bathroom door stood open.

She went in, turned on the light, locked the door and used the toilet. Then she checked herself in the mirror.

Not bad.

Except that her skin seemed unusually flushed and she had a strange, rather frantic look in her eyes.

Thanks to Mary, more than likely.

When she applied fresh lipstick, she found that her hand was trembling.

Man, I'm a nervous wreck.

That gal really must've shaken me up, she thought.

What is it, my fault Ronald latched on to me? They having an affair or something? What is this, Grand Beach or Peyton Place?

"*Every* place is Peyton Place," she muttered.

Look on the bright side, she told herself. Mary's probably the reason Ian noticed me. Maybe I should be glad she caused all that trouble.

She smiled at her reflection.

I wonder what he *does* look like, she thought. If his face is as nice as his bod . . .

Maybe *he's* why I'm flushed and shaking.

I'd better go out and find him.

She checked her hair in the mirror. It looked fine, kept in place by the red bandana tied around her head.

Maybe I should lose the headband. Makes me look like Willie Nelson.

Nah, leave it on.

She turned away from the mirror and opened the bathroom door.

Mary's snarling face was streaked with tears and mascara.

"Fucking whore!" A red arm lashed out.

Janet staggered back and the fingernails missed her eye. They raked her cheek instead, leaving hot trails as if she'd been burnt.

"Stop it! Christ, what's . . . ?"

Mary grabbed the front of her doeskin shirt, swung her around and slammed her back against the door frame.

Mouth close to Janet's lips, she whispered, "Fuckin' bitch, yer gonna get yours now."

FIFTY—SIX

THE GUNSLINGER

"Lester, how nice that you could make it. Helen told us you weren't feeling well."

"I took a nap after she left. Felt a lot better when I woke up, so I figured I might as well come on over."

"Can't keep a good man down," Dale said.

Lester smiled.

Good man, my ass. Who does she think she's kidding? She hates my guts.

"Helen's around here someplace," Dale said. "She'll be so surprised to see you."

"Won't she, though?"

His sarcasm seemed to anger Dale. Her mouth tightened. He smiled.

Who's she, anyway? Helen's friend. An enemy.

Probably knows all about Helen and Ian.

Everyone probably knows, he thought. They probably encouraged it, too.

Lester's such a loser, after all.

"The bar is out on the patio," Dale said, her voice cold.

"Thanks."

In the living room, Lester scanned the crowd. He saw a man dressed like a seaman, a couple of hobos, a guy in armor with the visor down, and many others.

There! There she is! Wearing her goddamn poodle skirt!

He made his way toward Helen and bumped into someone with a glass in each hand. "Sorry," he mumbled.

"No harm down." A hideous mask muffled the man's voice. "Nothing spilled."

Helen saw him. At first, she looked shocked. Then angry.

She broke away from a small group and came toward him, her eyes narrow, her lips pressed together in a tight line.

Lester smiled. "Surprise," he said.

"What in God's name are you doing here?"

"You know how I love these faculty parties."

"I know how you *hate* them. What're you doing in that stupid tie?"

"I know how much you like it."

"You look like an idiot."

"So what?"

"You're embarrassing me. Why don't you just leave now, okay?"

"Can't leave yet."

"Need to humiliate me a little more? These are my *co-*workers, you moron."

"Before I go, I want to finish things between us." Grinning, he patted his holster.

She looked down at it.

And at the revolver it held.

"You've got to be kidding," Helen said. "You brought your *real* gun?"

He smiled. "Can't be a cowboy 'less'n I got the pig iron on my hip."

"That thing had better not be loaded."

"How will I shoot Ian if it isn't loaded?"

She sneered at him. "You're not going to shoot anyone and you know it. You haven't got the balls. You're a gutless wonder. You always have been, always *will* be. That's the problem with you. You're a fucking *wimp*."

"Think so, huh? Well, we'll see about that. Where's lover-boy?"

"For God's sake, Lester. You'd better cut this out and leave before you get yourself into some real trouble. You want to end up in prison?"

"Where's Ian?"

"He's not here."

"You're lying. I saw his Jaguar out on the street."

"He's not here," she repeated, this time using her firm tone, her teacher voice.

"Don't worry," Lester said. "We'll find him. Then we'll all have a quiet little talk. Then I'll put a bullet in his head. See how much you wanta fuck him when his brains are blown out."

"Are you out of your mind?"

"If I am, you made me that way. Let's go find him. And don't try to cause any trouble or the first bullet'll be for you."

FIFTY—SEVEN

THE FIGHT

Walking through the living room with a drink in each hand, Ian couldn't find Janet. Lester, in a big hurry to get somewhere, bumped into him, but Ian managed not to spill the drinks. Curious, though, he watched Lester rush across the crowded room and confront Helen.

Who didn't look very happy to see him.

She seemed to be giving him a rough time about something.

On your high horse with your husband? You're the one sleeping with one of your students, you bitch.

Shaking his head, Ian turned away and saw Dale sitting alone near the door. He went over to her.

"I don't know how she puts up with him," she told Ian. "Insufferable. . . . brat. He's a brat. A cowardly, whimpering brat."

"Lester?"

Dale smirked. "Who else?"

"Ah. Well, maybe he has his reasons."

"I expect behavior of his sort from a child in a classroom, but heavens, Ian, from an adult?"

"Have you seen Janet anywhere?"

"Janet? Oh, she must be around here someplace. I'm certain she isn't the type to go sneaking off. Besides, I've been at the door the whole time. I just can't get over that man," she muttered.

I feel sorry for the poor bastard, Ian thought.

But he kept silent, knowing such a comment wouldn't be appreciated by Dale—or by just about anyone else on the faculty, for that matter. They all considered Helen to be a highly talented professional married to a guy who just couldn't get it together.

"Guess I'll go look for Janet," Ian said.

"She might be in one of the restrooms."

"Thanks."

"Somebody!"

Ian jerked his head toward the hallway. Susan Parsons was rushing forward, the cardboard chimney jumping around her.

"Somebody help! A fight! In the bedroom!" She flapped an arm behind her, pointing down the hall.

Ian ran. Susan was blocking the way. He turned his shoulders to leap between her and the wall and got by without knocking her down. Then he was in the master bedroom.

It was Janet on the floor, arms up, trying to ward off blows from the growling, half-naked woman straddling her hips. Tangled hair hid the face of the woman, but Ian knew it had to be Mary. Her nightgown was torn from one shoulder. A breast, dislodged from its bra, swayed and jumped as she swung her fists.

Ian grabbed one of the red-stained arms and twisted it behind Mary's back. Using her arm for leverage, he forced her to her feet.

"Somebody take her," he snapped, and shoved her away.

Ronald Harvey stepped out of the group in the doorway, his visor up, a look of shock on his face.

Mary ran to him, her loose breast leaping. She threw

her arms around him and blurted, "Take me home! Take me home right now! It's all your fault! You had no *right* to dump me for that skinny bitch!"

Ian pulled off his mask. Wiping the sweat off his face, he knelt beside Janet. She was sprawled on her back, crying.

"Get out of here!" he shouted over his shoulder. "Everyone out!"

A few people turned away. Others stayed, peering in through the doorway. Ian sprang up, rushed to the door and shut it. Then he returned to Janet.

Her cheek was scratched and bloody. Her nose and lips were bleeding, too. She sniffed.

"You," she said.

"Me?"

"The guy from the football game." She sniffed again and licked some blood off her upper lip. Then smiled.

FIFTY—EIGHT

SHOWDOWN

Lester knocked lightly on the bedroom door.

"Who is it?" The voice sounded angry.

Lester didn't answer. He opened the door, pulled Helen inside by her elbow, and took a final look down the hall. Nobody seemed to be watching. He shut the door.

Ian was coming from the bathroom with a dripping washcloth in one hand. He glanced at Helen and Lester, then knelt over the girl.

"I have a few things to say to you," Lester said.

"Fine." Ian didn't look up. He continued to clean blood from the girl's face.

"Look at me when I talk to you!"

"I'm busy right now, Lester. Why don't you save your talk for another time?"

"Ian," Helen said, "you'd better listen to him. He has a gun. He's planning to shoot you."

This time, Ian looked up.

Lester drew the revolver from his holster and pointed it at Ian's face.

"What the hell's going on?" Ian asked.

"He knows about you and me," Helen said.

"You and me?"

"He knows the whole thing. I'm sorry, Ian. I . . . I told him last night. I was angry and upset and I told him."

Ian began to stand up, face calm, eyes steady.

Lester felt fear crawl into his stomach. "Stay down!" He thumbed back the hammer. "Stay down!"

Ian stood up straight. "What is all this, Lester?"

"He knows you've been screwing me," Helen blurted.

"Is that what she told you, Lester?"

"That's it."

"*I'm* screwing her?"

He nodded.

"And you believe her?"

"Ian, for God's sake, be man enough to admit . . ."

"Shut up!" Lester snapped at her. To Ian, he said, "Yeah, I believe her. I guess I do. Why shouldn't I?"

"Why *should* you?" Ian asked.

"It figures, that's why. She sure as hell isn't interested in *me*, and you're the most likely candidate. Besides, she confessed. Why should she lie?"

"You'd better ask her about that."

"Don't listen to him, honey."

Lester glared at her. "Shut up."

She called me honey? Man, I must really have her scared.

"Ian's trying to trick you," she said.

"And I said to shut up."

"He's making a fool out of you."

"I'm not interested in Helen," Ian said. "I never have been. I think she's a cold and arrogant bitch, her career has gone to her head and she has weaknesses of character that make her unfit to be either a teacher *or* a wife. She's barely fit to be a human being."

"You fucking bastard!" Helen spat at him.

"He sounds pretty sensible to me," Lester said.

"Don't be such an asshole!"

Lester turned the pistol on Helen.

Her face blanched. She began to shake her head in tight, trembling nods, but her eyes looked scornful. "Don't you point that thing at me," she whispered.

"Tell me the truth," he demanded. "Have you been *doing it* with Ian?"

"Stop pointing that gun at me."

He shoved the muzzle closer to her face. *"Have you?"*

Looking him hard in the eyes, she said, "No. I haven't beeen 'doing it' with Ian. Okay?"

"Who then?"

"No one. I made it all up."

"Lying bitch! I want truth! Who's fucking you?"

"Nobody."

"I happen to know different."

"Oh, yeah? How?"

"Stains."

Her face went scarlet.

"Tell me whose," Lester said, "or I'll blow a hole through your face!"

"We only . . . we hardly . . ."

"Who?"

"Charles. You know. Charles Perris."

"Your *student?* The poet?"

"Yes."

"You've been *making it* with one of your students?"

"Yes! Okay? Damn it, I needed *some*one. I had to have someone."

"And that was the best you could do, huh?" Lester pointed the pistol at the bridge of her nose. "Say your prayers, Helen, you're about to meet your maker."

"Please!"

An arm swung up. Ian's. It struck Lester's wrist with a hard, numbing blow. The pistol jumped free and dropped to the floor.

Lester started to reach down for it, but Ian stepped on the barrel. "Just leave it."

Lester rammed his shoulder into Ian. The tall man staggered, his foot coming off the pistol.

"Don't!" Ian warned.

Crouching, Lester reached for it. His hand closed around its grips.

Then he cried out as Ian stomped on the revolver, mashing his fingers against the floor.

"Get off!" he cried out. He looked up at Ian in time to see a fist swing down at his face. The blow knocked him to his knees. The crushing pressure left his fingers. He pulled his hand out from under the pistol.

Ian had him by the shirt collar. Lifted him. Dragged him to the bed and threw him onto it.

"Stay there."

The bed felt good. Lester knew he'd been defeated: tricked and humiliated.

Not by Ian.

By Helen.

Doesn't matter. I'm done with her. The hell with her. Fuck her. Never want to see her again, the filthy slut.

Then he rolled onto his side and threw up.

FIFTY—NINE

THE PARTY'S OVER

Turning, Ian saw Helen staring down at the revolver on the bedroom floor.

"You can leave, now," he told her.

"He tried to kill me," she said, her voice quiet as if she were talking to herself, trying to understand a twisted puzzle. "He really tried to kill me."

Ian picked up the pistol. With his thumb, he lowered the hammer to half cock. Then he flipped open the side port and gave the cylinder a spin.

"It isn't loaded," he said. "Lester didn't want to kill anyone. No ammo. See?"

Helen stepped closer. She pulled the weapon toward her, turning Ian's hand, and scowled at the empty holes as Ian spun the cylinder.

"No bullets," she muttered.

Ian watched her step toward the bed. She moved slowly like someone in a trance. For a long time, she stared down at her husband. She shook her head slowly. "You miserable piece of shit," she said. "Didn't even have the balls to load the fucking gun. You worthless . . ."

"Take off, Helen."

She snapped her head toward Ian and fixed him with fierce eyes.

"Take off," he repeated. "I'll take care of Lester. Don't you even think about calling the police. If they get in on this, I'll tell them all about you and Charles."

For a moment, he thought Helen might try to attack him. Then the rage seemed to pass from her. She walked to the door and left.

When she was gone, Ian knelt beside Janet.

"How are you?" he asked.

"Not too bad, I don't think."

"Sorry about all that. Something always hits the fan at these parties. Usually nothing like this, though. Cat fights and gun-toting cowboys . . ."

"*Cat* fights?" Janet asked.

"Bad choice of words. Sorry about that."

"I didn't start it, you know."

"I'm sure you didn't."

Janet sat up, holding the washcloth to her face. "I'll be black and blue for a month." She wanted to smile, but knew it would hurt.

"Anything feel wrong inside?" Ian asked.

"I don't think so. I was afraid . . . she'd do something to make me miscarry."

"You're pregnant?"

Janet nodded. She could feel his concern for her.

"That crazy bitch," he muttered.

"What'd she think," Janet asked, "I was horning in on Ronald?"

"Guess so."

"He's not my type."

"But it did look like you were with him," Ian said. "He had his hand on you. I was starting to feel a little jealous, myself."

Her heart speeded up. She felt heat rush through her body.

"*You* going with Ronald, too?" she asked, trying to smile. "He's a popular fella."

"I don't care for him much," Ian said.

"Oh."

"But I care about *you*, which is pretty weird."

Oh, my God!

"Not that weird," she told him, staring into his eyes. Her lips felt dry. She licked them.

"We just met," Ian said.

"How long is it *supposed* to take?"

Ian's face turned crimson. "I guess first sight can do it," he said.

Did he just say what I think he said?

Heart racing, Janet said, "Looks that way."

Ian grimaced, smiled, shook his head. "Anyway," he said, "maybe we'd better get out of here and take you to an emergency room."

"Yeah as to getting out of here," she said. "No as to the emergency room. I'm okay. Just a few scratches and bumps."

"But if you're pregnant . . ."

"I feel fine. Really. Except for my face. Why don't we just get out of here?"

Ian helped her to stand. After she was up, he still held on to her arm.

On the bed, the man named Lester groaned.

"What about him?" Janet asked.

"I'm not sure. My Jaguar only holds two."

"I've got a Maverick."

Ian hesitated.

"I wouldn't mind," she said. "Really."

"Okay." Ian stepped to the bedside. He put a hand on Lester's shoulder and gently shook him. The shut eyes squeezed tight. Then one opened.

Lester groaned. "Huh?" he murmured. "What?"

"Let's get you out of here," Ian said.

"Huh?"

"We'll drive you home."

"Home? No. Haven't got one."

"Somewhere else? A motel? A friend's place?"

"Emily Jean's."

"What?"

"Take me to Emily Jean's house."

"Mrs. Bonner?" Janet asked.

Lester nodded.

The teacher I'm subbing for? The one whose daughter got at-tacked?

"Maybe we'd better phone her first," Ian said. "She was absent today, so she might not feel up to . . ."

"S'okay. I gotta key. I'm staying at her place. Take me there, okay?"

Ian helped Lester to sit up. Then he turned to Janet. "That all right with you? Emily Jean's house is only a couple of miles from here."

"Fine. Let's go."

SIXTY

THE VIGIL

Albert sat by the window of an upstairs bedroom and watched the street. Every so often, a car went by, headlights pushing through the fog and darkness.

One slowed down as it approached. Albert stopped chewing his mouthful of Swiss cheese until the car turned and pulled into a driveway across the street. Then he continued chewing, though his mouth was suddenly dry. The cheese became a tasteless wad and he had trouble swallowing it. He set the remaining block of cheese on the windowsill beside his knife.

A cat trotted silently across the street and disappeared under a parked Toyota.

An old man with a cane and a cigar walked by. He wore a beret like a Frenchman and swung his cane in a jaunty way.

Later, a woman in a bathrobe came out of a house across the street to let her poodle squat. The tiny dog got too close to the Toyota and the cat sprang out. Headlights lit its side as it scampered into the street. One of its eyes flashed an eerie yellow. Then the cat was out of danger.

The car slowed and began its turn.

Albert grabbed the cheese and knife, straightened his

chair, and left the room. He hurried down the hallway to the other bedroom, the bedroom with the poster of a rock star on its wall. The daughter's bedroom, he supposed.

May Beth's.

He dropped the cheese into a dresser drawer. Then he stepped between the open bedroom door and the wall.

And waited.

SIXTY—ONE

EMILY JEAN'S HOUSE

In the driveway, Janet stopped her car, shut off its lights and killed the engine. "Guess we're here," she said.

"Let's make sure Lester gets inside okay," Ian said from the passenger seat. Then he opened the door and climbed out.

"*Who* are you?" Lester asked from the backseat.

"Janet."

"I don't think I know you."

"I'm a substitute teacher," she said. "This was my first day."

"A substitute?"

"For Mrs. Bonner."

"Emily Jean?"

"Yeah."

Ian, now on her side of the car, opened the door for her. As she climbed out, the back door swung open.

The three of them followed a walkway toward the house's front porch.

"Do you know Emily Jean?" Lester asked Janet.

"No."

"I do. We're very close. I'm house-sitting for her while she's away."

"Where'd she go?" Ian asked.

"Denver."

"To see May Beth?"

"How'd you know about that?"

"May Beth's making a movie in Denver, isn't she?"

"Was," Lester said. "But not anymore, I guess."

"She's not?" Ian sounded upset. "What happened?"

"She got hurt, somehow. Cut up. The doctor told Emily Jean that she's in critical condition."

Ian looked stunned.

"She's going to be all right," Janet quickly added. "Emily Jean called Harrison today. The daughter's going to be fine, but I'm supposed to sub for Emily Jean all next week. I guess she's planning to stay away for a while."

Making no comment, Lester unlocked the front door.

"How did it happen?" Ian asked. He followed Lester into the dark foyer. Janet stayed close beside him.

In the living room, Lester turned on a light. "I don't know," he said, and dropped heavily onto the couch. "Emily Jean got a call yesterday. They didn't say what happened. Just that May Beth had been cut. I don't know."

"It was a sexual assault," Janet explained.

Ian looked sick.

"Maybe you can call the hospital," Janet suggested. "She'd probably like to hear from you."

"Anybody know which hospital?" he asked.

Janet shook her head.

Lester nodded and rubbed his forehead. "General . . . County General, I think."

Ian picked up the phone near the couch.

"Excuse me," Lester said. He got up. "I'll be right back."

As Ian dialed for directory assistance, Lester walked to the stairway.

SIXTY—TWO

PUNISHMENT

At the foot of the stairs, Lester flicked a wall switch. A light came on at the top. His legs felt heavy as he climbed.

Terrible night, he thought. But it's over now. I'll never have to see any of those people again.

Helen, maybe.

Not necessarily. Maybe I'll just disappear.

I can stay here for at least a week, anyway. That'll be nice.

He stopped at the door to May Beth's bedroom. His heart quickened, making blood throb through his aching head.

May Beth.

A patch of pale glow from the hallway light fell on a corner of her bed.

He had made love on that bed, but not with her.

Maybe it's a punishment.

Punishment for Emily Jean, for doing the daughter act.

Punishment for me.

My fault she got cut up.

He muttered, "I'm sorry, May Beth," into the dark of the room.

Then he crossed the hallway and entered the bathroom. He turned on the light and shut the door. In the medicine-cabinet mirror, he saw his own reflection.

Mussed hair, sallow face, eyes that looked tired and sad . . . and the bolo tie.

It *does* look silly, he thought. No wonder everyone thinks I'm such a loser.

"Fuck 'em all," he muttered.

I should've taken ammo and blasted everyone.

But I didn't, he thought. Because I'm a gutless, nutless wonder just like Helen says.

Worthless.

He looked down at the holster below his right hip. It was empty.

Who's got my gun? he wondered.

Who cares. Who needs it? Wherever it is, the fucking thing isn't loaded, anyway.

Story of my life, he thought. *I'm* no better than an empty gun.

His image slid away when he opened the medicine cabinet. Inside, he found a green plastic bottle of Excedrin. He shook two tablets into his palm, but decided that wasn't enough. Not for a headache this bad. He dumped out two more tablets, then washed them down with water cupped in his hand.

He turned off the faucet. He dried his mouth on a towel.

Then he stepped over to the toilet and urinated.

As he held his penis between his thumb and forefinger, Emily Jean came into his mind.

The feel of her fingers, of her mouth, of her slippery snug vagina.

He started to grow stiff.

Things could be a lot worse, he told himself. At least I've got Emily Jean. If I want her.

Maybe May Beth, too, if I get real lucky.

He managed to push his erection back inside his underwear, then zipped up his jeans and flushed the toilet. At the sink, he washed his hands.

Maybe tonight I'll sleep in May Beth's bed.

He opened the bathroom door.

A naked man stood there. A boy, really. His face was distorted by a crooked grin.

Lester saw the blade for an instant before it went into his belly. A very long, wide blade.

He tried to get his hands there in time to stop it, but he wasn't fast enough.

It disappeared completely into him and he couldn't believe it even when he felt its white-hot stiffness inside, even when he saw it slide out dark with his own blood.

He couldn't believe it.

Impossible.

This isn't happening.

He reached out to stop the floor from smashing into his face, but his arms didn't work.

SIXTY—THREE

FALLING

"Thank you." Ian hung up.

Janet, sitting beside him on the couch, had taken hold of his hand and leaned against him so he could feel her warmth against his arm.

Now she turned her head and met his eyes. "Sounded like good news," she said.

He nodded. "May Beth's off the critical list. She's been upgraded to serious."

"That *is* good news."

He nodded and settled against the back of the couch. Janet eased back against it with him. "They wouldn't let me talk to her. Understandable, of course. It's about midnight there. They said I should try again in the morning."

"She must be very special to you."

"Who? May Beth?"

Janet nodded.

"Never met her."

"You've never *met* her?"

"Her mother's a good friend. Emily Jean."

"Ah." Janet smiled and looked relieved.

Ian lifted her hand onto his leg and looked down at it. A small hand compared to his. Smooth and delicate. "May Beth's an actress. Stage, mostly. Anyway, they're filming one of my books out in Denver, so I pulled a few strings and helped her get a role in a film. That's what she was doing there." He shook his head slowly. "I almost got the girl killed."

"No, you didn't."

"She'll live, anyway. Apparently. No thanks to me."

"You shouldn't feel guilty, Ian."

"It's not guilt, really. I just feel sorry. Hell, you can't live without making decisions and every time you make one you start a chain reaction. You affect lives. In ways you never figured. Or wanted."

"Some of the effects aren't so bad," Janet said.

He looked at her. Her face was very close to his. He put his arm around her shoulders and she tucked her face into the curve of his neck.

"Those strings you pulled," she said. Her breath was warm against him. "They're why I'm here right now, you know."

"I guess so," Ian said.

Janet lifted her face away from his neck and looked up at him.

With a fingertip, he traced the curves of her lips, her chin. Then he kissed her. Her mouth was moist and yielding and she clutched him as if she wanted the kiss never to end.

He glided his hand over her doeskin shirt, found the rise of her left breast, and cupped it gently.

She untucked the back of his shirt. Then her hand went underneath it and roamed his skin.

He let go of her. "We'd better not . . . uh, I'll tell Lester we're leaving."

"Okay."

"Then we'll go . . . I don't know, someplace. My place?"

"That'd be great."

As Ian got to his feet, so did Janet. "One more kiss," she said and stepped into his arms.

Ian held her tightly, kissing her, feeling the curves of her back, feeling the urgent press of her body against his. Then he eased her gently away. "Back in a minute," he said.

"Hurry."

Smiling, he went to the stairs. He climbed them two at a time until he reached the top.

There, he saw fresh wet bloodstains on the carpet.

He went cold inside.

Beyond the soggy patch of carpet was a shut door.

Ian stepped over the blood and knocked. "Lester? Lester, you in there?"

He gripped the knob.

It wouldn't turn.

"Lester!" He pounded the door with his fist.

"What's wrong?" Janet called.

Ian stepped away from the door and looked down the stairs at her. "I don't know. There's blood up here and a locked door."

"Oh, no. You think he might be trying to . . . hurt himself?"

"Wouldn't surprise . . ."

He turned at the sound of an opening door.

A naked, blood-soaked boy rushed out with a butcher knife.

As Ian lurched away, his foot swept empty air. He reached for the banister and missed.

He seemed to fall a long time before a stair pounded the back of his head.

SIXTY—FOUR

DOC

With a sudden shock of fear, Janet watched Ian stumble backward. She dashed up the stairs hoping to stop his fall, but she'd hardly begun when his head slammed one of the carpeted steps. He twisted sideways, legs against the wall. His left arm, caught between two upright bars of the railing, snapped.

Dropping to her knees, Janet fell across Ian and stopped him from falling farther. As she tried to free his broken arm, she heard a squeak of wood above her.

She looked up.

The boy's bare skin was splattered and smeared with blood. He grinned as he stepped silently onto the stairs. Down low at his side, next to his erect penis, he held a butcher knife upright.

Janet felt as if her breath had been kicked out.

"Ian!" She shook him.

He didn't react, just lay motionless on his back.

The boy came slowly down the stairs.

"Ian! Wake up!"

Still nothing.

Janet grabbed the shoulders of his black silk shirt. Hunched over and scurrying backward, she dragged him headfirst down the stairs. Quiet ripping sounds came from his shirt. His boots dropped off the edge of each step and landed on the next with twin thuds.

The boy didn't hurry. All the way down, he stayed one step higher than Ian's boots.

Smiling.

Erect.

Ian's shirt came apart a button at a time, a seam at a time. Afraid it might tear off him entirely, Janet wanted to let go and clutch his arms. But she didn't dare release her grip on the shirt even for a moment; the slightest change in her own actions might trigger an attack by the kid.

The shirt was wide open and torn around her clutching fingers by the time Janet dragged Ian off the final stair. She pulled him across the smooth granite of the foyer.

The front door was just behind her.

I might get away if I let go of him.

But she clung to his shirt and continued to tow him.

When her rump met the door, she let go with one hand and reached back for the knob.

Squatting, the boy grabbed Ian's right ankle and grinned at Janet.

For the first time, she realized that he wasn't completely naked. Around his neck, he wore one of those cowboy ties . . . a thick string with a polished brown stone decorating its slide, the weighted ends of the string dangling down the middle of his chest.

Lester had been wearing a tie just like it.

"Howdy," the boy said. "What's your name?"

"Janet."

"Howdy, Janet. I'm Doc Holliday."

She nodded.

"Who did that to your face?"

"Some girl."

"Fingernails?"

"Mostly."

"You still look pretty, though."

"How about letting go of my friend, Doc?" she asked. "Please?"

He reached forward and pushed the point of his knife against the inseam of Ian black trousers. "You want, I can make him a girl."

Janet shook her head. "Don't. Please."

"Who's gonna stop me?"

"What do you want? I'll do whatever you want. Okay? Just leave him alone."

"We'll see. How about you let go of him and stand up?"

"Okay."

As she released her grip on Ian's shirt, the boy called Doc let go of his ankle. They stood upright, facing each other.

"Now come here," Doc said.

"Why?"

"Just come here."

She stepped around Ian, her legs so weak she expected them to collapse.

"Closer."

When she took another step, Doc grabbed her arm. He swung her toward the stairway. "We're goin' upstairs," he said. "You first."

She climbed, keeping her eyes forward and holding the banister to steady herself.

She could hear the quiet thumping of Doc's bare feet on the stairs just below her.

We're going to a bedroom, she thought. He's going to rape me. Then he's going to kill me.

He's going to kill me!

And you, too.

She touched her belly through her soft leather shirt.

Both of us. Oh, God!

Her legs gave out, but she caught herself on the banister. Doc hurried up to her side, took hold of her arm and helped her to stand.

"What . . . what're you going to do?" she asked.

"Have me a good time. Maybe I'll even *operate* on you."

"The real Doc Holliday was a dentist," Janet said.

"Not me. I'm a gut surgeon." He laughed.

Keeping the grip on her arm, he led her to the top of the stairs. There, she saw the blood-soaked area of carpet. Just beyond it, on the bathroom floor, lay the body of

Lester. He was sprawled on his back, his mouth open, a blank look in his eyes. His shirt was ripped in front, sodden with blood and clinging to his belly.

"Operated on *him*," Doc said. "Removed his *life*."

The hand on her arm steered Janet to the right, then down the hallway.

SIXTY—FIVE

CUTS

Albert turned on the bedroom light. He pushed Janet toward the bed. She caught herself against it, turned and faced him. She was breathing hard. Her scratched face was flushed and shiny. So was her chest where he could see it through the wide V-neck of her white leather shirt.

"You been playing cowboy 'n injun with that guy in the john?" Albert asked.

Her head jerked slightly from side to side. "We were at a party."

"Ah! A *Halloween* party, I bet! And you all played dress-up?"

"It was a costume party."

"It's *fun* to play dress-up! Look at me!" He laughed. "I'm Adam. Like in Adam and Eve."

"Yeah, sure."

"Who was that other dude supposed to be, Zorro?"

She shrugged and muttered, "Guess so."

"I don't reckon he'll be cuttin' any more Z's." Albert laughed. "And *you're* an injun squaw?"

"Something like that."

"Or Willie Nelson with tits?"

"Whatever you want."

"I want you to be the injun."

"Fine."

"Thing is, you don't look much like an injun with *blue jeans* on."

She stared at him.

"Take 'em off," Albert said.

She shook her head.

"Reckon you speak with forked tongue."

She just looked at him.

"Downstairs when I was all set to operate on Zorro, you promised you'd do whatever I want. Remember?"

"I guess so."

"Was that a lie? 'Cause if it was, we can go on back downstairs and I'll open him up. That what you want?"

"No."

"Then you better do what I say."

"Okay," she muttered.

"Get the jeans off."

With trembling hands, she unbuckled her belt. She opened her waist button and lowered her zipper. Bending, she pulled the jeans down around her ankles. She stepped out of them, keeping her moccasins on.

Her bare legs were slender and tanned. The front of her leather shirt hung slightly lower than her groin, and long white strips of fringe swayed across her thighs.

Albert felt a warm flow of excitement.

"Now your panties," he said. He saw her eyes lower to his erection, then quickly turn away. "Take 'em off."

Her hands went up beneath the fringe at the sides of her shirt. Bending at the waist, she slipped her panties down. Then she stepped out of them.

"There," Albert said. "That didn't hurt, did it?"

Though she looked the same with the panties off, Albert felt different knowing she was bare under the shirt.

Nothing under there but Janet.

Albert stepped toward her.

She started to back away, but the bed stopped her.

Albert switched the knife to his left hand. He slipped his right hand between her thighs and moved it upward. He could feel her trembling. He slid his hand higher. Suddenly, she knocked it away and clutched the wrist of his left hand—the one with the knife.

With his right, Albert struck her face.

She cried out, but still held his other wrist. Before he could punch her again, she grabbed his right wrist, too.

She drove her knee up.

It pounded Albert's thigh and he grunted with pain.

She tried again.

This time, he moved his left hand and the knife jerked as she drove her leg upward into the point of its blade. She sucked in a quick gasp of pain and surprise.

Albert shoved her backward onto the bed.

She squirmed there, clutching her stabbed leg, blood spreading out through the spaces between her fingers.

Albert clamped the knife in his teeth. Both hands free, he bent over her and shoved her legs apart.

Janet still pressed a hand against her bleeding wound.

Albert grabbed it and jerked it away. Clutching her thigh, he dug his thumb into the split skin.

She screamed.

Sitting up, she attacked him with a flurry of punches. He blocked most of the blows, but some got through and hurt so he took the knife from his teeth and slashed at her.

She kept her hands up, trying to stop the knife. It sliced her fingers, her palms, her forearms, but she continued fighting him.

"Stop it!" he snapped.

He clenched the knife in his teeth again, grabbed her flailing arms and lay on top of her, pinning her to the mattress. She struggled under him, bucking and twisting.

He felt the warm flow of her blood against his thigh, the thrust of her pubic mound against his erection, the softness of her leather shirt under his chest, the slippery wetness of her bloody wrists turning in his hands.

Letting go of one wrist, Albert pulled the knife from his teeth and pressed the blade to her throat.

"Lie still," he gasped. "Move and you're dead."

Janet stopped thrashing but couldn't stop gasping for air, couldn't stop whimpering.

Albert pushed himself up. Sitting across her thighs, he leaned forward and slid the knife down the neck of her shirt. He cut through the thong laces, then sawed the shirt open all the way down.

As he spread it apart, Janet's arms moved quickly to cover her breasts.

"Don't." He pressed the knife point to her belly.

She went rigid. "Please," she gasped.

"Please what?"

"I'm pregnant."

"No kidding?" Albert grinned. He scratched her belly with the tip of his knife and watched tiny droplets of blood form on her skin. "Right in there?"

"Please. Don't hurt me. Don't hurt my baby."

With his other hand, he smeared the red droplets.

"I'll do anything," Janet said. "Anything. Just don't hurt us. Okay?"

"What're you gonna name it?"

"I don't know."

"Boy or girl?"

"I don't know."

"Wanta find out?"

"No!"

"Let's have a look at it."

"NO!"

Albert laughed. "Maybe I will, maybe I won't. You be real nice, maybe I'll leave it in."

"I'll do anything . . ."

He pushed the knife.

Janet cried out and jolted stiff as its point slipped into her belly half an inch. Blood welled around the gash.

Moaning, Albert watched the blood pour out over her

skin. He clamped the knife in his teeth, then lowered himself onto her, pressing his belly to hers. The blood was like oil between them. Warm, slick oil.

His fingers probed and found the gash.

He raised himself off her slippery belly.

She'll scream. They all scream when I do it.

He pulled the pillow over her face and pressed it there with his right hand so nobody would hear her screams.

He used his left hand to spread the edges of the cut.

Then he lowered himself slowly.

He pushed at it. Head down, he watched the swollen knob of his penis sink into the bloody slit. He pushed and it went in deeper. She was all warm and squishy in there. He pushed again.

The knife in his teeth suddenly jerked, slicing into his tongue and cheeks. His mouth filled with blood.

The knife leaped free.

Letting the pillow go, he reached for Janet's hand. Caught it.

Too bloody.

Too slippery.

Her hand twisted out of his grasp.

The pillow tumbled away. Instead of its suffocating heat, she suddenly had blood cascading onto her face from Doc's mouth.

She turned her face away from the falling blood and saw the butcher knife in her own hand.

Saw her hand pull out of the boy's grip, felt its freedom, and struck at him with all her force.

The point jammed Doc's temple. Its impact knocked his head sideways. The blade deflected off bone, skidded over his skin and tore through his right eye.

Screaming, clutching his face, he tumbled off the bed.

Knife in hand, Janet crawled to the edge.

The boy lay on his side, moaning, hands tight against the place where his eye used to be.

Janet climbed down and squatted beside him.

She pressed the knife against his neck.

One quick slash.

I'd be killing him!

But he's *a killer!*

He had murdered Lester . . . no telling how badly he'd hurt Ian . . . he'd cut Janet herself and . . .

What the hell was he planning to do *to me?*

"You sick bastard," she muttered.

He whimpered and writhed.

My God, look what I've done to him.

I'd better just call the police, she thought. Let them take care of . . .

"JANET!"

The shout came from far away—probably down in the foyer where she'd left him unconscious.

"Ian?" she called out. "I'm upstairs!"

"You all right?" He didn't sound very good, himself. Janet could hear the confusion and pain in his voice. At the very least, he had a broken arm. Maybe a concussion, too.

"I'm okay!" she yelled.

"Hang on, I'll try to . . ."

"Why don't you stay down there and call the police? Lester's dead, but I've got this guy down. We'll need a couple of ambulances."

"Don't you need a hand up there?" he called.

"It's under control."

The moment "control" left her mouth, pain flashed up her arm from her twisted wrist and she dropped the knife. Then Doc was rolling, shoving his shoulder against her forearm, throwing her sideways from her crouch.

She landed on her back, her left wrist still trapped in the boy's grip.

She jerked it free.

The kid let out a cry of agony.

Janet flipped herself over and rolled away from him. She

rolled over and over, then shoved herself up on one elbow and looked at him.

He was on his hands and knees.

Sobbing—or giggling.

The weighted ends of his bolo tie hung toward the floor, swinging like pendulums.

He had the butcher knife in one hand.

His head turned and he looked at Janet with his single remaining eye. Blood spilled from the socket where his other eye had been and poured from his ripped mouth.

"It's over, Doc," Janet said. "Just lie down, okay? The cops'll be here in a couple of minutes. Ambulances, too. They'll take care of you."

"Janet?" Ian yelled.

"Yeah?"

"Phone's dead. Guess I'll have to visit a neighbor. You sure everything's okay up there?"

Giggling, Doc lurched to his feet.

"Not *really!*" Janet yelled.

SIXTY—SIX

RESCUE

Not really?

Janet's answer made Ian's heart lurch. Pain pulsing through his head, he raced up the stairs. He took them two at a time, pumping with his right arm while his left arm, swollen and stiff and useless, swung by his side.

"What's going on?" he yelled.

As if in answer, a door somewhere above him banged shut.

"Janet!"

Leaping up the final stairs, he saw Lester across the hallway, sprawled on the bathroom floor.

He rushed to the body and stopped.

Lester's eyes had the empty stare of a dead man. His shirt was ripped in several places and drenched with blood. The brown leather holster on his hip was empty.

Has the kid got the pistol? Ian wondered.

No, I took it away back at the party.

Where is it?

I must've left it in Janet's car, he thought.

Doesn't matter. Isn't loaded, anyway.

Raising his head, he looked into the bathroom and wondered if he might be able to find a weapon.

Like what, toenail clippers?

He lurched away from the bathroom and called, "Janet!"

No answer.

Earlier, her voice had seemed to come from the left. So that's the way he went.

All the doors along the dark hallway were shut.

But up ahead, a strip of yellow light glowed across the bottom of one.

He ran to it.

With his right hand, he grabbed the knob. He tried to turn it. The knob was rigid.

Locked? Bedroom doors don't have locks!

Obviously, this one did.

Emily Jean and May Beth, living together in the same house, probably wanted their privacy. And their safety.

Ian pounded the door with his knuckles.

"Janet!"

"Don't come in," she said.

"The door's locked."

"I know," she said. "I did it."

"Unlock it."

"In a minute."

"What's going on?"

"I don't want him getting away."

"Janet?"

"Don't worry, okay?"

"What's *he* doing?"

"Coming at me with a knife."

"Shit!" Ian stepped back, then hurled himself against the door and rammed it with his right shoulder. The impact shot pain through his head and across his body to his broken *left* arm.

"Ow!" Janet gasped. "Don't do that! I'm here!"

"Well, move!"

"Stay out!"

SIXTY—SEVEN

IN THE ROOM

Janet's "Not *really!*" had just slipped out, her quick reaction to Ian asking if things were all right—and seeing that they weren't.

She'd wanted to take it back.

But you can't take back words. When they're out, they're out.

So Ian was probably on his way up the stairs to rescue her.

With his battered head and broken arm.

I'm in better shape than he is.

I'm in damn *better shape than Doc.*

All she had were the scratches from Mary, a nasty stab wound on her thigh, the gash on her belly, and maybe seven or eight cuts on her hands and arms.

Doc's mouth was ripped open, he had a gash across one temple and one eye gone.

But he has the knife.

As he staggered toward her, she pushed herself off the floor, whirled around and ran to the bedroom door.

I could run out and just keep running!

She imagined herself hurrying down the stairs, pulling Ian by his good arm. *Come on, let's get out of here!*

And maybe Doc catches them.

But maybe he doesn't. Maybe they get away and run next door to call the cops.

And maybe Doc vanishes.

For a while.

Instead of rushing out through the open bedroom door, she slammed it shut and thumbed down the lock button.

She turned around fast.

Doc had stopped coming toward her. He stood a few paces away, his feet apart and his arms out slightly as if he might be having trouble staying up.

"Put down the knife," Janet said. "Okay? You're really hurt. We'll get you to a hospital."

His split, drooping cheeks gave Doc a bizarre grin. He tried to say something, but only managed to spit out blood.

"Let's just stop," Janet said. "Please."

He shook his head slowly from side to side, then slashed the air with his knife and took another wobbly step toward her.

She pulled off her shirt, stepped backward until the door stopped her, then wrapped the bulky leather garment around her right hand and arm just as she'd seen it done in the movies.

Doc stopped coming toward her and fixed his single, bulging eye on her breasts.

Someone knocked hard on the door.

She flinched, startled, then realized it must be Ian.

"Janet!"

"Don't come in."

Doc's eye flicked from side to side as he looked at her right breast, then her left, then her right again.

"The door's locked."

"I know. I did it."

Doc's penis, small and limp a few seconds ago, began to rise.

You've gotta be kidding, Janet thought. But she felt herself go cold and squirmy inside.

"Unlock it," Ian said.

"In a minute."

Doc's eye roamed downward and stopped at the cut he'd made in her belly.

That's where he wants to nail me. In my cut, not my . . .

"What's going on?"

"I don't want him getting away."

"Janet?"

Gazing at the gash, Doc looked as if he were drooling blood. His penis was now jutting upright, rigid as a pole.

"Don't worry, okay?" Janet said.

Doc took another slow, unsteady step toward her.

"What's *he* doing?" Ian asked through the door.

"Coming at me with a knife."

"Shit!"

She raised her leather-wrapped arm.

The door suddenly jumped against her back and buttocks. "Ow!" she yelped. "Don't do that! I'm here!"

"Well, move!"

"Stay out!"

Doc's head tilted sideways as if he didn't understand what was going on. Why was she trying to keep Ian out?

"Just you and me," Janet told him. "If I let Ian in, one of you'll end up dead. I don't want *anybody* else dead, okay? Not even you."

He stared into her eyes.

"Why don't we try to work something out?" Janet asked.

His single eye moved slowly down her naked body, lingering on her breasts, her cut belly, her groin.

"No more stabbing, okay?"

Nodding, he lowered the knife to his side.

"That's good, Doc. That's very good."

The knife still down, he took a step closer to Janet.

"It's all right," she said. "Just no knife." She spread her arms so they wouldn't be in his way.

Doc slid his bloody left hand over her breasts, then down to the slit in her belly.

She flinched and groaned as he fingered open the wound. Writhing with the pain, she grabbed his wrist.

He made a sound like a growl.

"Here, Doc." She shoved his hand downward. Guided it between her legs. "Here. It's better here."

At first, he tried to pull his hand free. Then he began to caress her. She felt his fingers glide gently, spread her open, slip in. As he panted and quietly whimpered, he rested his forehead against the side of her neck. He slid his fingers deeper.

"It's fine, Doc. It's very nice. You don't need the knife anymore. Why don't you drop it, okay?"

She heard it thump against the carpeted floor.

My God, he did it!

Somebody up there likes me.

Somebody here in the bedroom likes me, too.

"Yes," she said. "Thank you." She shook her arm until the doeskin shirt fell off. Then she put her hands on Doc's shoulders and eased herself against him.

He was *so* hard. How could he possibly be so hard with such awful wounds?

"Here's what you get for dropping the knife," she said.

Clutching his shoulders, she pushed him backward across the room until he fell onto the bed. Then she climbed onto the mattress. Knees on both sides of his hips, she eased herself down, slowly impaling herself.

As she sank lower, she felt the rigid thickness push its way higher, deeper.

Then it was suddenly jumping, pumping, spurting.

Doc grunted and whimpered under her.

And Janet saw a single tear slide down from the corner of his remaining eye.

★　★　★

When they were done, she climbed off the bed. Seeing herself in the closet mirror, she realized she was still wearing the red bandana around her head. She pulled it off and tied it around her thigh as a makeshift bandage for the stab wound there.

She had plenty of other wounds, but decided they might as well wait.

She put on her panties, her jeans, and then her doeskin shirt.

Doc stayed on the bed, crying softly.

In front of the door, Janet crouched and picked up the butcher knife. Then she turned the knob. The lock button popped out with a *ping*, and she opened the door.

Ian was sitting on the floor on the other side of the hall, holding his left arm and looking up at her. He raised his eyebrows.

"It's over," Janet said.

"You all right?"

"I'll live. How about you?"

"Okay." He struggled to his feet, then looked past Janet and into the bedroom. "What happened in there?"

"I fucked him up pretty good."

Ian grimaced. "Looks like it."

"He won't be any more trouble," Janet said. "Why don't I stay here and keep an eye on him, you go find a phone?"

Ian turned toward her, frowning.

"What?" she asked.

"Are you sure you're all right?"

"A few cuts."

"Why didn't you let me in?"

"I had it under control."

"I wanted to help you."

"I know." She shrugged. "Anyway, it worked out."

"You sure you're okay?" he asked.

"I'm fine. Really."

His eyes suddenly went shiny with tears. "I was so worried about you," he said. Then he put his one good arm around her back and pulled her in against him.

She tilted back her head.

His face lowered slowly, becoming very large, and Janet stared into his eyes until she felt as if her own eyes might cross if she kept looking.

So she shut them.

And then she felt his lips.

PART TWO

AUGUST, 2000

SIXTY—EIGHT

MALIBU, CALIFORNIA

The ringing doorbell woke Lisa up. Rolling onto her back, she opened her eyes. Her bedroom was bright with sunlight. The curtains above her head swelled outward, filled with a cool morning breeze. She heard the squeal of seagulls, the smooth *shushhhh* of the surf.

The doorbell rang again.

Frowning, Lisa sat up and looked at the alarm clock on her nightstand.

8:17.

Who would be coming to the door this early on a Saturday morning?

None of her friends even knew she was staying here.

She climbed out of bed and slipped into her moccasins.

Whoever it is, she thought, let him wait. Maybe he'll get tired of waiting and go away. Him, her, whatever.

She certainly had no intention of answering the door in her nightshirt.

The bell rang again.

Insistent son of a bitch.

She pulled off her nightshirt, folded it and stuffed it into her dresser drawer. Then she took out a pair of faded red shorts and put them on. In the closet, she found the blue work shirt that she liked to wear around the beach house.

The doorbell rang again.

"Hold your water," Lisa muttered.

She put the shirt on and buttoned it. On her way to the door, she rolled its sleeves up her forearms.

"Just a minute," she called.

She opened the oak door. Through the mesh of the outer security door, she saw a man standing on the front porch. His gray hair was pulled back in a ponytail; he wore dark sunglasses and had a thick mustache and beard. His white knit shirt hugged a pumped-up torso and flat belly. A beeper hung on his belt. His tan trousers looked brand-new. So did the white Top-Siders on his feet.

Has to be a movie guy, she thought.

"May I help you?" she asked.

"I'm here to see Evan Collier," he said. There was a thickness, a sluggishness to his speech as if his tongue didn't work quite the way it should.

"I'm afraid he's not here this morning."

"Oh? This *is* his residence?"

"It's his beach house, but he isn't here. Was he expecting you?"

"I *thought* he was. I'm Wayne Kemper. I'm here to interview him for *Film Weekly*." He shook his head. "There must be some sort of a mix-up."

"Looks that way," Lisa said.

"Would you know how I might reach him?"

"Far as I know, he's at the other house."

"Oh, dear. I suppose *that's* where I'm supposed to be. I'm afraid I don't even have the *address* for the other house." He glanced at his wristwatch, then shook his head. "I'm *already* late. Oh, this is awful. I'll be in *so* much trouble."

"Let me give Dad a call," Lisa said. "I'll let him know . . ."

"Dad?"

"Yeah."

"Then you must be Lisa!"

She nodded.

"I didn't recognize . . . well, of course, I can't *see* you through this door. But I haven't laid eyes on you since you were . . . oh, four or five years old, I should think."

"We've met?" she asked.

"Why, of course. I knew your father and mother *very* well. In fact, I knew Janet before she married your father."

"You knew her *before?*"

"Oh, yes. Very well. They've never spoken of me?" he asked. "Wayne Kemper?"

Lisa shook her head, then realized he couldn't see her through the door's mesh. "I'm not sure. The name *does* sound a little familiar."

"Anyway, I *am* late for our interview. Your parents must be wondering why I haven't shown up yet. *Would* you give your father a call, explain the situation and tell him I'll be over as soon as possible?"

"Sure. Glad to." She unlocked the security door and swung it open. "Why don't you wait inside while I call?"

Wayne smiled. "Oh, there you are." He entered the house. "And what a lovely young lady you've turned out to be."

"Thanks."

He stepped into the house and pulled the security door shut behind him. "So," he said, "how does it feel to be the daughter of two such famous writers?"

"It's all right," she said.

"Do you have ambitions in that direction, yourself?"

"No way. But my little sister might turn into a writer."

"And what do *you* do?"

"I'm a teacher."

"Oh, that's wonderful. Your mother was a teacher, wasn't she? Before she became an author?"

"Yeah, for a few years. But you're supposed to be interviewing Dad, not me. I'll . . ."

"You bear a *striking* resemblance to your mother," Wayne said. "*Astonishing*."

"Well, thanks."

"I knew your mother when she was just about your age. She was a stunning beauty."

"She still looks pretty good," Lisa said.

"You could be her *clone*." Wayne took off his sunglasses. "Such a beauty," he said.

She tried not to stare.

He looked as if he'd had a very bad accident at one time—an accident that destroyed his eye and scarred his face from the corner of his eye almost to his ear.

The left eye was obviously fake. Not a good fake, either; it gazed downward at a lower angle than his real eye so that it seemed to be studying her breasts.

"I'd better make that call," she said, and turned away.

She took only one step before the sunlight started sliding out of the foyer. She looked back. Wayne was shutting the main door.

"You don't have to shut that," she said.

"Yeah, I do," Wayne said. "We don't want anyone hearing your screams."

Lisa went cold and numb.

Wayne reached behind him, took something out of the seat pocket of his trousers, and raised it in front of his face. A blade suddenly flicked out and snapped into place.

A long, thin blade that tapered to a point.

"Hey," Lisa said.

"Hey, yourself."

Her heart pounded hard and fast as if trying to smash its way out of her chest.

"What do you want?" Lisa asked.

He grinned. "I'm Albert Mason Prince."

"Big whoop."

"You don't *know* about me?"

"What am I supposed to know?"

"Your mother did this to me." He swept his empty

hand in front of his face. "She never *told* you about her encounters with the infamous killer, Albert Mason Prince?"

Infamous killer?

"I never heard of you," she said.

"Ever see *scars* on your mother? On her hands and arms, on her leg, on her *belly?*"

"She walked through a plate-glass door."

Laughing, he said, "*I'm* the door."

"*You* made those cuts on her?"

"With my little knife." He gave his switchblade a twirl. "And I fucked her, too. Her *and* you."

"Huh?"

"I fucked *you*, too. You were *in* her when I did it. So I got both of you at once."

"She was pregnant with me?" Lisa asked.

"And *so* scared I'd hurt you, her precious little fetus." He gave his knife another twirl. "I was all set to cut you right out of her. Sure glad I didn't, though. I'd done that, we wouldn't be having our little fun this morning."

"*I'm* not having fun," Lisa said.

"Let's see what you look like naked."

"Let's not."

"Oooo, you're a fiesty one. I like that. Your mom was fiesty, too. She nailed me good." He grinned again. "But now it's payback time. She only *thinks* she won. She'll have another thing coming after I get done with you. Now take off your clothes."

"You don't want to do this," she said, trying to keep her voice steady.

"That's what you think."

He stepped toward her.

She stood motionless, trembling.

"When I get done with you," Albert said, "your mom's gonna wish she was never born. She'll wish *you* were never born, too."

"Don't do this, Albert."

He slid the knife down the front of her shirt. After slicing off every button, he raised the knife toward his mouth. For a moment, he looked as if he might clamp it between his teeth. Then he let out a tiny huff of laughter and moved the blade close to Lisa's eye.

"Take it off," he said, "or I'll take your eye out. Just like your mom did to me."

She spread open her shirt, slipped it off her shoulders and let it slide down her arms.

Albert lowered the knife slightly. As he pressed its point against her cheek, his other hand began to fondle her breasts. He moaned. His good eye slid shut, but his glass eye remained open and seemed to be watching the activities of his hand without much real interest.

"Know the last time I felt one of these?" he asked.

She didn't answer, but she winced as he squeezed her right breast.

"I was just seventeen, and it was your mom's. She had the last set of tits I ever saw . . . or felt." His good eye opened and peered at her. "She was the last gal I ever fucked, too."

"Been in prison?" Lisa asked.

"Something like that."

Oh, God, he's probably got AIDS!

He twisted her nipple, laughed as she cried out in pain, then said, "Loony bin." He pinched it. "Thanks to your mom." He released her nipple and shoved his hand down the front of her shorts. "But now I'm out." He spread her, fingered her. "I'm all well and free as a bird."

"Stop that."

"I don't think so."

"Stop right now. Please."

"Oh, honey, this is just the start. This is gonna be *so* sweet."

"Somebody's going to get hurt."

"I know, I know. That's the fun part."

"Don't do this, Albert. Get your hand out of there."

"Mmmm."

His fingers slipped into her.

"Don't," she said.

They slithered in deeper.

"I'm not my mom," Lisa said.

"Oh, you're *better*. I can already see that. I can already *feel* that. You're so smooth and juicy and . . ."

She clutched his knife hand and twisted it. As Albert gasped with pain and surprise, the knife flew from his fingers. Then she *broke* one of them, snapped it backward so it popped like a twig. Before he could get his other hand out of her shorts, she'd popped two more of his fingers.

"Mom's the *nice* one," Lisa said.

She drove a thumb into Albert's good eye and gouged it out.

"This time you picked the wrong babe . . ."

As his knees pounded the marble floor, Lisa drove her right knee into his nose.

". . . to fuck with."

He slammed down on his back.

Lisa pulled off her moccasins and picked them up. Holding them in one hand, she stepped out of her shorts. She picked up her shorts, then her shirt. She took her clothes and moccasins into the living room, dropped them to the floor and came striding back into the foyer naked.

"Don't get excited, Al. I just don't want to get blood on my stuff."

He writhed on his back, clutching his bloody face.

"Oh," Lisa said. "Forgot. You can't *see* me, can you? Too bad. I'm bare-ass naked. Guess you'll have to use your imagination."

She stepped past his feet, jerked his legs apart and knelt between them.

"I *do* know who you are, by the way. Mom and Dad told me all about you."

She drove a fist into his groin. He grunted and his knees jumped up.

"Why do you think I let you into the house? Did you think I was a fool? I don't let *strangers* in."

She grabbed one of Albert's feet and jerked the Top-Sider off it. She tossed the shoe over her shoulder, then went after his other foot. "I always thought you should've gotten the death penalty."

She scurried across the marble foyer, snatched up the switchblade and hurried back to him.

"For that matter," she said, "I thought *Mom* should've killed you when she had the chance."

She picked up one of his bare feet and slashed through the Achilles tendon.

Albert screamed.

"Mom's always been too nice."

She picked up his other foot and slashed the tendon. Albert's howl of agony made her ears hurt.

"Mom thinks *I'm* mean-spirited. Do you think so, Al?"

He didn't answer.

"I think I'm just *practical*," Lisa said. "I didn't cut your tendons to be *mean*, just to keep you from getting away."

Lisa tossed the knife across the foyer.

"This time, Albert, you don't go anywhere."

Slipping and sliding on the bloody marble, she made her way around to the side of Albert's thrashing, writhing body.

"Mom and Dad aren't *at* our other house, by the way. They're on a three-week cruise to Hawaii with their good friends Meg and Mosby. My brother and sister are spending most of the summer in New York City with May Beth Bonner. The actress? I guess you know who *she* is, don't you? Hell, you helped launch her career. All that publicity . . ."

Lisa squatted, reached out and unfastened the buckle of Albert's belt.

"Life works in strange ways, doesn't it?"

She opened the waist button of his trousers.

"The upshot is, everyone's far, far away for the next

three weeks, I'm on summer break from school, and *I* have the only key to the house."

She slid his zipper down.

"Just you and me, Al. Won't this be fun?"

From Horror's greatest talents comes

THE NEW FACE OF FEAR.

Terrifying, sexy, dangerous and deadly.

And they are hunting for YOU...

WEREWOLVES

SHAPESHIFTER by J. F. GONZALEZ
JANUARY 2008

THE NIGHTWALKER by THOMAS TESSIER
FEBRUARY 2008

RAVENOUS by RAY GARTON
APRIL 2008

BRYAN SMITH

It was known as the House of Blood. It sat at the entrance to a netherworld of unimaginable torture and terror. Very few who entered its front door lived to ever again see the outside world. But a few did survive. They thought they had found a way to destroy the house of horrors…but they were wrong. A new house has arisen. A new mistress now wields its unholy power—and she wants revenge. She will not rest until those who dared to challenge her and her former master are made to pay with their very souls.

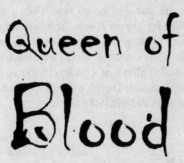

Queen of Blood

ISBN 13: 978-0-8439-6061-7

RICHARD LAYMON

SAVAGE

Whitechapel, November 1888: Jack the Ripper is hard at work. He's safe behind locked doors in a one-room hovel with his unfortunate victim, Mary Kelly. With no need to hurry for once, he takes his time gleefully eviscerating the young woman. He doesn't know that a fifteen-year-old boy is cowering under Mary's bed....

Trevor Bentley's life would never be the same after that night. What he saw and heard would have driven many men mad. But for Trevor it was the beginning of a quest, an obsession to stop the most notorious murderer in history. The killer's trail of blood will lead Trevor from the fog-shrouded alleys of London to the streets of New York and beyond. But Trevor will not stop until he comes face to face with the ultimate horror.

ISBN 10: 0-8439-5751-4
ISBN 13: 978-0-8439-5751-8

RICHARD LAYMON

They call it Beast House. Tourists flock to see it, lured by its history of butchery and sadistic sexual enslavement. They enter, armed with cameras and camcorders, but many never return. The men are slaughtered quickly. The women have a far worse fate in store. But the worst part of the house is what lies beneath it. Behind the cellar door, down the creaky steps, waits a creature of pure evil. At night, when the house is dark and all is quiet…the beast comes out.

THE

CELLAR

ISBN 13: 978-0-8439-5748-8

RICHARD LAYMON

The Beast House has become a museum of the most macabre kind. On display inside are wax figures of its victims, their bod-ies mangled and chewed, mutilated beyond recognition. The tourists who come to Beast House can only wonder what sort of terrifying creature could be responsible for such atrocities.

But some people are convinced Beast House is a hoax. Nora and her friends are determined to learn the truth for themselves. They will dare to enter the house at night. When the tourists have gone. When the beast is rumored to come out. They will learn, all right.

THE BEAST HOUSE

ISBN 13: 978-0-8439-5749-5

RICHARD LAYMON

For years morbid tourists have flocked to the Beast House, eager to see the infamous site of so many unspeakable atrocities, to hear tales of the beast said to prowl the hallways. They can listen to the audio tour on their headphones as they stroll from room to room, looking at the realistic recreations of the blood-drenched corpses....

But the audio tour only gives the sanitized version of the horrors of the Beast House. If you want the full story, you have to take the Midnight Tour, a very special event strictly limited to thirteen brave visitors. It begins at the stroke of midnight. You may not live to see it end.

THE
MIDNIGHT
TOUR

ISBN 13: 978-0-8439-5753-2

A STRANGER WALKS INTO A PLACE OF BUSINESS...AND STARTS SHOOTING.

Three of horror's most terrifying authors challenged each other to write a novella beginning with that simple idea. But where they each went from there would be limited only by their own powerful imaginations. The results are incredibly varied, totally individual, and relentlessly horrifying. Prepare yourself for three very different visions of fear, each written specifically for this anthology and available nowhere else.

JACK KETCHUM

RICHARD LAYMON

EDWARD LEE

TRIAGE

ISBN 13: 978-0-8439-5823-2

MICHAEL LAIMO

The church waits in darkness. It looks abandoned, forgotten. It has no congregation, but it is not empty. Under its floor, in a pit dug long ago, lies a wooden crate that was never meant to be unearthed. But the church is finally being renovated and workmen have found the pit. How could they realize what they have done? How could they know the forces they've unleashed?

Father Pilazzo's dream is to see the church restored to its former glory. But his dream is becoming a nightmare. He's begun to see horrific visions, unholy images of death and warnings of terrors to come. And within the church forgotten men fight to survive against impossible demons, while sides are drawn for the ultimate battle...

FIRES RISING

ISBN 13: 978-0-8439-6064-8

BRIAN KEENE

Something very strange is happening in LeHorn's Hollow. Eerie, piping music is heard late at night, and mysterious fires have been spotted deep in the woods. Women are vanishing without a trace overnight, leaving behind husbands and families. When up-and-coming novelist Adam Senft stumbles upon an unearthly scene, it plunges him and the entire town into an ancient nightmare. Folks say the woods in LeHorn's Hollow are haunted, but what waits there is far worse than any ghost. It has been summoned...and now it demands to be satisfied.

DARK HOLLOW

ISBN 13: 978-0-8439-5861-4

THE DELUGE

MARK MORRIS

It came from nowhere. The only warning was the endless rumbling of a growing earthquake. Then the water came—crashing, rushing water, covering everything. Destroying everything. When it stopped, all that was left was the gentle lapping of waves against the few remaining buildings rising above the surface of the sea.

Will the isolated survivors be able to rebuild their lives, their civilization, when nearly all they knew has been wiped out? It seems hopeless. But what lurks beneath the swirling water, waiting to emerge, is far worse. When the floodwaters finally recede, the true horror will be revealed.

ISBN 13: 978-0-8439-5893-5
